DARK EYES

Books by Nina Romano

Darby's Quest Series
The Girl Who Loved Cayo Bradley

Novels
Dark Eyes
The Secret Language of Women
Lemon Blossoms
In America

Story Collection
The Other Side of the Gates

Poetry Collections
Cooking Lessons
Coffeehouse Meditations
She Wouldn't Sing at My Wedding
Westward: Guided by Starfalls and Moonbeams
Faraway Confections

Poetry Chapbooks
Time's Mirrored Illusion
Prayer in a Summer of Grace

Nonfiction
Writing in a Changing World

Coming Soon!
Darby's Quest Series
Book 2: Star on a Summer Morning

DARK EYES

Nina Romano

SPEAKING VOLUMES, LLC
NAPLES, FLORIDA
2023

Dark Eyes

ISBN 978-1-64540-799-7

For Nico

Prelude

In a while, he'll come to you with sweet words, kiss your lips, and like a refrain from an old love song, he'll caress you, and the world will wing away. A velleity. If only it could be.

Underneath the city of stars, *Piter,* on this last of the white nights of summer . . . the hours of darkness were still, heavy with opaque shadows, seemingly concise, controlled, vigilant.

Standing by an ashcan filled with twigs and burning logs, the flints and sparks thrusting heavenward like firecrackers, Anya leaned in to warm her hands, her light Chinese silk duster open so her ballerina body clad in a leotard and tights could be seen by any passersby. A car slowed.

She peered over the trash bin to see the driver leaning out the window beckoning her. His handsome face, his sweet demeanor, his eyes crinkling into a smile. Why couldn't she find someone like that to love her? It could be him. It might be him. She walked closer, bent to see how he was hungry for something—something physical, perhaps, but not love. She saw it clearly in the fistful of rubles he held out. Then in the flash of headlights from another car, she gazed into his soulful, tender green eyes. She jumped back and instinctively glanced over the car. Official. *Mylitsya.*

She waved him away. "Good night, officer—be sure to dream of me," she said, wrapping the duster around her lean torso as she retreated toward the flames.

Chapter One

I awoke from my dream of snow falling softly, amassing next to the twisted dead body of a woman wearing a red and green floral babushka partially covering her face, a pasty white, more ashen than the snow.

Looking out the window, flurries assembled in an immense milky sky. Through the frigid windowpanes, my sense of snowfalls perceived whispers of snowflakes that would soon cascade, perch, and bank—the way it always does in fairytales and dreams. I sensed the rhythm—the pulse, the throb of the descent, snow falling as petite discordant angels: geometric, concentric formations to blanket earth.

I gazed out, feeling cold, wishing warmth, intuiting every fallen flake as a perfect unit, an inconceivably inordinate shape, impossible to fathom, unadorned, yet magnificently haloed.

Who was the woman?

The afternoon of that same day, Anya Ivanovich Andreyeva walked alone along the streets covered confectioner's white, a downy fleece blanket with the scent of more snow brimmed in the overclouded sky. She was careful where she stepped, evading cracks in the pavement and avoiding anything that could break her step or cause her to fall. Her ideas of becoming a ballerina had been dashed, but she didn't need to break another leg because of a misstep on a dark, poorly lit street where so many lanterns should be turning on, but instead the electric-powered bulbs were dead and out.

Monuments and buildings buffered by a frozen landscape—would it ever cease to be winter? Would she ever feel warm again, seeing wintertime dissipate in the sprouting of spring foliage? Muffled yet echoing steps kept her turning around, reminding her of when she was young and living alone in the basement of the building where her uncle did repairs. She'd really been followed then. It had been the maestro. She recalled how he'd looked at her in that lascivious way. She hated him. She feared him. She wanted to know what it would be like to kiss him, taste the hair of his moustache above his lips. Oh how he reminded her of someone, but whom? She remembered nothing of her father, except one night his shadow bent over her. He had kissed her goodnight, his scratchy mustache tickling her. After that kiss, she never saw him again.

Back then she had quickened her pace. But now she slowed. Every time she did the slightest maneuver to pick up speed, someone in the not far distance did the same, or was it only in the back of her mind? She understood she was being followed. *But why? By whom?* By ghosts of her past, or maybe that lout Grigory she'd been hypnotized by. Walking alone, her body recalled arched ankles, screaming legs, hurt pelvic area, abdominal muscles. Stress injuries caused in ballet. Although Anya would never dance in public again, she practiced. She danced. And danced.

As she slowed to step off of the curb, a man and his dog passed. Nothing to be afraid of, yet she was always alert and constantly fearful, having to convince herself she could handle anything—even and especially Grigory Sergeiovitch Kirillov. She pictured his handsome face as she reached her destination. How she'd like to claw that face.

In the plaza near the Sacred Blood Cathedral, as she approached a seller's stall, Anya kneeled down to pick up a *matryoshka* doll, which had fallen off a vendor's cart. It rolled to her feet. The woman vendor, whose name Anya couldn't recall at the moment—a friend of her quasi mother-in-law, Calina Petrovna Kirillova. The vendor was most upset about the doll falling, and came from behind the stand, flailing her arms, screaming, "Oh you blundering girl, heavens, not that one—that's for a very special customer—on order it was." The woman went at Anya, almost attacking her. Anya was now acutely aware of two things—she couldn't place the woman's accent, and nearby market hawkers had stopped in the middle of their commerce to stare at her and the fat–cheeked screamer.

"I know you?" the fat lady said.

"Did you think I'd pocket it?" Anya said. *Why had the vendor left the doll out if it were such an expensive commodity and if it had already been sold?*

"Important doll," the woman said, her voice an octave lower.

The nesting doll had opened and several inner dolls had spilled out.

"I'll pick them up, don't worry," Anya said in a harsh voice, annoyed with herself and the situation. She continued, trying to sound more cordial. "Calina sent me around to look at your work. In fact, the exact message was for you to give me a doll to bring to her. She told me how lovely your—"

"What did you touch?" the woman snapped.

Anya had stacked the doll and put it in the first line. "This doll was here in front—"

"No, it wasn't. Don't trouble yourself," the woman said out of breath from the exertion of reaching down for one part of the doll.

Carefully Anya put together another doll's top and bottom parts and fit them one inside the other until all nine dolls pieced together perfectly. Just as she was about to replace it, the seller snatched it from her hand and said thanks, repeating, *spasibo,* maybe as a way of asking pardon for being so gruff. "You said Calina sent you. What about her son?"

"Haven't seen him in quite some time. We're divorced," she lied.

"The girl—what's her name?"

"My daughter? Iskra."

"How's she doing?"

"Calina watches her. She—"

"Have you found a job yet? Want to come here and work for me? We should connect—after all we're all involved anyway—"

"Involved?" Anya pointed to the dolls. "I'm afraid I haven't talent for this. I have no creative spark for making things, except a mish-mosh of my life—"

"Do you know how to sell?"

"Forget selling altogether. I've become anti-social. I couldn't convince anyone to buy such a pretty item." Her reflections ran amuck. Only a tourist would buy such a useless article.

The woman was eager to engage Anya in a conversation that would take her where she wasn't willing to go. Yet the woman already discerned so much about Anya. An image leaped into her mind of the last time she'd seen Grigory; it made her shiver.

Anya looked over the dolls. "Which doll do you want me to take to Calina?" When she looked back up the doll seller was talking to another merchant.

Peeved, Anya started to walk away. The wind picked up and she tied her kerchief tighter under her chin. She stopped dead in her tracks as police cars with sirens blaring seemingly from all directions approached and surrounded the square. Two police cars parked on either side of a Gaz 69. More police sirens. More police cars. A black Packard drove onto the square and parked. The driver got out and opened the back door. Anya didn't wait to see who exited the car. A wave of nervous tension hit her and made her feel at once hot and cold, wanting to vomit the little she had in her stomach.

"Wait," the seller yelled. "Come back, girl. Please!"

Anya turned.

The woman, wrapping something in brown paper, beckoned her with a furious hand motion and kept wrapping with the other hand.

Anya began a slow stride back, wondering what she wanted.

"Quickly," the fat lady said. "Here. Take it," she urged, thrusting the wrapped doll into Anya's hands.

"I haven't any money to pay for it." Anya brushed stray hair from her eyes, dark eyes that held sorrow and fear.

"For Calina. No rubles in your pocket? Ha. Doesn't matter. You couldn't afford it. I must go—you go, too." The woman was already passing her hand above the dolls, knocking them over one by one.

Anya counted at least another ten for sure. And for the first time, she looked at the dolls carefully. They weren't painted the usual garish red, oh no, these were etched and burned and carefully carved and the colors went from a muted beige to brown to burnished gold, the eyes like dull jewels. There was one tall one that caught Anya's attention and she passed her hand over it, like the head of a small child.

"This one must hold thirteen dolls at least," she said, admiration in her voice. "She's beautiful."

"Ah! You like? Here, take it too, with my blessings. Now go."

Anya turned her coat pockets inside out for the woman's close inspection.

"No time now, never mind," the woman said and grunted. "You come back when you have money. Ha! Come tomorrow to see if I'm still here. Ha!"

Several policemen fanned the outer fringes of the square, questioning the owners and workers of stands close by the perimeter.

"But wait, girl. Here," she said, hurriedly. "Here," she repeated. "Too late for me to go now. Take this small one. For luck."

"Oh, I couldn't, really."

6

But the vendor wasn't listening, and instead she started to wrap the innermost squat doll in a piece of newspaper. Anya read the date: December 14, 1956. Three days ago. The vendor must have reconsidered, probably not wanting to smudge the beautiful face and dress in the unpainted portions with newsprint because she whipped off her kerchief and wrapped it around the doll's face, and handed it to Anya. "After tomorrow, I'm a dead woman. Take them and go, say the prayer to Saint Ephrem for my soul."

She couldn't be serious. Did Anya even know the prayer?

Then the woman sniggered. "Ha." Again, the mirthless laugh. The bone-chilling wind gusted through Anya's thin, worn wool coat, and she couldn't remember anyone asking for prayers in this god-forsaken city in a long, long time.

"Go now," the woman said, "leave before police question—you innocent. Go. Fly." She made a shooing movement with her hands.

"Thank you," Anya shot back over her shoulder, rushing away before the policemen approached the stand where she had conducted such an odd business transaction.

"Not thanks I need, but a bodyguard and prayers. You keep dolls, missy. I made myself with Calina. Special for special official customer. Better you than the police. Worth big money, you hear?" The woman held up her hand, covered in a gray mitten, the tops of the fingers cut off, and drew her hand in front of her neck. "Go, fast!"

As Anya walked away at a swift pace, she ducked between two stalls, and walked even faster. She stooped down and squinted, noticing in periphery a tall man in a black coat loom over a boy at a stand.

The gray-haired vendor of the stall she was behind said, "Can I help you, Miss? Are you unwell?"

"Fine," she murmured and pointed to the tall man on the outer fringes of the plaza.

"Probably routine police check, but there are more of them than usual today," the gray-haired man said.

Anya stood and turned away from him. Walking briskly, juggling the dolls, she stuffed one glove into her pocket. Struggling to open her coat at the neck, she crammed the two bigger dolls on top of her breasts. Buttoning the coat, but never stopping, she must look like a nursing mother with huge breasts. The tiny doll, she shoved into her pocket, with her ungloved hand. She stopped, pulled on her glove, looking all around. Anya unwound the long shawl she had around her neck folded like a scarf. She threw it around her shoulders to cover the straining buttons and bulging breasts, crisscrossed the ends and tied it at her back. She increased her pace, but stopped short at a screeching sound and people yelling. Afraid to look back, she jogged a few feet and then continued her rapid walk.

Well out of sight of the police cars and the plaza, she stepped into the shadow of a building entrance, looked around to see nobody was near. She whipped off her rucksack and unzipped it, leaving on her shawl. Kneeling on one knee, she took the dolls out of her coat, and shoved them into the pack, and pulled it on once more. She spun into the wind and crossed the Neva River, buttoning her coat, feeling the raw winter Leningrad day fade fast from sunset. What little light had seeped through the clouds went out quickly like pulling the single light bulb chain above a toilet bowl.

Anya stepped over puddles, pushing along feet swathed in felt boots, avoiding the slush that gathers near the curb in respect for the holes in the boot's worn soles. Despite the fact that she'd lined the bottoms with tightly folded newspaper and an old piece of oilcloth for an inner wrapped layer, they leaked in the frigid street water.

All the way to the tram stop, she kept remembering the way the woman had toyed with the dolls, first in such a loving fashion, then knocking them over like so many toy soldiers in the front line of a child's make believe battle. *Were the police cars there for the woman? Did the woman think they'd arrest her? Kill her?* The doll-seller changed immediately from gruff and rough to scared—and what else? The police cars flooded the outer reaches of the square, and the woman's shoulders slumped in resignation to a terrible fate. *Were they after that old lady? What crime against the State could she be guilty of— dangerously making dolls? Making dangerous dolls? What could they possibly hold? poison? homemade bomb parts? drugs?*

Dolls are dolls, nothing precious about them, although there are some famous artists who sign them. No, these had been made from the old one's own hands, hadn't she said so? Calina had painted these colorful ones in delicate shades. Anya had seen her paints and brushes, but couldn't recall if she ever had seen her actually painting. These dolls were the woman's pride and joy, like so many different children. But that awful fake laugh, Ha! And what did she mean by that horrific gesture of slitting her throat? Would she attempt suicide if she were jailed or sent to Siberia?

Anya boarded the trolleybus and took a seat. She slipped off the glove of her left hand and let fall four kopeck coins into her lap. Luckily she'd removed the other glove when she was grappling with her coat to stuff the dolls inside. She'd forgotten about the coins in her glove, her safety net, just like she'd forgotten the vendor's name. Tamara, that was it. How could it have slipped her mind when that's all Calina seems to speak about of late? She looked at the pathetic coins; still they wouldn't have covered the price of a doll, let alone three of them.

If only she had a permanent job. She'd have a monthly Government Issue Pass: tram, bus-trolley, metro, and underground rail issued at any Tabak kiosk or newsstand. It would allow her to board any conveyance at all. She remembered last Sunday how Calina had talked about Anya's getting a GI pass and also getting work in the Hotel Astoria where Calina worked, and where customers often tipped the maids for cleaning their rooms.

Hotel guests gave her foreign currency or rubles. Sometimes they'd give her remains of a box of chocolates, or skin cream, a pair of torn pants, a shirt missing buttons, or even cigarettes and half-empty bottles of perfumes. Calina had practiced begging without seeming to until it became an art. It was a sweet job. Tourists passed her in hallways with her trolley full of scented sheets and she made sure to greet them with a smile. She'd go from room to room cleaning, sometimes finding food left on a tray, or an open bottle of liquor. She'd spirit away a portion of these things, always leaving remnants to cover her thieving. She hoped for tips or even better found articles she'd later use, barter, or sell.

Anya got up and paid the conductor, then sat back down. The doll seller had asked for a prayer to Saint Ephrem. How did the prayer go? She'd heard it as a little girl in one of the onion domed churches, but when? Some feast or holiday. A ceremony. No, not in a church, but in someone's basement. She'd been praying during Great Lent with her mother in some hidden ceremony she was told never to speak about in public. What were the words of supplication? Anya's lips began to move in a silent sing-song rhythm. *O Lord and Master of my life, take from me the spirit of sloth, despondency, lust for power and idle talk. But grant unto me, thy servant, a spirit of chastity, integrity, humility, patience and love. Yea, O Lord and King, grant me to see mine own faults, and not judge my brothers and sisters. For blessed art Thou unto Ages of Ages. Amen.*

Anya was astounded she remembered the prayer in its entirety, and then her mind filled with a title: The Ladder of Divine Ascent. Then two other saints' names came to her: St. Basil the Great, St. John Chrysostom. These had been in the recesses of her brain for a long time, but only now after so many years had they come back to her because Tamara had asked for a prayer.

The seller's words replayed in Anya's mind: *After tomorrow, I'm a dead woman.* Anya's ears deafened like a change in pressure climbing up a mountainside. Her ears popped open when she heard the scream of the wheels turning as the trolley car pulled into Nevsky Prospekt. Soon she'd pick up her daughter from Calina and go to the small, neighborhood market to collect the honey she'd paid for in the morning and left with the pretty braided salesgirl in one of the stalls at the back. When Anya got home, she'd give Iskra the little doll and make herself a good cup of strong black tea, and lace it with vodka and honey. Then the chill would work itself out of her, and she'd feel her blood warm and want to dance like a whirligig, a whirling dervish, dance like she had last weekend with the Gypsies near the military cemetery—dancing like she still had a ballet career ahead of her.

Chapter Two

Andrei Aleksandrovich Garin, a photographer, worked for the *militsiya,* a police force unit. He'd been so preoccupied by the events of the afternoon that he'd inadvertently forgotten the extra film for his camera. He'd made himself a dinner—a bastardized version of his mother's *kasha varnishkes,* and while washing the pots, his mind retraced the afternoon and evening of choreographed chores. That's when it dawned on him he'd forgotten the extra film in his shared office. He dried his hands, went into the bedroom and, just to be sure, searched his satchel. No film. His mind spelled the word: дерьмо, and he said it out loud: "*Der'mo.*" He repeated crap, three times, and tossed his satchel on the unmade bed. He'd have to go back and get it. He needed it for tomorrow morning and his partner Nikolai Vassilievich Fomin would be irate if he showed up for the shoot without it.

Andrei juggled and separated the coals and wood in the little burner, then shrugged into his jacket, threw a woolen scarf around his neck, pulled on a knitted hat. He checked his pockets for gloves, keys and cigarettes, and slammed the door to his two-room rental that had been sectioned off from a small apartment. He skipped down the steps, one gloved hand gliding down the banister, the other hand pulling out his car keys. It had stopped snowing, but the wind had increased and he punched his way forward with alternating thrusts of his shoulders. Key in the ignition, he pumped the gas pedal a few times before turning the key, hoping it wouldn't flood. A miracle. The motor turned over and he pulled out of the parking space. Not a living soul on the road.

Approaching the office building, he turned the corner and pulled to the rear. Nikolai's vehicle was parked in his usual spot. What in hell was he doing here at this hour? Andrei glanced up. Too many office lights on at this hour. What was going on? He gained entrance, flashing his identity card to the familiar guard on duty. "Forgot something upstairs," he said never stopping. He punched the elevator button, but feeling *derganyy*, too antsy to wait, opened the door near the elevator and ran up the stairs to the second floor. About to put his key in the lock, he heard voices and turned the knob. The door to the outer office was unlocked. Lights flooded the hallway as he closed the door behind him.

For some reason, he moved with caution. He walked toward the light. He could see a young man sitting across from Nikolai. *Greet him or just walk on by?* He walked passed Nikolai's open door. Andrei waved, giving the two men a cursory glance. He called to Nikolai. "Working late?" Not waiting for a response, he added, "Forgot the extra film for tomorrow's shoot." He backtracked his steps to stand in the doorway. "Need any help?"

"Just questioning this thug," Nikolai said. "He looked up to no good so I brought him in. But," he glanced at the man, gesturing a thumb towards the door, "You're free to go, Kirillov," Nikolai said, and in a somewhat hushed voice added, "stay clear of that pawnbroker."

With alacrity the man jumped up and scurried out past Andrei. He was tall, almost as tall as Andrei, but leaner and scruffy-looking with mousy brown hair and squinting eyes—like he needed glasses. Andrei pictured the skinny guy wearing horn-rimmed glasses. Bookish-looking. Had he seen him before? Perhaps with the glasses on?

Still standing by Nikolai's office, Andrei unbuttoned his jacket. "What was that about?"

"He looked suspicious—maybe going to try a break-in. Caught him peering in a window. A hood. He had a cover story so I let him go."

"I'll get the film. We can leave together."

Nikolai shook his head. "I want to jot down some notes. In case. You go. I'll lock up."

Andrei went through the door of the next office, found the film where he'd left it on his desk. Retracing his steps toward the exit, he waved the film at Nikolai. "Got it. See you tomorrow. You picking me up early? I want to be done by noon so I can develop the film."

"Hm? Oh sure," Nikolai said, distracted with what was on his mind.

"What time's early for you?" Andrei insisted.

"I said fine. I'll be there."

"Can you make it by eight?" Andrei tried to keep the annoyance out of his voice and leaned on the door opening.

"Only if you bring a thermos of tea." Nikolai looked up as if from a bad dream.

"You bring the sugar."

Driving home, Andrei deliberated on the man he'd seen being inter-rogated by Nikolai, and his first strange impressions, drawing mental pictures. The word reptilian came to mind and for some reason, eyes that oddly enough reminded him of isinglass. Andrei had noted the clothing. The guy wore a black sports coat, a black turtleneck sweater. What was odd about it? Dark green corduroy patches on the sleeves of the coat. What was Nikolai doing interrogating the bum at this late hour? Some-thing didn't square. Nikolai's attitude, almost friendly towards the *prestupnik*—the perp—in custody when Andrei first appeared in the doorway, changed abruptly. Why was Nikolai questioning him? About what? Just because he was peering in a window? Made no sense. When did this take place? Nikolai had lowered his voice to say, "that pawnbro-ker." Dozens of pawnbrokers all over the city. Where? Did Nikolai spot the thug on his way home? Why did he let him go so abruptly? He wasn't writing notes—he gave the impression to be day-dreaming. Why didn't he leave with Andrei?

From there Andrei's ideas bounced back to just a few months ago when he worried over the fact he still might be drafted to fight in the Hungarian Revolution. Ever since then he'd upped his resolution to secure a firm post in the police department. The Hungarian Uprising had been crushed in merely a matter of days from October 23rd to November 10th. Hard to believe that a month had passed or that the Hungarians had made a firm assertion of hate in the Olympics polo match less than two weeks ago on December 6th. He heard news transmitted on radios in the police station. Radio Free Europe and the BBC calling it the "Blood in the Water" match. Hungary's star player, Ervin Zador, and others admitted to the tactic of cursing and insulting the Russian team players in their own language, hoping they'd get angry and lose control. That's precisely what happened. The Russians got physical and blood did flow, and the Hungarians won the semi-final match 4-0. Andrei recalled it was as if a pall had fallen over Headquarters. How could we surpass them but lose in a red pool of water? Andrei kept his ideas to himself—easy with an army and tanks to crush a people fighting with sticks and stones, but something else when it was man to man athletes combating.

Chapter Three

The day after her meeting with the doll seller and after yet another unsuccessful day of job-hunting, Anya went to pick up her daughter, Iskra from Calina, the mother of Iskra's father, Grigory. Anya, a single mother, always referred to Calina as her "mother-in-law"—sometimes even "mother" as Anya didn't remember her own very well. It was late afternoon, and Anya was tired and cold, and it was later than her usual pick-up time. She hoped Calina would give the child something to eat, a collation of sorts, to stave off the child's hunger. Anya had forgotten the honey yesterday. She'd have to go with Iskra to fetch it today.

As she approached the building, there was a hub of people near the entrance. A policeman was trying to get them to disperse. Anya kept her head down and walked on by, retreated a few steps, side-stepped a crush of people, and from the right side walked in the open entrance door while the cop was occupied. Odd, the door being open so she didn't have to use her key. She pocketed it and climbed the three flights of stairs to her "mother-in-law's" apartment, hoping that lout, Grigory, wouldn't be there mooching off his mother. Anya didn't have to knock on the apartment door. It stood ajar, and strange loud voices came from within. Men's voices. And a neighbor sobbing. A sense of dread settled into Anya's soul.

She yelled out to the rubbernecked neighbor in the hallway, "My daughter? The old lady? What happened? Are they hurt?"

Something flashed inside the corridor. It was the bulb of a police photographer's camera. The man's face looked shadowed with a beard he'd never had time to shave.

"Step back, please. Hey, miss, where the hell do you think you're going?" he asked.

"This is my mother-in—my mother's apartment. She tends to my child while I look for work. My little girl is in there with her. What's happened, officer?" she asked with politeness that revolted her, wanting to say, *Ment! Musur!* Filthy copper!

Another officer, a bovine man, came out of the apartment with broad yellow tape, black printed letters spelling out: *OSTOROZHNOST*, caution, as he started to pull it across the doorway.

"Just a minute. I've a right to go in there. That's my daughter and my mother. You can't treat people like this." Anya tried to push past him, thinking, You hunk of sausage.

"Hold your skinny ass right there," the heavy-set man in uniform said.

"Watch your mouth," she said.

"Pipe down, miss." The guy holding the camera said.

"What's your name? Where do you live? What's your, what was your mother's name?" the police photographer asked.

"Was? What's happened? *Bozhe moy*. Oh my God. Is she dead?"

"I didn't say that," the photographer said, pulling a pad and pencil from his back pants' pocket. He turned to the beefy officer. "Right away, they jump the gun. I've got this, Nikolai."

"Well, she is dead," the hefty cop said in a flat voice. "Can't hide a corpse."

"No! No! That's impossible. We were together talking just a few hours ago," Anya cried out, trying to force her way past the huge hulk blocking the doorway.

"Smooth, Nikolai, very smooth," the younger copper, the unshaven *ment* not in uniform said to the monster.

"Who are you to reproach me? And by the way where were you when I needed you yesterday, Garin?"

"What?" Garin said to Nikolai's back as he reentered the apartment.

"Not here. I'll see you in my office," Nikolai said over his shoulder.

"Out of my way. Let me in—my little girl!" Anya cried out, "You brute." She shoved him, muttering, "Beast."

The photographer intervened, stepping between Anya and the cop.

"Calm down, lady. Here," the photographer said and slung the camera over his shoulder. He took out a card from the wallet in his back pocket and called to the other officer, "Give me one of your cards for the lady," but apparently he didn't hear. The photographer turned back to her. "My name's Garin. Andrei Aleksandrovich Garin," the name rolling off his tongue, almost as if it were rehearsed.

She looked at the card and read his name. Disoriented, she looked up into his green eyes. She had to steady herself to reach for the banister. *Where had she seen those eyes?*

"What's your name?"

"Anya Ivanovich Andreyeva."

"Your surname isn't your mother's?"

"My professional name." In a soft voice, barely audible, she said, "The truth is I never married Calina's son, Grigory Sergeiovitch Kirillov. I'd have had to print my intent to divorce in the newspaper and then wait ten years for a divorce."

"Kirillov? Now I know why it's familiar—I've heard that name recently during an interrogation. Not your brother?"

"Brother? *Niet.* My ex—it's a miracle how he evades someone's knife or prison."

"Do you know what your surname Andreyeva means?"

She shook her head. "I can't even think."

"It means 'property of Andrei.' That's my name," he quipped. "Sorry. Are you all right?" Garin asked.

"I feel like I'm drowning. This isn't real." *Is this guy flirting with me? Where had she seen eyes that intense color green before? He looked familiar. A woman could make a living batting long eyelashes like his.*

She took hold of his card. "What's happened here? I implore you to—was it *prestupniki?*"

"We don't know if it was criminals or something else. Wait," Andrei Garin said, and pointed. "See that man? He's my partner Nikolai Vassilievich Fomin. I'll introduce you. He'll tell you more."

Anya stood by, tears stung her eyes. Something awful had occurred and she still wasn't privy to it.

"Have a heart, Fomin," Andrei Garin said to the other officer, and nudged his head toward the inner part of the apartment.

Raising her voice, Anya said, "What's going on?"

"There's been a break-in and—" Garin scratched the back of his neck.

"Please I beg you. Tell me everything," Anya said.

"This is now a crime scene because—" the hefty officer started to say.

Just then there was a distracting movement from inside the apartment.

A little voice called, "*Mamasha.*"

"Iskra!" Anya screamed. The little girl ran, arms outstretched and flailing down the ill-lighted hall toward her mother and into her waiting arms.

"Your Mama's here. What happened, darling?" Anya said, brushing back the hair from Iskra's face. The mother wiped the daughter's tears from the child's blank and expressionless eyes. "What happened, sweet girl?"

"As I was saying," the husky officer said with an edge to his voice, "because a murder was committed."

Instinctively, Anya covered her daughter's ears. *Had she heard? Did she know? Understand?*

"My *Babushka*," Iskra said, and then hesitated.

"Your Grandmother what?" Anya coaxed.

"She said it was too cold to go to school this morning. Someone was coming to see her. Maybe the trams aren't working because it snowed so much."

"Go on, dear." Anya brushed hair out of the child's eyes.

"Ma'm, please, don't ask her any more—she'll need to be questioned again," Garin said.

"Again? Can't you see the poor child has an infirmity and she's traumatized?"

"Orders are orders—" Garin shook his head.

Anya held her daughter close and rocked her.

Garin said, "You have a beautiful name, Iskra, do you know what it means?

"Mamushka says it means 'spark' because I lit up her life when I was born."

"Tell your *Mama* what happened. Come on, baby girl, tell me, *malyska*." Anya finger-combed the child's messy hair.

"Every day after school I wait for Babushka—"

"That would be her Grandmother, right?" Garin interrupted.

Anya nodded, and rubbed the child's shoulder so she'd continue talking.

"She comes to get me from school and then sometimes I hide under the bed until after Papa leaves on the days he comes. I always hide with my things until he's gone. But today Babushka didn't think I needed to, but just in case it's a strange *mal'chik,* maybe I should hide just the same. She told me, Put your things beneath the bed as if Papa's coming. So my things were already hidden under the bed. Lunch pail. Pinafore. Coat. Galoshes. And books."

"A lad? A man? Who?" Garin asked.

"Maybe she said *gangstery*? Sometimes she uses that word. Not sure if that was today or yesterday," Iskra said.

Anya looked up at Garin and gave an exasperated sigh, shaking her head slowly from side to side.

She turned back to her daughter. "Why should she think it was gangsters? Go on, love," Anya enticed the child.

Iskra looked puzzled. "Once she told me she secrets away valuables. What's valuables, *Mat*?" Not waiting for an answer, Isrka continued. "Babushka heard steps on the stairwell. She looked scared, put her finger over her lips—our sign for quiet and go like a mouse under the bed. So I did. And I stayed. Quiet. A long time. Even after the screams. I put my hands over my ears so I wouldn't make a sound. Not when the man stood in front of her dresser pulling out her clothes. Then *kerwhack*. And again *kerwhack*. Here and there and more till all seven dresser drawers smashed. How will she fix them?"

"Was the man your Papa?" Garin asked.

"No." Iskra shook her head.

Apparently overhearing, the bullish policeman's approach, the ununiformed cop asked with kindness, "How do you know, little girl?"

"Babuska told me Papa was held in the arms of the devil before he was born. That's why God punished him and he walks with a club foot sometimes when he's tired. He walks with one foot a bit dragging. After he steps with the good foot he erases it with the bad one."

Fomin raised his eyebrows at Garin, and stepped in back of Anya.

"Now, ma'm, I'm sorry but we really have to bring her down to our headquarters," Garin said. When someone pulled Anya's arms back-

21

ward, she looked over her shoulder to see Nikolai Fomin. She yelled, "What the hell are you doing?"

"Fomin, let her go," Garin said.

Iskra stamped her feet. "The *kerwack* man not my Papa. He walks straight. And has different shoes. Not like Papa."

"What's she babbling about? We'll find out later." Fomin shoved the little girl forward and stormed off. "Garin, I'm inside if you need me."

Another officer whisked Iskra into the air, but the child struggled like a slippery fish out of water so much so she fell from his arms like the *matryoshka* doll in the square but Garin caught her.

"Hush now," Garin said softly, and put her down and squatted next to her. "Don't be upset. I'm listening to you. Tell me like it's a secret. Whisper in my ear. What kind of shoes was the man wearing?"

"Mmm." She looked down at Garin's feet, shook her head, and then looked around at the other men's feet. She put her hand in front of her mouth and said into Garin's ear, "Like that man's."

"Which one?"

Iskra took her hand down and pointed to the police shoes Nikolai wore. Then she began to cry. Anya picked her up and cradled her, crooning. Soon the child stopped crying. In a voice meant for the officer but sounding as though she were singing a lullaby to the child, Anya crooned, "Now you see, now you see what comes of trying to force my baby?"

Just then another cop came out of the apartment. Another *ment*—maybe this time Anya would learn something.

"This is Sasha, oh sorry, I mean, Alexandr Abramovich Sokolov, a senior officer," Garin said. He asked Anya for his card back, wrote his number on it and then handed it back to her. "Whenever you can get her to this address, we need to ask her a few things. Call me if she says anything more about this *ugolovnoye delo*."

"Criminal case?" Anya covered Iskra's ears. "You cold-hearted bastard," she mouthed, still cradling the child's head on her shoulder. Garin stood and tried to hide the shock, saying through gritted teeth, "Watch your mouth. I get you're upset, but these men aren't so understanding. He pulled his face back but took a step closer to Anya. He punched his clenched fist into his other hand, and shook his head as if to say, Get my meaning? He said aloud, "Look, lady, it's been a long day for us. We had another case today before this one."

"Sorry." Anya put her head down and stepped back. "Let me ask her. Tell me what you need to know and I'll get the answers." In a low voice now, she said, "Don't frighten this helpless darling anymore. My poor hapless halfwit. I beg you."

Garin scribbled something down on paper and handed it to Anya.

"I'll call you with this information, but first tell me exactly what happened in there," Anya said, nodding toward the apartment.

"The lady who lived in the apartment—"

"Calina."

He leaned toward her. "Yes, Calina. Was murdered." His voice softened as he whispered near Anya's ear. It was obvious he didn't want the child to hear. "I'm sorry to say, she was bludgeoned to death. I don't think the child knows she's dead. I told her Grandma was in a profound sleep. She's an observant little tyke for she asked me why Babushka wasn't in bed sleeping but on the floor covered in an old blanket. I told Iskra that Grandma was so exhausted she fell asleep on the floor and we covered her, but she must not be disturbed."

Anya covered her mouth with one hand and put the other on his chest to steady herself, imagining blood all over the place. Such horrid words, such warm breath near her ear, and the clean scent of him. She tore her hand away from him.

Garin stood above them. Anya picked up the child and set her down, the two of them on the step below Garin. Anya read the question from the paper and asked Iskra. "How do you know for sure it was a man by the dresser if you were under the bed?"

"I peeped."

"Peeked. And?"

"He had long trousers of heavy rough stuff—and heavy shoes of a man. Not that man," she said, and pointed to Sokolov's shoes this time. This cop wore boots different than the shoes of the beefy one, and said to Garin, "Perhaps Iskra saw these men after the perpetrator left and is confused."

"How do you know for sure it wasn't your Papa?" Garin asked, his tone gentle.

"Papa has small feet and was carried in the devil's arms. He doesn't have those shoes."

"What the hell does that mean?" Nikolai loomed above them.

"She means the man didn't have a damaged foot," Anya interpreted. "Watch the language, please." *O, Khristos! Oh Christ, and here I'm telling him not to curse when I even think in curses.*

Andrei Garin, the officer with the camera, had moved away. Was that in deference to the brusque officer who'd interrupted?

To clear the area of more on-lookers who had gathered, Nikolai Fomin said, "That's it, folks, main attraction's over. Scurry along now."

It welled-up in her before she had time to think and she blurted out, "Nice bedside manner you have."

"Just doing our job, comrade," Fomin said.

In spite of herself, Anya smiled, thinking, What a dickhead. Nikolai Fomin had already turned and started walking away when Garin returned. Under her breath, she said, "What is it with you guys? You're supposed to be the good guys, but you're as tough maybe even meaner than the *Bratva,* the brotherhood."

"Whew. Quite a mouthful," Garin said. "Comparing us to mafia-type bandits? Careful what you say, Ma'm."

Garin turned and called out to Sokolov, "Hey, what's the story, Sasha? Close to finishing?"

Alexandr Sokolov nodded and stepped back inside the apartment for a minute. He came out and closed the door. "Guys from the morgue are on their way," he said. "The rest of the team also. Let's hope they've not all been drinking shots, honoring the souls or the dead they've already picked up earlier, and they're in fair condition to take this situation under control."

Garin said, "I want to be notified on fingerprints and evidence—"

"Sure, but what's it to you? You're not on the force."

Garin glared at him as though he wanted to gut-punch him. Anya didn't understand what had transpired, but the animosity weighed in the air. She didn't understand why this man was questioning her if he wasn't part of the police crew. *And why wasn't he in uniform? Undercover?*

Garin said between his teeth, "As a favor then?"

"I'll make sure you and Nikolai both get a copy," Sokolov said, and added, "as a favor. Of course."

"*Konechno,*" Garin repeated.

Anya caught Andrei looking down at her just at that moment. *How much had her strange little girl, eyes almost yellow in the sickly hall light seen and understood?* Anya returned his look.

His voice softened. "Want a lift somewhere? It's late. You don't have to get the kid down to headquarters today."

Anya balked at the word headquarters, thinking, the *mentovka,* the cop shop.

Both Alexandr Sokolov and Nikolai Fomin came out of the apartment, speaking in hushed tones.

Garin interjected, "Look, I'm taking the missus here home with the kid. I'll pick her up and bring her around to the office tomorrow first thing. She needs to get a bite and put the doll to bed."

Sweet reference to Iskra, but at the mention of doll, she touched her breast, remembering she had removed the dolls. *Was that only yesterday? More like a century ago.* In a rush yesterday, she'd forgotten her rucksack at home before picking up Iskra. Today Anya had intended to give the dolls to Calina, who appeared anxious to have them. However, Anya had showed them to her neighbor and had inadvertently left them with her. The cold and damp of the steps seeped through, and now she was glad she hadn't taken off her coat.

Sokolov looked at Garin and gestured with his thumb toward Anya. "Yeah, be the good guy, why don't you and get her something to eat, Garin?"

"Get the kid's things inside," Fomin said to Garin.

Garin handed Anya his camera. "Don't mess with the evidence," he said, patted Iskra's head, and winked at her mother. Then he ducked underneath the tape and walked into the apartment. Garin bent down to pick up something near the wall. It looked like a pack of cigarettes. A few minutes later he came out, arms loaded with Iskra's hidden paraphernalia. "Everything was still under the bed." He smiled a lopsided grin.

"I hate to ask, I should have before, but did Calina leave something cooked? I haven't eaten and bet Iskra hasn't either," she said.

He nodded and went back into the apartment. He came out a few minutes later with a glass jar wrapped in a cloth and handed it to her. "Here, soup."

"Thanks, Officer Garin," Anya said, in a polite tone, thinking of her ex-husband Grigory for the first time in a long time without an epithet before or after his name. *How will he take his mother's death? Could he have been involved?* Anya pictured the way he looked standing on the bridge after they'd become lovers, a cigarette dangling from this mouth, smoke trailing heavenward. She dizzied at the remembrance, recalling how she walked toward him tipsy as though the earth had slipped from its axis.

"The least I could do," Garin said.

"How did the cops know she was killed?"

"Door was wide open. A neighbor found her and reported it. Iskra had fallen asleep under the bed."

She stood up gently tugging Iskra's hand so she'd stand too. She dressed the girl in coat and galoshes, and tied a scarf around her head. She put the soup jar in her rucksack, hefted the books, and they walked down the three flights of stairs and exited the building. An old battered navy blue Peugeot was parked across the wide boulevard.

Chapter Four

It had been cold when Anya went into the building and now when she exited it, the wind picked up and the air was glacial. Juggling Iskra's articles, Anya awkwardly pulled her coat collar up and closed the lapel at the neck. How Anya longed for the warmth of a car heater. They walked across to Garin's car, obviously not the Peugeot, but a jalopy, a 1946 M20 "Pobeda." Some Victory model, a *razvaluha*—a falling apart car—surely rescued from a junk heap on the outskirts of town. He was steering them straight for it. As for a heater? This heap had four doors and windows that might roll up.

The smashed, dented, rusted out car had been dark forest green, but still had a visible license plate number 3NT 2736. In its heyday, Anya had read somewhere that it did 105 km per hour. This one would be lucky to hit 37 km/h.

Snow began to fall. As the first large flakes swirled in the headlights of the car, Andrei said, "It won't stick."

"Wait till the flakes get smaller with bigger intentions," Anya said. The child in her lap was already asleep.

"Snow's too wet." Andrei wiped off the inside of the fogged-up window. "We've got about twenty minutes to go. Need to stop somewhere?"

"No thanks. Hey, look there. Ahead under the street lamp. See. The flakes are smaller and they intend to blanket this city before daybreak. Bet on it?" Her dark eyes flashed.

The wind picked up the fairy-like fluff and deposited a great gust-full on top of the windshield.

"*Der'mo.* Crap," Andrei muttered. He got out of the car and with his arm wiped off his side of the windshield and then ran to the other side and did the same.

"Damn wipers," he announced, getting back in behind the wheel with a cold blast as he slammed the door.

There was hardly any traffic. Andrei slowed for a red light, looked both ways and downshifted, sending the small car into a bit of a spin which righted itself as he tore across the intersection.

"Forgive my gruffness before. Sorry about your mother. They'll take her to the morgue. I can accompany you if you'd like. Tomorrow. You said you're out of work, if I—"

"I can't stop thinking about Calina. Why would somebody murder her?" Anya flicked away tears. "I can't understand why someone would rob her. She wasn't rich. Calina was—"

"Calina? Your mother."

"Not my mother."

He decelerated the car to a dead stop, and looked at Anya. "But you said—"

"She's—she was Iskra's father's mother. I'm a single mother. Haven't you ever told a lie to get what you wanted?"

"Not married. So your professional name is your real name then?"

Anya nodded. "I needed to see what happened to Calina and if my daughter was all right. She was kind to my daughter—you can see the child's not right. Her father abandoned us when he understood the girl would always remain backward."

"You know the dead woman's friends and acquaintances—got any idea who might have something against her?"

Anya shook her head with vehemence, thinking back and remembering Tamara, the doll-seller saying that Calina was what you'd call a pistol, not to say, pisser. Visibly shaken, Anya said, "Calina came up nard. Took care of her son by herself. Born in blood and unwanted, she sweated and cried over him. He's just—"

"Look, it's ok if you don't want to talk about it now."

She looked out the window.

"This isn't a line, believe me when I say it, but you look familiar," Garin said.

Anya was quiet, thinking she couldn't consider it a line. Hadn't she supposed the same thing about him earlier outside Calina's apartment?

"Here. Pull up here, Garin." Anya pointed.

"No one's around to hear. You can call me Andrei."

"We can walk from here, Garin."

"What about sleeping beauty?" Andrei said. "Want me to carry her?"

"I'll throw her over my shoulder like a sack of new potatoes. I always do. I'll manage. You've been kind. I didn't expect it from your manner before."

"Hey, that wasn't me that was Nikolai—don't confuse us. Let me help you with her."

His eyes were startling—in this light they were the soft color of moss on a shady side of a rock just hit by a sunburst.

"*Spasibo,*" she said, thanking him.

"*Pozhalujsta.*"

"But no. You'll want me to answer more questions, and I need to drink some tea . . . oh—"

"What is it? Forget something?"

"I was going to take Iskra to the market for some honey."

He laughed.

"What's so funny?"

He reached into his pocket and brought out two brown sugar cubes.

"A miracle."

"There's never any sugar in the office. I like to sip my tea with the cube in my mouth like a good Russkie."

"Like? Aren't you one?"

He let the question hang in the air. "I'll tell you something about me if you make me tea. A cube for you, and one for me."

Anya hesitated. The wind picked up. She should say no and trudge through the snow and up the five flights of stairs to the top floor of her tenement building alone. But she was tired and disconcerted by earlier events and somehow tonight she wanted to be in the company of a man. Any man would do. However, this was one night she couldn't go out in search of a connection or score. She couldn't leave Iskra sleeping with the door open so the neighbor lady Yelizaveta could hear the child cry out. *Net podklycheniye*—no hooking up—to help pay for some food and heating materials. Anything to stave off the loneliness that always engulfed her at night. Too bad this one was *politsiya*. But for once, maybe she'd feel safe, having someone from the police close to her.

"You offered to carry her," she said, her tone indifferent, wondering if he were part of NKVD, recalling what the initials stood for: *Narodny Komissariat Vnutrennih Del*, The People's Commissariat for Internal Affairs. This one night, dangerous or not—although he was a police photographer. Did that mean he was a copper, too? A law officer? Did he have the same authority as that lout Nikolai?

Andrei got out of the driver's side, opened the passenger door and Anya handed Iskra up to him. "A rag doll." Awkwardly, he took the burden.

Anya shivered against the cold blast as she clambered out of the car with all of the bundles, and the rucksack.

When they got to the top floor, Anya opened the door. She let the bundles fall to the floor, placing her pack more gently, as she remembered the soup. In the dim light shafting in through the kitchen window from the street, she fumbled for a match on a sideboard to light a candle.

"There. Let there be light." She removed the eviction notice leaning on the candle and pocketed it. She beckoned Andrei to follow her. He trailed behind her. Anya looked back. He was tired from the exertion of carrying the child up the many flights of stairs. She was well acquainted with that feeling. Precisely.

Anya pointed and he dumped his package unceremoniously on the double bed. Anya undressed Iskra. "Here," she said to Andrei, "I'm like a cat used to doing things in the dark. Take the candle and hunt us up something to eat. Put water in the kettle for tea." She waved toward the hallway which led back to the kitchen.

When he came back to the bedroom he'd taken off his coat, and run his fingers through his wet, shiny hair. She did a double take. He had the face of a chiseled statue of a god she'd seen somewhere—a museum, perhaps.

"How did you manage to get this *khrushchyovka* apartment in a block and not a communal one?"

She gave a wry smile at the name, knowing it was a combination of Krushchev for his invention of the poorly but quickly constructed buildings plus a name for a Russian slum.

"I lived in a communal when I was with Grigory, but he stole from the others—robbed whatever he could to pawn it. They had us evicted when Iskra was born and then he decamped. Escaped. Like a pigeon, flew the roost! I might get evicted from here, too, if I don't pay *vzyatka* to the man who set himself up as the concierge/handyman."

"A bribe? That's illegal?"

"Really? Don't sound so indignant. Have you ever been desperate? Taken chances for loved ones you can't support? Hidden things from our precious government—oh but no, of course not, you're a part of it.

32

There's much you need to learn about how the real citizens live here in Leningrad, copper."

Anya shed her coat now and the *matryoshka* doll she'd set on a wooden box tumbled to the floor with a clattering noise. She picked it up and righted it on the box next to the bed that served as a night table.

"No money for food, but you buy dolls?"

"Uh-uh." She shook her head.

"What, you stole it?"

"You police think you know everything. No," she said, a tinge of annoyance in her voice. "A vendor gave it to me. In fact, she gave me three of them. Really beautiful ones, not the run-of the mill you see on all the tourist stands here and in Moscow. She was frightened by something yesterday when police cars came from all sides into the plaza, and—she's a friend of Calina's."

"You said she had no friends."

"I lied."

"Police cars?"

Anya covered her daughter with her coat. She sighed. "Doesn't matter anyway—does it?" She could have kicked herself for giving away innocent information, but how would he construe it?

"Odd," he said.

"What?"

"Oh nothing—it's probably a coincidence, but there was a murder committed yesterday evening, perhaps late afternoon—can't remember where exactly, but it was a woman and she had a vendor's license to sell from a stall."

"I'm sure the police wouldn't have killed her with people mingling on the streets."

"No. Something else." He plopped down on the bed next to Iskra. "There's been a small lead to a smuggling ring—I doubt there's a connection. The dolls would've had to be a meter high to be able to transport Turkish hashish."

Anya remembered her own thinking about the dolls. "Some of them are a bit large—it's not possible." Why had she spoken so unguardedly?

"How high was the biggest one, really?"

"Oh maybe fifteen or twenty centimeters," thinking more like half a meter. Pleased with herself at the quick lie. She'd shown them to her neighbor, meaning to take them to Calina, but had accidentally forgotten them in Yelizaveta's apartment.

Anya stood awkwardly for a moment, and Garin, too, looked down at the sleeping child as if they were adoring parents until the blare of the teakettle whistle.

He shrugged his shoulders. "You're lying. Even I know they make larger ones. Never mind," he said, his attitude sheepish. "Conjecture gets me into trouble every time, too. Coincidence? Although, perhaps not hash, what about pure dope?"

"Did I not say the dolls were empty? Not exactly empty, one nestled inside the other to the smallest one." Her response came out too gruffly.

"What did the policemen look like?"

"I didn't stay around long enough to find out. It was none of my business." She walked toward the kitchen.

She lowered the gas flame under the kettle, which continued to whistle, and then she lit another candle. Anya looked around. *Can't even tell the place needs a painting in the dim light.* She removed the kettle but didn't extinguish the flame. "Warmer this way, don't you think?" She stifled a yawn.

She swished boiling water around in a cracked porcelain teapot and unceremoniously tossed the water into an unwashed pot in the sink. She reached into a tin canister and brought out one scoop of loose tea, placed it in a strainer angled into the pot and poured boiling water into it. She set out the last two of her glasses that had metal holders. After ⸜ minutes of silence, steam rose from the pot, both of them entrenched in their own thoughts. She poured the tea into one glass, and then the other.

Like a child at school recess, Andrei took out his hoarded treasure and handed one of the cubes to her. She took it, placed it in her mouth and holding it in between her teeth, clinked glasses.

"To good Russkie, one and all." He smiled and took the steaming glass in his hand and brought it to his lips. He blew on the hot liquid and took tiny sips, until the sugar had melted and there was no more weak tea in his glass.

Russkie. She hadn't heard that expression in a long time. She fidgeted. He was sizing her up—but for what? Ah . . . she may as well tell him now and end the mystery. She took hold of a bottle of vodka from underneath the curtained sink and waved it.

He nodded. "Ah, yes, some Vitamin V."

She took down two tiny upside-down bell-shaped glasses, a "wedding present" from her ballet instructor, and poured for both of them, making furtive glances his way. He had dirty blondish hair and freckles on the backs of his huge hands. His nails were clean. He had a broken nose, which hadn't been reset correctly and which gave him a tender yet tough demeanor all at once. The nose, a little flattened, must have been quite nicely formed before. His eyes, this very second, were as cold as dawn. This man had been hurt. Physically for sure, but there was another kind of hurt he wore like a mantle, the kind that said, I've got this chip on my shoulder and I dare you to knock it off, World.

She drained her glass. "More?" Not waiting for an answer, she tipped in more vodka into their glasses.

He cleared his throat and moved the glass across the small table till it touched hers. Andrei Garin took out a pack of cigarette papers, a pouch of tobacco, rolled himself a smoke, lit it, and took a drag.

"Why don't you smoke one of the cigarettes from the pack you found at Calina's?"

"Ah," he said, reaching into his shirt pocket under his sweater. He tossed her the pack. "For you . . . a bribe."

Anya took hold of the pack. "Calina didn't smoke and Grigory doesn't smoke either—he's a health fanatic. Perhaps these belong to one of the brigands who killed Calina, or," she hesitated, "maybe your investigating officers."

Andrei looked at the pack as if he were trying to recollect something. "Belomorkaval cigarettes," he said, deliberation in his tone.

"Something to keep in mind for your case," she said. "That's it, isn't it? What you're trying to do is solve this. Why?"

"To get a promotion to the force. Maybe. I need you to tell me everything you know about Calina. Before we go to the station tomorrow. Can you do that? With honesty?"

"How long do you intend to stay, Garin?" She pointed to his cigarette.

"As long as it takes. Will you please call me Andrei?"

Anya sighed. "On the afternoon I came home from the hospital, Calina began to nurse me. It was after Grigory, my ex, her son beat the living crap out of me. All during the rest of my pregnancy with Iskra, Calina nursed me and told me her life story parsed out piecemeal. Some people have photographic minds, but I have the knack of hearing a thing once and pretty much have it memorized. I think it has something to do with music. This is what I know from Calina."

Garin kept his eyes on Anya as if she were acting on stage and he needed to catch her every movement. "Tell me."

"Calina was sixteen. An orphan. Her father had been killed in an undercover operation for the Military Police. Her mother died in childbirth. Calina spent most of her childhood being shifted and shuffled around from aunt to uncle, to cousin, to orphanage. Finally she had finished some schooling and had learned enough to become a baker's apprentice, having baked every day for four years in the school orphanage. One day when enough was truly enough, she walked out the front door, never turning back and never again speaking to any of the rotten relatives who had abused and used her as a sex slave or servant. She had pondered on only one thing in those last four years, freedom, and to be her own person, to be on her own, to survive or die, but doing it in control of herself. Calina was one of the lucky ones, who fell through the cracks of Russian Communist rule.

"Near the bakery where she worked, boys raped her in back of an old fenced-in-wreck-of-a-building, still not completely demolished. Boys from the neighborhood. They were street smart, savvy about how the strong could prey upon the weak. They were undisciplined, unruly and a gang who could expect to spend part of their life in the *Glavnoye Upravleniye Ispravitelno-trudovykh Lagerej i kolonij,* our well-known Gulag.

"Calina lay in her own blood for an eternity until one of the neighbors who had witnessed the scene from a window rushed to unearth her husband's hunting knife buried in the slats of the floor under the kitchen sink. Then she dashed to a friend's apartment for help and went running out to Calina. The older woman arrived on the scene armed with the hunting knife and in the company of another, a younger woman behind her, holding a broomstick.

"The woman with the knife wanted to know what happened, but she already could well-imagine. She stood over Calina and bent to help her sit up. Calina didn't know whether to laugh or cry, thinking about the defense these two women offered. But they were women and they had come to succor her. The woman told her she was a mess and asked if she was a virgin.

"Calina almost laughed again, but it hurt her too much. She could only shake her head and tell the woman that those ruffian boys had followed her every day after work at the bakery, but nobody would listen. They mocked and called her names, threw things, jeered, hissed in her ears, told her they'd get her and have her front and back. Pigs. She told the bakery owner, but he only said to walk or run faster when they pursued her, and then he pursued her more, and cornered her like a rat in his stinking basement among the flour sacks.

"I remember Calina telling me one of the women had said, That bastard, Rykoff. I'll walk a kilometer from now on, but I won't buy his stinking bread. The lady with the knife wrapped the blade in a handkerchief and put it in her apron. At that precise moment, Calina asked, 'Am I going to bleed to death? Am I dying?' Needless to say, she was overwrought and distraught."

Anya's voice changed as her recitation of Calina's story continued. It was like she inhabited the lives of all the participants.

"Then the other lady with a babushka tied beneath her chin stepped forward."

'I'm Rada, a nurse. You're still bleeding, but can you walk to that building there where Ludmilla sighted you—see the open window? My rooms are below. Can you make it if you use us as crutches?'

Calina indicated her belongings. 'How will I carry my bag of things?'

'What bag? Where is it?' Rada asked.

'They threw it over there somewhere. My *avoska* also.' Calina pointed again.

'Wait,' Ludmilla said. 'I'll get it.'

"Out of the corner of her eye, Calina saw the woman bend down and stuff the items which had fallen out back into the bag. She then picked up the smaller *avoska*, known as a serviceable *perhaps bag*, closed with a tied string. Its uses many and for whenever needed. She carried it over to where Calina was and said, 'I'm strong. I can manage these and you.' She put her arms through the cord handles of the hemp bag. 'Looks like a flour sack,' she said.

'It is,' Calina said.

'Let's lift her,' Rada said to Ludmilla. 'Grab her from under the arm; then turn into her and let her lean on us, ready, count: *odin, dva, tri.*'"

~

Anya watched Andrei pour another tot of vodka for himself. She took another swig of hers.

"Continue the tale? More of the story?"

"*Da,*" Garin sipped his drink.

~

"Stretched out on the couch in Rada's apartment, Calina experienced a safe feeling she hadn't in a long time. She told me Rada gave her a cup of strong tea followed by a shot of vodka and then another, telling her to drink it, because she was going to need it.

Rada said, 'I'm going to have to sew you up with some stitches. You've been brutalized badly—I'm also giving you a tetanus shot.'

Stunned, Calina asked, 'How do you have all this medical equipment?' She raised her hand toward a tray of instruments and vials.

'Stolen from the hospital. They put me on night duty after six weeks of straight days and no break. I was exhausted and . . . how do you say that, Ludmilla?'

'Pissed off,' Ludmilla said. 'Rada doesn't curse or swear—I do it for her, married to a trucker and a hunter made me feisty.' She clenched her

39

fist in the air near her ear and shook it. I don't take none of his crap, not since the first beating.'

'Worse. You caught all his bad habits,' Rada said.

'You two could be a theater comedy act,' Calina said, feeling a bit woozy.

'Here,' Rada said. 'Drink.'

'No more vodka, please.' Calina shook her head.

'*Da, da*, more vodka. Then lie back. I'm going to wash and shave you down there and sew. So if you need to, just go on and faint. But hand me that glass first,' Rada said.

Calina handed back the jelly jar glass.

'Ludmilla, get me the hot water, soap and razor.' Rada lifted Calina like a baby about to have its diaper changed, and placed a rubber mat beneath her. Calina shivered. Rada lifted the girl again and this time, placed a warm, fluffy towel between her buttocks and the rubber mat.

'No need for modesty here,' Ludmilla said, carrying in the basin of hot soapy water and a man's razor.

'How come you're both not working now?' Calina asked, by now her words a little slurred.

'I'm on sick leave,' Ludmilla said. 'Good and sick of being over-worked, and she's on probation from the hospital. A horny doctor made a pass at her, and she, stupid girl that she is, denied him his secret passion. Lucky she wasn't fired.' Ludmilla cocked her head a bit toward her friend.

'A savage. Probably related to those gang boys who did this. One of them could grow up to become chief surgeon and marry a country girl to make a lot of babies and become so tired she doesn't give a hoot if he messes with every nurse in the hospital. Now, I'm finished shaving you. Take a deep breath, child, what's your name?'

'Calina.'

'Hold that breath, Calina, as long as possible, then let it out slowly.' Rada took the threaded needle from the tray and began to sew. She turned slightly, 'Hold her, Ludmilla.'

Calina whimpered but did not cry out at first. Then, in distress and pain, her eyes wild with fear, Calina was about to scream, but Ludmilla clamped a hand over the girl's mouth.

'Ach, it wouldn't do, dearie, to let the neighbors know about our little operation, now would it?' Ludmilla crooned.

Calina fought to raise her shoulders and struggled to remove the iron-clamped hand over her mouth, but Ludmilla kneeled beside her and placed her forearm across the girl's chest and pushed her down.

'She's blessedly passing out,' Calina heard Ludmilla say as if from down a well, stroking the patient's wet forehead and then in a soft voice, 'There, there now, almost done.'

When Calina awakened, Ludmilla had gone and Rada was cooking something in the kitchen. The smell of boiling vegetables reached Calina. She tried to sit up, but was too weak. She flopped down on the makeshift bed, covered with a blanket while a pillow propped up her head and shoulders.

Rada's two little boys were asking their mother questions, like bullets flying from firing squad rifles.

~

Anya coughed. She reached into her pocket and pulled out a handkerchief, wiped her eyes and settled down. "I'll tell you the rest of Calina's story, but first I need to use the WC."

When Anya returned, she eyed the contents of the bottle and poured a thimble full of vodka and sipped it.

"Calina listened to Rada's boys and then more closely to the rumbling noises her stomach was making. She was hungry and the broth smelled delicious. She was so used to eating bread that the pleasant perfume of the vegetable soup made her mouth water. She looked toward the window. She'd been out for quite a long time. The afternoon had bequeathed a sullen evening sky that darkened quickly. Less street noise came through the open window in the kitchen. Calina could almost smell the warm bread baking in the *pekarnja,* the bakery where she worked."

~

Calina called out, 'Please,' and one of the boys turned. 'Hand me that bag over there on the floor.' The boy did so. Calina extracted a paper wrapped loaf of bread. 'Here,' she said to the boy. 'Give this to your mother.'

Rada came closer. 'Thanks so much,' she said.

Calina turned toward her and grimaced. 'I'm sorry, I've nothing else to give you and you've been so kind. I must be going now.'

'This is wonderful.' Rada sniffed the fresh bread. 'A real gift. And you're not going anywhere. Do you even have a place to go to?'

'I live in an abandoned building near here,' Calina's face flushed.

Still holding the bread, Rada said, 'This would've been your supper then? I insist. You're having hot soup with us and you'll stay here tonight so I can medicate you.' Rada leaned in close and like a conspirator murmured, 'It'll sting when you urinate. The WC is down the hall. Think you can manage on your own? Wait.' Rada brought her a glass of warm water. "Use this when you pee. Might help. There's no paper. Take this gauze. Bring it back and I'll wash it. Don't rub, just pat yourself dry."

Calina nodded again, and swung her legs off the couch. 'What about your husband?'

'Never mind now. Good. It's settled. You'll stay.' Rada called after the children, 'Boys come here I want to introduce you to my friend Calina.' Rada leaned over and whispered, what is your patronymic?'

'Calina Petrovna Kirillova, my father was Colonel Kirillov, have you never heard anything good of him?'

'No.' Rada shook her head.

'Neither have I—that is, I've heard things, but nothing good. Oh yes, much about him—all bad. He died in the Gulag.'

Rada's two sons came near the door.

'Hello, young men. Do you have names?' Calina tried to sound gay.

'Yes,' they said in one voice.

'This is Anton, he's nine and this is his older brother Petya, he's eleven,' Rada said, with a note of pride, patting his head.

The boy pulled away from Rada. 'Mamma wants to keep me a baby by calling me Petya, but my name is Pyotr.'

'Go on now, boys. You have time to play and then wash up for supper,' Rada said.

'Nice.' Calina leaned back.

'What is?'

'To have a family.'

'You will too someday.'

'Can you guarantee that? My mother tried to abort me but died in childbirth.' She waved a hand down the length of her stretched out body. 'This, I'm afraid is the result. I was abandoned when my father was arrested.'

'Oh dear. Sorry. Didn't mean to offend you.'

'Thin skin for a nurse. No offense taken.'

~

When Anya finished recounting, she told Garin that Calina, pregnant from the rape, had remained close friends with both of these women and after Anya met them, so had she. "It will be shattering for them when they learn about her. They found her in blood, and she died in blood." She pointed to his empty glass. "More?"

Andrei handed her the glass. "Please."

Anya took a long breath and let it out slowly. In a serious voice she said, "Calina married shortly after and her son, Grigory, was born. Somehow her husband never bothered to count the months, became a father, but shortly after they divorced. She gave his name as a patronymic to Grigory, but kept her own name. Rada got Calina a job in the Astoria Hotel where she's worked ever since. I think that's where she met Tamara. End of story."

"Tamara?" he asked.

"The doll-seller. Tamara used to go the hotel to sell lacquer boxes and dolls to the tourists. I think she taught Calina how to paint the dolls, although I never observed her doing it. Perhaps my little one did."

Garin's manner appeared absent. *What was he thinking?* She had a feeling it wasn't about the narrative she'd just recounted.

"Thank you," Garin said.

"Don't you sometimes just wish for days of nothing to remember?"

He shook his head. "No. I want to remember everything."

"What is it? You're trying to place me, aren't you?" Anya asked in a shy voice that made her seem younger.

"I promised to tell you something, but you must tell me something too."

"I just did."

"I mean about you. Personally."

"You first," she said, "after all it's your idea."

"He cleared his throat and moved the glass across the round table till it touched hers. Garin took out a pack of cigarette papers, a pouch of tobacco, rolled himself a smoke and took a drag. Blowing out the smoke he said, "I'm a Jew." He puffed again. "Knowing that," he hesitated, "you could get me kicked out of my job, never to become a cop. Even imprisoned or killed."

"Why would I? You're doing such a fine job protecting little girls and grandmothers from killers," her tone sarcastic, almost caustic.

He grabbed both her wrists. She recognized the look of someone wanting to hurt her, or at least frighten her and he was succeeding. But she wouldn't drop her facade or show how scared she was; instead she jutted out her chin.

He dropped her wrists. "Tell me about the doll. Where did you get it?"

"I told you. The important thing is: who killed Calina? And why? Officer Andrei Garin? Why?" She repeated. "Do I need to fear for my child's life? What if the killer knew Iskra was under the bed, not so hidden as she imagined? Is she in danger? Do I need to fear for my child's life?"

"I don't know." He shook his head. "I don't think so."

"Think, Officer Garin," she snarled.

He shook his head. "If the killer was involved with Calina personally and knew that she cared for Iskra, and if he understood the child was under the bed—then maybe. But maybe not, because the child is—"

"Backwards? Maybe he didn't need to kill her, too? That's a lot of conjecturing, isn't it?"

He didn't answer right away. A minute passed. "You said there were three dolls. I saw only one."

"My you're a good investigator, searching for dolls now?"

Anya went to the bedroom and brought back the little doll from her pocket. "I'll get the others tomorrow. I hid them."

"Now."

She wasn't going to screw around with this copper. He had bloodlust in his eyes and he wasn't afraid of prison or death. He'd told her his secret—that he was a Jew. *Why? What did it mean?*

She went next door and got the dolls from Yelizaveta.

When she came back, she said, "I forgot them at my neighbor's that's why I didn't bring them to Calina."

He opened all three dolls and there in the last one was a tiny blue paper packet containing a fine white powder that wasn't sugar or flour.

Still holding the satchel, she watched him hold up the little stash to her, giving it a slow shake as if it were an old-fashioned school chime. "Ring a bell?"

Realizing the implication, she looked stunned. Her eyes opened wide, a petrified animal on a country road caught in bright headlights.

"You wouldn't be so stupid as to give me evidence against you, so I take it, you never opened this doll.

"I opened two of them, the little one and that other one. I wasn't looking for anything. Besides that isn't exactly a kilo—barely a few grams."

"How did you know so much about the weight?"

"Any moron who cooks could tell you that." She glimpsed him scrunch up his lips. *Displeased? Pensive?* "Besides, this has nothing to do with me. I didn't put drugs in a doll, and show it to you to incriminate myself in something I know nothing about."

"Maybe—" he started to say.

There was a soft knock on the door. Anya jumped up. "I'm not guilty of anything except dreaming of a dead woman," she blurted out.

"What?"

Anya pushed the rucksack under the table.

Andrei raised his head and jerked it toward the door as if to ask, at this hour? He made an instinctive move, opening his jacket, passing his hand across the gun's holster.

"Just my neighbor," Anya whispered. "Relax." She made a move to get up but he wrenched her arm and she sat again.

"It's all right," she hissed. "I told you. It's my neighbor. She's not used to hearing voices at this hour."

He nodded and Anya walked to the door. She put her ear to it and more to calm the cop at her kitchen table than herself she asked, "Who is it?"

"Who could it be? You just left my place. It's me. Yelizaveta. Who's with you? Is it that hooligan, Lazar? Kick his ass out, do you hear me?"

"No, it's not him. It's a friend who gave me a lift home from Calina's."

"A friend with a car?"

"Yelizaveta, go to bed."

"How can I when you woke me?"

Anya stepped back from the door. "We'll talk tomorrow."

"How's Calina? Did she like the borscht I sent the other day? You never said."

"She . . ." Anya straightened behind the door and looked to where Andrei sat. He shook his head.

"She wasn't well," Anya said. "Now go to bed and we'll talk in the morning."

Andrei produced another cube of sugar. Anya stifled a laugh with her hand. Then she said to the door, "I've a gift for your tea tomorrow morning if you go to sleep now."

"Ach, the trouble you put me through and then no satisfaction even hearing if my soup was good," Yelizaveta said. "Goodnight then."

"Goodnight." Anya sat down again at the tiny table. "Do you want me to heat Calina's broth?"

He nodded. Placed the cube of sugar on the table.

"Why did you tell me such an important secret?"

"I want you to trust me."

"Why?" Anya rubbed her arms. She got up and moved toward the stove, took the soup and poured it from the jar into one of the dented pots. She lowered the flame beneath it so as not to scorch the soup or pot. "I asked you, why?"

"Call it instinct," Andrei said.

"A piece of bribery sugar. Call it whatever you want. What are you talking about anyway?"

She went toward the bedroom. Andrei called after her, "Who's Lazar?"

"None of your business."

"Who was the dead woman you dreamed about? Do you have special powers? Are you what they call psychic?"

Walking away, she called over her shoulder, "I didn't see the dead woman's face. It was hidden by a colorful babushka."

"Ah, so you dream in color. Interesting."

She came back with a knitted shawl over her shoulders, her legs in woolen ballet calf-warmers.

"I'm a cop photographer. I never get to investigate a crime . . . because I was never promoted."

"They can do that to you? What reason?"

"I want to solve this case. I'm not a member of the party—"

"You cops are all NKVD. I use different words for those initials and they aren't complimentary. I don't know anything about this case, as you call it. I can't believe you're talking about that poor, dead woman as a case."

"Not NKVD, but I messed up on a case involving some Afghanistan imports—I said I wanted to join the party, but my supposed-partner Nikolai suspects me. He tampered with evidence and blamed me. Said I messed up on a case involving smuggled—"

"Drugs?"

"Imports, at least that's the way they referred to the goods. And the Chief . . . never mind. It's complicated."

"He lost money in the deal, didn't he? These dirty commissars—all on the take. They smuggle and get rich and think people are stupid because things don't come out in the newspaper—everything's all hushed up."

"Forget it. Don't put me in that category. This case. She was beaten. Someone tortured her to get something."

"Christ crucified! About what? Taking my little girl to day care? Or maybe picking her up and giving her hot chocolate and cookies? You cops—if this wasn't so sad, I'd laugh." She caught herself and said aloud, "I don't think the dead woman of my dream was Calina."

"What are you talking about?"

"I dreamed of a woman dead in the snow. And now I know it wasn't Calina."

"Think. Calina was slaughtered in her own home. A hunch, but probably for information about something she knew—the hotel guests she worked for, her friends?"

Anya sat stonily still, biting her lower lip. She shook her head slightly.

He finger-combed his hair, folded his hands in back of his head and rocked the chair. He sat upright and took his hands down. Abruptly, he leaned forward. "If you help me solve this case, I may have a chance at getting a desk, or at least a beat. It'll mean I'll finally have some clout."

"I don't know anything about it and can't believe you keep talking about Calina as part of a mystery to solve. How can I help you get what you want?"

"She was beaten. Someone tortured her for whatever they were after—whether it was an object or information."

"About what? Possibly Babysitting?"

"Either you're hiding something or know more than you're saying. Even if you know nothing, you could inadvertently tell me something that might lead to capturing her murderer. Your mother-in-law's killer. You'd like that wouldn't you? You look like the type who'd be vengeful."

"Garin, eat your soup and get out." She poured soup into two bowls and set them on the table. "Leave me and my daughter alone. We know nothing, and I could care less if you never got a promotion. What a shit job. Taking pictures of dead, mutilated bodies."

Garin picked up his spoon and ate as if he'd not had a meal in three days. He said nothing, and when he was finished eating, stood, picked up his bowl and spoon, deposited them in the sink, and walked into the mouse-sized living room, picked up his coat and hat. "How do you know she was mutilated?"

"You said so."

"No, I didn't. I said she must have been tortured—I never said mutilated."

"Earlier. You said bludgeoned—isn't that mutilation? This is ridiculous. Are you accusing me? Out! Now! If you don't go, I'll scream and my neighbor will attack you with a frying pan. She's football-player size—a meter, ninety centimeters. I wouldn't mess with her, were I you." Anya opened the door. "Now," she repeated.

50

He made a sudden movement and Anya was pinned against the door. He kissed her fiercely. She struggled, pushing and punching his shoulders and arms. Then, she bit him.

He backhanded her and wiped his mouth with his shirtsleeve. "Only for money, I suppose, eh?" he said, his voice mean, his demeanor menacing. He pulled out his wallet and threw a bunch of kopecks and rubles in her face and stormed out.

"*Idti! Ubiraysya,*" she said and slammed the door in back of him. She listened to his retreating steps. She quietly opened the door, looked over the banister, hoping his back was the last she'd see of him. "Sick bastard," she muttered, wondering if he knew for sure, or was guessing she had tried to drum up a trade on the streets. *Had she been followed? Maybe that's where she'd seen him—when she was out hustling weeks before the big storm hit. Better to go hungry and let Iskra starve then ever do that again. But the way his eyes shine with mirth—almost like he's laughing at the absurdities of life— yet something more, perhaps sagacity.*

That night had been almost over when she'd been approached by a pimp for bustling in on his regular girls' turf which gave her a mammoth fright. At first he threatened her, and then propositioned her for a free trial with an offer to become one of his protected women. Anya swore to him it was a one night deal only because she was desperate to feed her child and she'd beat a hasty retreat, but not before having her arm twisted. She handed over some of the money she'd made. He ran his hands over her breasts to see if she had any concealed cash. A feeling of relief washed over her because she'd put most of the money under a rock behind the huge tree she'd been standing by instead of inside her boots. Sure enough the whoremonger made her take off her boots. As she stood barefoot in a smattering of snow covering the frozen ground, her mind was cognizant of two emotions: hate and fear, strong emotions that can incite people to kill. Counting her money, he left in a chauffeured car. She retrieved her hidden money, and thanked two other women of the night who'd been her companions for not revealing her hiding place.

"He'll be back, better move along, ballerina," a hooker said. As Anya began to walk away, another streetwalker, strung out on drugs, heckled her. "Hey, dancer, don't strut those shapely legs here again."

Wasn't it enough she no longer could do what she was born to do, dance? She washed the dishes, then heated more water in the kettle which she poured into a basin in the sink filled with already cooling water. She pulled a chair over to the sink, pulled a towel out from beneath it and placed it on the chair. Anya kneeled on it and stripped to the waist, leaned over, and splashed her breasts and underarms, bathing them with the warm water. With the soap, she made a rich lather in her hands. It was the last piece of perfumed soap Calina had taken from the hotel where she worked and gifted to Anya, which made her eyes tear up. Calina was the only mother she ever had. Shivering, she remembered how she'd washed over the kitchen sink, when she lived in the basement dwelling before being accepted to ballet school. She rinsed and toweled off. Then she threw on a sweater over her skirt and went out of the tiny apartment, down the hall to use the WC.

She heard a train whistle's lonely sound and wondered if it was still snowing and thought about the snow and ice sculptures she'd seen in Lithuania a few months past in late spring. Forever ago, like Garin's fading brutish kiss.

~

Lithuania a year ago. She'd envisioned herself back then at the Glavny Station in Leningrad, getting on the train. She'd never questioned why Calina had asked her to drop off a package to a stranger in the Vilnius

rail station in Lithuania. Why hadn't Anya asked? She'd been so relieved to have two days of rest just traveling, going and coming on a
fast-moving train, absentminded and relaxed. She never inquired what
the urgency was, or how Calina had money to pay for train tickets. What
was in the package? Why hadn't she looked? Trying to recapture the
memory, Anya repeated the conversation in her head. "You have to do
this for me. I can't leave. I may be followed. You must deliver a package
for the pawnbroker. The man picking it up will pay you in American
dollars."

"Watched by whom?"

"Never mind that."

"Never mind! If you're in danger, am I also a suspect for something
I've no knowledge of?"

"Of course not. You have no part of this."

"This what?"

"Listen to me. I watch your daughter—now I need you to do this for
me. We'll all benefit from it."

"Will I need to count the money in public?"

"There's a small eatery in the station. He'll take you for tea and pay
for a light repast and discreetly pass you the money under the table. Put
it in your bag and go to the WC to count it."

"How much?"

"Two thousand American dollars."

"So much?"

"Enough. Oh, and make sure he gets you something to pack in your
bag to eat later and also to give you money for tea. And a bottle of vodka
for me and cigarettes for a friend. I want to get something out of this
risk."

"But I'm the one risking."

"I'll get your pay from Yasha."

"Yasha? The pawn broker?"

"*Da*. Grigory's partner—I mean friend."

"You'll never have to worry for you or my little Iskra. I'll take care of you both. Always. But Yasha will pay you a little money, some clothes for Iskra, and some canned goods."

When she'd boarded the train, Anya wondered if she could sleep or daydream long enough for the ride, or would she become bored. She was about to put the package above her head in the storage bin, but thought better of it, and set it underneath her seat where she could feel it with her foot. She sat down and made herself comfortable, but something jabbed her hip on the side of the window. She looked over and reached for a hard crammed-in object. Wedged between her seat and the window was a package, which she struggled to wrench free. It was a gift wrapped in cloth and tied with a bow. Anya opened it, all the while doing so she'd already made up her mind she wouldn't give it to the conductor in case the owner came back. She pretended it was her birthday and wound the ribbon around her fist and folded the cloth wrapping and put them inside her bag. She held in her hands a book. The volume bound in deep sienna leather. The embossed cover bore four gold glyphs, one in each corner and the arched word in the center above the title read: Tolstoy. Underneath the author's name was the title: *Anna Karenina* in straight bold print letters beneath which was another detailed, intertwined and scrawling gold glyph. She opened the book. It was a first edition, printed in 1878. Who could have carelessly left such a treasure behind? Her first thought was that she'd never read anything by this author, and her second thought was of its value—how much was it worth? Who would buy it from her? In a flash she knew it would grace the shelves of Yasha's pawnshop at the right moment. But for now, it was her possession and she was going to read it. She always considered herself unlucky, but this accidental find would make her rich in every sense—intellectually and monetarily. Perhaps her luck was changing.

The train's passing reminded her of Anna Karenina's sad story. Engine steam, fog and mist shrouding like foreshadow. No, she couldn't count on luck to change her destiny—she had to be careful with the choices she made.

Anya rinsed her hands and washed her mouth with trickling water in the sink and dried her hands on the rear of her skirt. Standing at the sink, her mind leapt to an image of the key islands dotting the canal and harbor. The representation came to her as if the islands were laid out before her. The land that blocks the sea on the way out of the harbor could have been manmade—all rocky promontory and trees—but the bushes now have come to cover it. But what was it like fifty or one hundred years ago? What thoughts? Why now?

Why does the mind boggle and jumble thoughts? Oh, but what wonderful workings of the mind we possess. Though sometimes of need or danger, does it help or hinder us? The mind must seek to aid a person and get them out of jeopardy, but what havoc and intricate spiders' webs weave our emotions? What went through Calina's mind when she was being beaten to death? A sudden shudder passed through Anya and she felt faint. Did Calina thrust, lunge, parry? Did she fence and try to dodge the murderer? Did she know him? Was it her own son, Grigory? Was it Calina's friend, the pawnbroker, Yasha? Terrified while being bashed and clobbered, did her mind rush back to when she'd been raped? She was expecting someone. Who?

Anya closed the door to the WC. She walked down the unlighted hall seeing Garin framed in her open doorway, leaning against the doorjamb, the kitchen candle-light haloing him. Her heart pounded so fast in her chest she thought she heard it in her ears. No place to run. Better to give in to him rather than have him hurt her.

He stepped aside. She walked past him. He smelled of the outdoors and cold snow and wet wool, and she remembered the faint scent of tobacco she'd tasted on his lips and smelled on his mustache when he'd kissed her. He followed her inside.

"Forget your keys, Officer Garin?"

He took off his gloves and stuffed them in his pockets. Took off the coat and fur hat and placed them on a sofa that had seen happier days. He pointed to the kitchen window and said, "It's blowing up a bloody blizzard out there. Can I stretch out on the couch?"

"Staying the night? You'll need to cover yourself with your coat."

He rubbed his hands together. "I, I want to say I'm sorry. I've never hit a woman before."

Anya laughed, but stopped when she saw him clench his fist. She picked his fist up with both her hands and brought it to her mouth. She kissed it. "Whatever you say, Officer Garin," and gently shoved him down into the kitchen chair.

"Do you have more tea? I'll be civil. I brought sugar—don't look so surprised. I have a stash in my car—just for occasions like this with pretty women I give rides to in the snow. Smoke?" He pulled out the pack of Belomorkanal cigarettes and offered her one.

"Thanks." She shook her head. "From Calina's apartment?"

He lit the cigarette and looked up.

"Could that be construed as evidence? Are you holding out clues from your colleagues?"

He looked at the cigarettes. "I was going to give these to Nikolai. His brand, too. Wonder if he dropped them."

"Cigarettes and sugar for the one who's obliged to put you up for the night?" Anya refilled the teakettle at the sink and put it on the stove. She lit a match to the gas beneath, and then blew on it and tossed it into the flame and put the box on the table. She held her hands up to the warmth of the fire darting out from under the kettle.

He leaned over and picked up the money where it still lay on the floor. He shook his head.

Ah. Two apologies. One with words, one by action.

He put the money on the table and ran his hands through his hair.

A woman could come to love that gesture.

"You really do look familiar," his voice trailing.

Anya thought back to the last of the white nights when she was desperate for money and out on the streets instead of borrowing from Calina with no intention of paying her back. She was about to tell a lie, but what she said was, "I'll tell you something. About me. I was on stage. You'd never recognize me from my performances—they were too few."

"An actress?" He cleared his throat and moved the glass across the small table till it touched hers. He furrowed his brow, and after several minutes looked at her as if his internal debate was over. "I was secretly adopted. Knowing that could get me an unwanted ticket to Siberia."

Ah, and now two secrets. What does he want from me? "Maybe it's not my face you recognize but my legs. See? She kicked off her felt boots, pulled off one leg warmer and pulled up her skirt. Balancing on one leg, she stretched out the other toward him, extending a pert pointed toe. She bent her knee and placed her toes on his thigh.

"I was a Kirov ballerina, but that was a lifetime ago. Now you have my secret," she said with remorse underscoring the statement. "We're even, if I can believe yours."

"That's not a secret. I could've found that information had I wanted to do a background search on you." The whistle blew, but before she picked up the kettle and put it on a cold burner, he ran his hand up her leg.

"That's one brutal scar."

"Here's your one word answer: Grigory."

"Your husband?"

"Ex. Lover." And for some reason she reiterated that he was Calina's son.

Anya retrieved her leg, making all the motions in reverse, gently kicking her boots under the table and sliding into a pair of fluffy old slippers she kept near the sink. She then picked up the kettle and poured. "We're even as far as secrets go, that is if I can really believe yours."

"Mine has more significance, don't you think?"

"You're not a cop or a murderer, are you? Or in the hated NKVD or is it the KGB?"

A smile played upon his lips. "That knowledge could get me kicked out of my job and never let me get into the force. As I said before, worse—it could mean Siberia. Death."

She blinked. Her eyes trying to mask fear. She nudged his hand with the spout. He moved his hand and she poured the boiling water into the glass, steam rising like a smoke screen.

She looked at him for a long moment, trying to make up her mind as she placed the kettle back on the stove. Then she kicked off her slippers and slid off the other leg warmer, took down her panties and dropped them on the floor. She pulled up her skirt and with one quick long-legged movement she straddled him. While he fumbled with the buttons of his fly, she plunged her fingers into his hair and pulled his head backwards and kissed his lips, then his throat and back up to his lips that yielded to hers. Her arms wound around his neck and she kissed his lips over and over, and then in earnest as if memorizing his face with her lips.

Andrei responded with his tongue riding the curve of her neck and taking possession of her with one quick thrust.

When he was done and she'd come back from washing in the WC, he said, "I'm starving. Nothing much to that soup."

"Then cook. Eggs are on the window sill. There's a potato and an onion in the bin underneath."

She hung her washed panties on a line strung in front of the window.

He found a frying pan under the sink. "Are you sure you won't need this to hit me over the head like your neighbor?" He smiled an uneven grin, and Anya's thoughts assailed her. *Calina's dead and I just fucked a volatile cop as if falling off the Earth into a void while my daughter's asleep in the next room—is there no place to run from this maddening world?*

While she put the leg warmers back on, he held up the pan. "Any grease to fry these eggs?"

Anya pointed to an old cocoa tin next to a square basket holding the eggs. It was filled with rendered bacon fat.

He sniffed it. "How old? From the year of the ark and flood?"

"Not quite."

While he cooked, she took out the bottle of vodka and rinsed the two small glasses under tap water.

After they ate, Anya digested each insight along with every morsel of food. They sipped tea and in between tossed back shots of vodka and talked long into the night. The candle burned low and then went out. Still they kept on talking. They took turns using the hall WC. But she knew, like he did too, they loathed the ending of the night. She felt an unburdening of soul when he touched her hands with his fingertips, as if fingering the petals of a delicate rose, and she was certain he felt something kindred to relief when she crept her hand into his. He showed her his wristwatch that read 7 am. "A couple of hours till dawnlight."

"You've got the couch. I move too much when I'm tired but can't sleep or have bad dreams. I may wake Iskra. If she gets up she may be frightened to see you. Tell her you are guarding us, won't you?" Anya patted his shoulder as she headed toward the bedroom.

"*Da*," he said, though it sounded like a question.

"*Dobroj noci.*"

"*Spokojnoj.*"

She stopped, put a hand on his chest and leaned into him. He kissed the top of her head, then raised her face and kissed her with the kind of tenderness she'd craved all her life.

He walked to the window and happened to look out. "Someone pulled alongside my car, and it's no ordinary citizen. I should've parked elsewhere. Shit. *Govno.* I've been followed."

Anya came back and stood next to him. "Your own people?"

"Indeed. But why, that's what I'd like to know. Why?"

They watched the black vehicle parallel to his car driving slowly forward and back.

"They'll follow up again—I've got to move my car from there—"

"I thought you said the snow storm wouldn't—"

"Car wouldn't start. I'll have to check relays and fuses. I've got extras."

"What are you going to do?" She saw something like remorse wash over him at his lie about the snow storm. "What if you're unable to start it?"

"I'll start it," he said, shaking his head as if to say, How could you disbelieve me?

"Ah. A confident man who knows mechanics."

They watched the unmarked car pull away.

"I can almost hear the slap, slap of their windshield wipers at top speed." Anya dried the frying pan. He gestured toward it. "Better keep this handy weapon out—never know when it might be useful." He smiled another crooked grin.

"Shit. Forgot something else in my car. Won't take me long."

"I hope it's food."

He didn't even bother putting on his coat. Was he daft?

She dressed in her sleeping togs—not quite pajamas: leggings, baggy soft warm-up pants, a sweater, and shawl for her shoulders. She sat on a kitchen chair she'd moved closer to the stove with every flame on it lit, and the oven door open for warmth. She poured herself more vodka and sipped some tea, thinking she'd have to use the WC again before getting into that lovely warm bed with Iskra.

When he got back, he was shaking. He placed a small covered basket with six eggs on the table, took the two from the sill and added them. He rubbed his arms briskly. "No need for grease to fry tomorrow morning." From his belted pants, he whipped out a slab of bacon.

"Oh my. Heaven! You're trembling. Soaked with fresh snow. Take off your sweater and shirt over here by the oven. I'll get you something dry to put on," Anya said, murmuring, "*Psikh*—crazy. *Chertovski sumasshedshiy.* Hellishly crazy! Running out without a coat."

When she came back holding a sweater, he'd already stripped to the waist and stood next to the gas flames, rubbing his hands and arms. He took the sweater and pulled it on. "Tight, but it'll do. Thanks. It's a man's. Thought I'd be stretching out one of your girlie jumpers."

He extended his arms, turned up his palms and looked at the sleeves that didn't quite make it to his wrists.

"My ex. I wear it sometimes—it's light but warm—maybe alpaca."

Anya placed an old tin of cacao next to the rectangular basket that held the eggs. "You can add more rendered bacon fat to the batch," she said with no hint of an apology in her voice. She took his sweater, shirt, and undershirt and draped each over the back of a chair.

He wafted the tin under his nose. "Not Kosher, but not bad. But I've something better," and he took a wax-paper wrapped chunk of frozen butter out of his pocket and wiggled it in front of her astonished eyes.

He reached into his other pants' pocket and took out a small jar.

Anya couldn't believe what he showed her. "Sturgeon caviar? You must live right."

"I stole it."

"Ah. That makes me feel so much better." She smiled.

"I'll make a small omelet, cut it in three and top it with the caviar for breakfast." We'll save the bacon."

"Sit."

But he remained standing and rubbing his arms by the open oven door.

"Success starting the car? Where did you move it?"

"An alleyway behind a block apartment one street over. I ran all the way back."

"Frigid." She picked up his hands in hers and rubbed them till the circulation came back. You could get frostbite like that. No gloves." He turned toward the open oven and she rubbed his back. He sighed.

"Tea?" she asked.

"With vodka."

"I've run out," she said, feeling guilty about the shot she'd poured herself while he was gone. With that he whipped out of his back pocket a flat, slightly curved flask.

She smiled, despite herself. "Will wonders never cease?"

"Saw you were running low."

"Tell me, is that little car of yours a grocery store? I'm surprised the back seat isn't lined with shelves."

She took off her shawl and arranged it around his shoulders, made tea and poured out the vodka.

"You've got an engaging smile—you should smile more often, An-ya."

She felt heat rise in her face. He was flirting with her. To make up for his previous violence or show he genuinely cared?

They took turns using the hall WC. Still unwilling to say goodnight, she felt an unburdening of soul and thought perhaps he felt some kindred relief. He went to the window, shook his head, and held up his wrist-watch. "We've lingered till dawn. Shall we get some sleep?"

She turned off the stove burners and shut the oven door.

Chapter Five

Wednesday, December 19, 1956

At ten in the morning, when the sun made a weak attempt to come up over Leningrad, Anya stretched in the bed. Iskra wasn't there. Anya heard her talking to someone and remembered Garin, the strange copperman, had slept on her living room sofa. He was now probably conversing with her daughter. Anya listened a little longer, trying to pick out some words, and realized Iskra was playing with the new nesting doll. Anya probably had been blissfully sleeping through this artless conversation. She closed her eyes just for ten more minutes.

An hour later, she was awakened to the smell of frying onions emanating from her kitchen. Iskra came in, so Anya pretended to be asleep. Iskra shook her mother, and then crawled in under the covers with her. "*Mat*, he's making you breakfast. I already ate. He's a good cook."

"What did you eat?"

"Tea with sugar in my teeth."

"Let's go, little one. We'll see what else besides tea there is for you."

Anya walked into the kitchen holding her daughter's hand.

"*Dobroye utro,*" he said too cheerfully.

"Good day to you. Did you get any sleep?"

"Like a tank off duty."

"What's that mean?"

"I fell into a coma, and a truck couldn't move me so I must be a tank."

"Iskra said you gave her tea and sugar. Thought the last of the sugar was for my neighbor."

He grinned and, raising his eyebrows, produced another cube from his pocket. And Anya had the distinct urge to go over and kiss him.

"Iskra also had fried potatoes. How can you live like this? A mouse would starve."

Anya picked Iskra up and sat down heavily with the child in her lap. "It's not by choice. Guaranteed. I used to pick up staples now and again from Calina. Her *negodyay* son, the scoundrel, drops her some money once in a while. You'd be surprised what the foreigners leave in their rooms at the hotel where she works, I mean, worked."

"Iskra, did you wash? Did you go to the WC?" Anya asked.

"I'm a big girl."

"Of course you are, my darling."

"I went to check on my car. It was covered by an avalanche two hours ago. Thought to borrow a shovel to dig it out, but it might be better to leave it hidden beneath all that snow. Someone tailed me last night for sure. Nothing's moving on the street. Not a trolleybus, tram, not a car or truck. I'm going to have to call in from someplace to say I can't get you to the office with Iskra. We're frozen in a winter wonderland."

"Read me a story." Iskra climbed down from her mother's lap and sat in another chair.

Garin smiled.

"All right, but then what?" Anya looked from Iskra over to Garin.

"You tell her a story and I'll use the WC to wash the sleep out of my eyes. When I come back you can serve me some of those delicious potatoes and onions and pour me some tea. No sugar. That's for my neighbor later. If I can get to the market, I'll get the honey." She hesitated a second. "Already paid for."

As Anya walked toward the door, towel and soap in hand, she heard Garin mumble, "Beautiful dark eyes." She wondered if he meant Iskra's or hers.

When she came back, she had a moment's panic. Garin stood at the window looking out. "Where's Iskra?"

"She got sleepy and so I put her back to bed."

Anya finished eating. "Temperatures are already freezing."

Andrei took her plate and fork, washed and dried them. "I'll bet the organizers of the art show are sorry they scheduled the exhibition so late. The Neva froze last week."

"What art show?"

"*Autumn Exhibition of Works by Leningrad Artists*" opened in the Exhibition Halls of the Leningrad Union of Artists. A friend of mine is showing his work, and I've not been able to get there. I'd planned on it today after bringing you in for questioning. But this heavy snow is impossible to believe. They should've had it at the end of September when we had *bab'ye leto.*"

She laughed. "I adore that brief respite of warm weather, the last window of soft sunshine before the cold of winter and it lasted a whole week this year. I took Iskra out every day into summer held in a goblet of winter—imagine, seven whole days of warm weather and sun."

"What shall we do today if we can't get to the police station?"

"If there's a break in the weather we could take in the art show."

"What show?"

"The one I just told you about at the *Leningrad Union of Soviet Artists Exhibition Halls.* Want to go?"

"To Bolshaya Morskaya?"

"Trams will be running later. After you and Iskra get sorted."

"What do you mean by that?"

"Let her sleep. It's pitch dark in there, like night. Here," he said and held out his hand. "Sugar for the nosey one next door."

"Ah. *Spasibo*. I'll go now." She took it from his hand and went to deliver it.

When she got back he said, "Did that placate her?"

"More questions. I'm not a good liar. I get confused and change my story too often. I told her I got a ride home from Calina's, which is the truth. I didn't say more." She looked around. Everything had been washed and put away. "Why do you want to go to the art show? Had a change of heart?"

"Beg your pardon?"

"No eggs and caviar."

"Ah—our brunch! I'll make it for dinner instead."

"What's with your interest in art?" Anya fidgeted, picking up her cup, placing it down, stirring the tea, rubbing her hands together.

"I saw *The Girl with a Bow* by Lev Alexandrovich Russov two years ago in of all places Lithuania. Most impressive. I'm curious to see if he's done anything else as classic. There are rumors of one called, *The Birth*."

Lithuania, she thought. Should I mention delivering the package to the strange foreigner at Calina's behest? Instead, she asked, "Who's your friend?"

"A minor artist, but he's got possibilities. I'm not a connoisseur. Can't afford it, but I know what I like, what appeals to me. I learned a great deal from my birth father about art and literature."

"Iskra will be nervous. Can you get us on the trams without fuss and calling attention?" Again, Anya recalled her travel by train to Lithuania. Why hadn't Calina sent Anya by bus, the cheaper route, which was the same amount of time: sixteen and a half hours. *Perhaps it was safer. What was in that package?*

"By all means," he said with a confident air.

"Sorry. Got a little lost in thought for a moment."

"Not to worry. We can go by trolleybus. I'll make her feel safe. I promise."

In fact, he would, she was confident. Iskra had taken a liking to him. "Then we'll go when she wakes," Anya said. "Were you invited?"

He lifted his camera from the table, and the shield hanging around his neck. He'd changed back into his own clothing.

"Why're you so interested in art? Especially because it seems you don't know a great deal about it?"

"When I was young I wrote something about Art, and I committed it to memory—I never shared it with anyone. Want to hear it?"

"Yes, though I think it will be painful for you."

He looked at her face, and then held her dark eyes with his. "Art, like life, like love when it encompasses and cajoles a soul into believing it exists, is a charm becoming a middle distance or balance, searching for a position like true north on a compass."

"What does it mean?"

"Art rests between dream and reality. A fantasy, magic, but in a sense, real, too, with each brushstroke." He pretended to paint in the air. "The artist skillfully, no, masterfully shades or lightens an effect into illusions created of dimensional shapes—designed imaginings bearing witness to something near or far, surreal, romantic in proportion, evocative, poignant in language: interpreted, translated by fluttering emotions—the essence of heart."

He looked at her face and she could almost swear he found in it something akin to awe.

She leaned forward and said barely above a whisper, "Repeat it. Slower this time." And he did.

Without realizing what she was doing, as he pronounced the word "fluttering," Anya's hand reached out for his and she set it down like a homing bird landing on its nest.

Chapter Six

Back when Anya had been teaching dance and gymnastics to pre-school children for almost two years, she was fired. One of the students, Dunya, a plump five year-old, was in tears because her father was late to pick her up one day. The next thing Anya knew was that she was harassed and in a compromising situation with this widower's unwanted breath blowing on her neck. She was disgusted by his inebriated actions and lewd suggestions in front of his daughter and finally broke from him with some very unkind words. She decided to report him to her director.

The next day, approaching the director's office, Anya had a bad feeling. As she walked toward the open door, the director stood to meet her. Without prelude, she said, "Anya, I'm so sorry, but he beat you to it and with the Big Company. He has already been here to complain that you seduced him." The director shook her head.

Anya stood stone still in shock. "He what? He practically attacked me in front of his daughter."

"He said you put a move on him and he wants you removed from influencing his little Dunya with bad moral principles. Sit down, Anya."

"The rat bastard," Anya spit out.

"The man—I'm terribly aggrieved but it's out of my hands. I have to let you go, dear. This man, Kuznetsov, works for *Izvestiya*— as you know the News of the Councils of Working People's Deputies of the U.S.S.R."

"Of course, who doesn't know our government's newspaper?"

"His superior is Georgy Maximilianovich Malenkov, who presides over a collective leadership, although rumors are always flung about that he's on borrowed time as to the party's First Secretary, Nikita Khrushchev."

"This information doesn't make me feel ecstatic, despite your commiseration— *negodyay*!"

"Scoundrel is right! But my hands are tied—"

"The fact is I'm now jobless again with my name probably on some incriminating list heading for the Gulag. Worse yet that *bomzh*—bum—my baby darling's father never helps me. Thank heavens his mother assists me whenever she can."

"I apologize, but no matter how profusely I say I'm sorry, we know this is complete bullshit that I can't change." The director took hold of Anya's clenched hands, and looked at her with pity in her eyes. "If there's anything I can do to help you find another job, please call upon me."

Anya hesitated a second. "For what? I'm not very qualified."

"Although I can recommend you for another position it doesn't mean he won't squelch my nomination. He's got that kind of power."

"Why did I have to be alone watching his daughter? Is my entire life destined to ill fate? I'm once again without an income. Who will feed my daughter?"

Anya trudged up the stairs to Calina's flat. The door flew open before Anya could knock. Calina greeted her with a huge grin, but seeing the dejection written on Anya's face, she said, "What? What has happened?"

Anya recounted the story of the occurrence the night before with the bigshot making lewd advances and how she was fired. "What will I do now to feed my baby, Calina?"

"God will provide."

"God? In this godforsaken communist country?"

"God. Look." She drew out a large diamond engagement ring from her apron pocket. "I found it under a rug cleaning in one of the rooms in the hotel yesterday. I couldn't wait to tell you."

Anya took hold of the ring. "Who knows its value, but where can you sell it anyway?"

"Come in and sit." They went to the kitchen and Anya peeled off her coat, hat, and gloves and sat down.

"I wasn't going to tell you just yet, but well, I've been meeting a pawnbroker sometimes in a cellar café. The other day he bought me a drink. Grigory knows him also, and some burly brute who passes himself off as a cop. I didn't want to say too much to Yasha, he's the pawnbroker. He does such business and can maybe buy the ring from me—I have a feeling he deals in diamonds. I know he's a diamond-cutter." Calina set the table with two cups and put the kettle on to make tea.

"Who can buy diamonds under the table here in *Piter?* You mean smuggling?"

Calina shrugged her shoulders.

"My dearest, Calina that will be a miracle and three quarters!"

"What do we need to make it two miracles?"

Anya looked puzzled. "What do you mean?"

"Look at this other little miracle!" And from her other pocket she produced a wedding ring with smaller diamonds.

"What if the person reports them lost or left behind to the concierge? You could get fired for stealing."

"*Moya dusha,* my soul! The room where I found it is part of an expensive, elegant suite that hasn't been rented in over a year. I was in charge of freshening it up because guests are expected. No one has ever reported missing rings in a year!" Calina poured the hot water into the cups, and swirled it around with a cinnamon stick.

"That smells so good."

"I took it off a tray left in the hall outside of Room 112. Not a room I clean. Took this, too." She set a small dish of sugar cubes on the table. "I left the sugar bowl. Didn't want the new girl to get in trouble."

"So kind of you."

"What's wrong?" Calina put a sugar cube in each cup and stirred again.

"I don't doubt Grigory knows this pawnbroker—he talks about doing business with a jeweler, but who's this other guy you mentioned?"

"Him? I heard Grigory refer to him as Kolya. My gut impression? The yellow-gold on his cop's badge needs some buffing up—it's quite tarnished."

"A dirty *ment*. Kolya, that's a nickname for Nikolai, isn't it?"

"I think so. Common enough name, though."

"A cop in league with your son. Sorry, Calina, but if the shoe fits . . ."

"I know my son, but don't rub my nose in his soiled diaper. I'm not exactly as clean as the first Leningrad snowfall either, my pet."

"This is *Piter*, after all—no one's pure. Get the rings to this Yasha. How will you know if he's given you a good price?"

"I won't. Unless I go to another pawnbroker first and get an estimate." She blew on the tea.

"Good idea. It's strictly commerce with him, right? Just business and nothing more?"

"And if it were? Would you deny me some pleasure?"

"*Bozhe moy!*"

"You said it, my God is right! Yasha will take them apart, he'll melt the gold, and fashion some other piece of jewelry. He'll be able to sell the stones separately."

"He'll never give you full price. Listen. I have something to sell also." Anya sipped her tea.

"You? What on earth could you have?"

"A rare book. In great condition. Over fifty years old for sure. I found it on the train ride to Lithuania."

"Political? A science book?"

Anya shook her head. "I've read it three times, but it's valuable. Literary and signed by Tolstoy."

"Bring me your treasure tomorrow and I'll take it with the rings."

Chapter Seven

Morning
Thursday, December 20, 1956

Anya left Iskra at school and went to visit Yelizaveta. After the two women cried once again over Calina's murder, Anya said she had to meet Grigory to give him his mother's key back, and as usual, Yelizaveta cautioned her to be careful.

~*~

Midday
Thursday, December 20, 1956

Outside of the shop, written in small fading letters, Pawnbroker. Grigory knew that the clever owner would never put his name, Lev Yakovlevich Gubenko, out on a sign. The people that the pawnbroker dealt with didn't know he was Jewish because he'd changed his first name to Yasha, very Russian sounding, and his last name was Slavic and common, so he could also pass for a *goy,* basically the only Jewish word Grigory knew.

Somehow Yasha had acquired the patronymic Ivanovich, although certainly Yasha never had a Russian father. What Grigory didn't know was that he himself had been given a patronymic by his mother when she married a man who wasn't his father. Grigory was sure the bastard Yasha had never had a legitimate father. The reason Grigory knew Yasha's real name was because he'd seen it on an old passport six months ago underneath a new forged one. He'd returned from Israel via

Germany. From there he took a train to Russia. Grigory figured Yasha must have paid a handsome sum to bribe someone in order to travel back and forth. Grigory had been snooping among papers in Yasha's desk while the pawnbroker sorted diamonds at his jeweler's workbench. The bench, about one hundred centimeters in height, should have prevented the old man from hunching over, but he was so tall that he did anyway.

Grigory thought back to a few years ago and how he'd met the pawnbroker. It had been an accidental meeting at an open-air market when he'd overheard the pawnbroker dealing to buy stolen goods from a hawker. Grigory tapped the man's shoulder, and slyly took out a pocket-watch he'd clipped off a well-dressed shopper minutes before. The pawnbroker lifted the watch by the chain and held it to his ear. He flipped it over, opened the back cover and read an inscription. He raised his eyes, inclined his head and quoted a price. Grigory accepted a handful of rubles. This forged their partnership.

Then his mother had pawned two diamond rings she'd found clean-ing. Thus a friendship between Calina and Yasha began and turned into something more, including a partnership of smuggling diamonds out of Russia. This illegal part of their intimate relationship, Calina kept secret from Anya. Although Grigory was privy to it, he couldn't fathom the romantic liaison between his mother and Yasha.

Grigory wondered whatever did his mother see in Yasha besides his pockets filled with rubles and the vodka they shared on cold nights in her flat? He couldn't envision his mother coupling with Yasha. But since Grigory was still living with his mother at that time, Yasha couldn't very well move in with her, so the vagabond son moved out temporarily. However, Yasha was only a guest at Calina's every once in a while. And now Grigory, who couldn't keep rubles in his pocket, was back in Calina's apartment permanently, claiming to authorities he'd never moved out.

Grigory looked at his watch, knowing Anya would be on time. He crossed the street to a small tea shop. He was seated in the back, perusing the menu. He looked up when the door opened, bringing with it a cold blast of air along with Anya, disheveled but still stunning.

He didn't stand, but patted the seat next to him in the booth. She hesitated and then sat opposite him, removing her hat, scarf, and gloves and unbuttoning her coat.

"How will you be able to stay in the apartment now that your dear mother is dead?" Anya asked.

"I've got plans to get a roommate who can afford not only the rent but to give me something on the side," he said, giving her a smirk for a smile. "I took the liberty of ordering you tea."

While the tea was served they were quiet. As soon as the waiter moved away, Anya looked up with a curious expression on her face. "And who is this generous person with deep pockets? Another thief or Yasha?"

"A person of good standing in the community. I believe you've met the investigating officer Nikolai Vassilievich Fomin."

Anya sputtered on the tea.

"Too hot?"

She placed the cup into the saucer, spilling some tea. "You're insane messing with the police. Especially that one."

"More clever than you give me credit. He's recently widowed and wanted a change, *moya dusha*."

"Keep your charm and endearments for him—you're going to need them."

"So what is it you wanted to discuss?"

"This," she said sliding Calina's apartment key across the table to him.

"Ah, so I guess you won't be coming to visit anytime soon?"

"My guess is they're going to requisition the apartment soon—so you'd either better get someone in there fast or take what you can and move it out. Make sure the neighbors don't see you."

"That's all you have to say to me after all this time?"

"*Niet.* There's also this—I hope never to see you again after we lay your mother to rest."

"What about my darling little daughter? You'd deprive her of seeing her daddy?"

Anya had already replaced her hat and scarf. "Speaking of which, now I won't have your mother's help, why don't you give me some of that easy money you've got so I can buy her a pair of boots that fit and a cup of borscht?" She stood and held out her hand like a pauper. "You have it. You're flushed, slurring your words on drugs." She waved a hand in front of his face. "Give me something for the child," she said through her teeth.

"*Moya dusha,*" he said, sarcasm dripping from the words, and reached into his pocket.

Anya held the money in her fist and slipped on her gloves.

"I'm off to get some more of where that came from," he said, his voice boastful.

She walked toward the exit.

"What? No kiss or thanks?" Grigory called to her as she opened the door.

Chapter Eight

Early afternoon
Thursday, December 20, 1956

As soon as she left Grigory, Anya ran across the street to catch the public conveyance, but slowed her pace when she saw the long line. She had intended to go home, but skirted the line to queue up. She placed her gloved hand without the money in her pocket and patted the duplicate key to Calina's apartment. Anya had had a spare made that morning before meeting Grigory. Intuition had kept Anya awake the night before insinuating the thought that the interlopers who killed Calina had been after something they wanted.

Knowing she had time and Grigory was off to do some shady dealings, instead of going home as she had planned, she couldn't afford losing the opportunity of rummaging through Calina's things. She went directly to the apartment to give it a thorough going over. *What had the thieves sought? What could a poor woman have that they wanted to steal?* Andrei had told her the police had come up with nothing of value, and the crime seemed to be one of mistaken identity. Anya stood shaking her head, knowing this was no coincidence. They were after something. She felt certain. But what?

Inside the apartment, Anya slipped off her rucksack, threw her coat, scarf, gloves on a chair near the door. She began to search every possible hiding place. When she'd finished, she sat down a minute, disappointed yet satisfied, knowing there could have been nothing of value. Anya packed a grocery tote bag with a few canned and boxed goods from the kitchen and looked over the produce in a wire-rack, deciding to take some but not all of it. She jammed into the bag: two potatoes, an onion, a wilted cabbage, and three beets. Under the sink, she found a bar of hotel soap and a towel from the hotel where Calina had worked. Anya popped these in the bag also. In the back of some pots, under a large soup kettle, she found an unopened old bottle of Rodnik Vodka. "Ah," she sighed, "a shame you never got to drink this, Calina."

Anya ransacked the bedroom closet. Calina's boots were too big, but Anya stuck her hand inside and pulled out the warm linings. She rifled the disorderly dresser drawers that had been replaced, the broken ones, too. Anya held up a warm nightgown two sizes too big, but took it, some toys and a book Iskra had left behind. She stuffed these in her tote, straightened everything she'd touched or messed, and was about to leave. But something prompted her to take another look around.

Anya knew Calina always had a stash of reserve money in a large bill somewhere for emergencies or to help Anya out with Iskra. *Where had she kept it hidden?* Anya went back to the closet and patted down all of the clothes' hems and pockets and the hotel maid's uniform. She ran her hands over furniture backs and undersides, and inspected beneath the mattress corners—too difficult to get way underneath, also too obvious. Anya's eyes swept the bedroom and came to rest on a photograph of Calina flanked on either side by her dear friends, Rada and Ludmilla.

Anya picked up the frame, turned it over and slid out the picture behind the glass. There it was—a five thousand ruble note. Anya took hold of it and a pawn ticket fluttered to the floor. "Interesting," Anya whispered, seeing that it wasn't from Yasha's pawnshop, which made her wonder exactly how much Calina trusted him. This may have been where Calina went to check on the value of the stones before selling them to Yasha. As Anya pocketed the note and the pawn stub, she calculated if she had time enough to get there and back home before dark. She replaced the picture, but a niggling feeling drew her back to the kitchen.

Calina had once said, "Thieves never look up or waste time climbing." Anya pulled over a chair. Disappointed there was nothing on top, not even dust. It had been wiped clean. Curious, she felt around the edges of the cupboards. At one of the angled joining corners, she saw a shiny object—probably a button. *But why hide a button?* She tried to ease it out with her fingernail, but it was jammed in too tightly. Anya stepped down off the chair and got a knife. She worked the object out and stood studying it in the palm of her hand. A faceted stone. Like the one she'd seen in the engagement ring Calina found. Anya did another quick hunt on the opposite joint to find yet another diamond of the same dimension—neither one of the precious stones small in size. The surface of each could almost cover a pinky nail. *Where had Calina gotten them? The pawnbroker? Had the thieves been looking for these?*

She stepped down, clutching the jewels in her left hand. She opened the cabinet door and ripped a piece of paper from the inside shelf lining, put the diamonds in it, wrapping them up and placing the tiny packet in her mitten with the money from Grigory. *Had he known his mother had hoarded two diamonds? Were there any others? Were they hers or was she keeping them for Yasha?* Noise from the staircase outside seeped into the apartment and a leaky valve hissed. She put the chair back in place. Then she dressed in her outer clothing, slipped on her rucksack, picked up the tote, turned off the lights, and stood by the door. When all was quiet she exited, closed and locked the door, and once more pocketed the key.

She decided not to go to the pawnshop to redeem the stub. It was late and she had the packages to trudge with her. By the time she got home, she was exhausted by the extra weight of Calina's groceries, despite the fact that she had transferred some of the foodstuffs to her rucksack. At the same time, she was elated by her find, yet confused. *Could Grigory have killed his own mother?* Anya knew in her heart he was capable of murder by the way he had sadistically beat her. *But his own mother? So cruelly? Brutally?*

Once more in her apartment building, Anya trudged up the stairs, careful not to touch the banister. There was a sign saying "WET PAINT." Boris was already on her floor and had painted the banisters below.

"Good evening, Anya," Boris said in his booming voice.

"Looks great. Where did you ever find paint?"

"My friend owns the auto shop to fix all those Packard cars and other fancy cars for a *bol'shoy vystrel*— I do handyman jobs for him."

"A payment in paint for doing jobs for a bigshot."

"I think there's more than one heavyweight. I've seen a parade of lots of fancy cars."

She decided on the spur of the moment to give Boris some of her groceries. "Boris, I have a gift for you—some beets. After you've finished the job, knock on my door. Please knock five times fast, and five times slow so I'll know it's you."

He nodded his head slowly in understanding. "I will, Miss Anya. Are you worried about robbers?"

Anya shrugged. "You can never be too cautious even if you have nothing to lose."

Before going to get Iskra from Yelizaveta, Anya went to her place and disrobed. She didn't put away the grocery items, made a cup of tea, and sat down with the unwrapped paper, which she'd opened. She looked at the diamonds. *Had she now endangered herself and Iskra? Who could she tell? Confide in? What could she do with these precious stones? People can't eat diamonds. Who could she sell them to? What if Yasha somehow was connected to the murderer and knew that Calina possessed them or was hiding them? Possibly for him or from him.*

Tomorrow she'd go to the other pawnshop and see what the article was that Calina had left there, possibly as a hiding place, but from whom? And now, faced with all of these dilemmas, where could she hide these jewels? She sipped the tea, and looked around. Why not the same overhead place Calina had used? The police hadn't found them, had they? But what if it wasn't Calina who'd hidden them? What if they belonged to Grigory? Yasha? Anya couldn't be sure but knew she surely should not use the same hiding place. Where? And if it were someone other than Calina who'd hidden the stones, could they figure Anya now was in possession of them? Could she trust Andrei enough? Hadn't he shared incriminating intelligence with her about his spurious identity which was far more intimidating? No way would she endanger Yeliza-veta—she couldn't burden her with this information or hide the stones with her. Where? For the moment, Anya placed the stones underneath a cloth in the basket of eggs on the windowsill. Perhaps she'd sew a false hem in her bedroom curtains towards the top like a pleat and insert them there. She decided to hide the five thousand ruble note the same way Calina had. She took hold of the only picture she had in the house—a picture of herself in a white ballet costume from Swan Lake. She placed the money behind the picture, but kept the pawn stub in her glove for tomorrow.

Late afternoon
Thursday, December 20, 1956

Anya and Iskra were picked up and escorted to Police Headquarters. Brought in for gruff questioning, not in the way Andrei would have liked Anya knew, she held her head up as he kept passing by to let him know that things were all right. She answered directly and with conviction, using a softer tone in her voice like he'd instructed her to do and keeping her eyes down in a submissive attitude. Nevertheless, their stories matched the information Andrei had gathered. On her way out, he told her basically, he was off the case, except for the photos he would take at the autopsy.

Evening
Thursday, December 20, 1956

When they returned from Police Headquarters, Iskra and Anya called on Yelizaveta to invite her to have dinner. Anya said she'd had a windfall and found money on the street to buy groceries.

"Hot soup sounds divine. Shall I help you prepare it?" Yelizaveta asked.

"First, Iskra's going to do some reading and then we'll knock to tell you when it's time to get ready—you can peel the potatoes and scrape the carrots."

Yelizaveta winked. "I've got a gift to celebrate this windfall. Black bread from an admirer." She nodded her head toward the staircase, and Anya smiled, understanding it was from friend Boris.

While Iskra sat at the kitchen table reading aloud, Anya sewed a false patch into the thin curtains of her bedroom, and replaced them high on the curtain rod. She looked down when the girl stopped reading, and stepped off the chair she'd used for a stepstool.

Iskra was staring off in space.

Anya touched the child's shoulder gently. "What's the matter? Did the police station scare you?"

"Not that."

"Did you have a good morning at school?"

"I did a bad thing, *Mat*."

"You did. What?"

"The teacher let us outside for recess today. It's been warm so snow melted near the bushes."

"And?"

"I played with the doll you gave me."

"That's all right."

"In the mud. She's filthy. My poor dolly. Are you mad at me?" Iskra asked, her voice contrite.

"Sometimes these things happen. Did you leave the doll in school?"

Iskra shook her head with vigor.

"Let me see her then. Perhaps I can clean her."

Iskra dug into her book bag and pulled out the *matroyshaka* covered with dried mud.

Anya took the doll and used a rag to dust off much of the caked mud. The eyes were still smudged. "Let's try some water." She heated some in a shallow pan, wet the rag and put a little bit of dish soap on it. "This isn't working. Oh, I know, I have an old toothbrush—that may do the trick."

"What trick?"

"The cleaning trick," Anya said. "Gently she rubbed one of the eyes, then put some dish soap onto the toothbrush and added a little more elbow into the cleaning. The mud came away, but also some of the pigment of the eye color, and with it, Anya did an intake of breath.

"What's wrong, *Mat*?"

"Nothing, my little love. I'll just have to repaint the eyes," she said, staring at the bright diamonds. A terrible sense of dread overcame her with realization of what she'd just discovered in the eyes of the *matry- oshka* dolls. She coughed to gain time before answering. "I'm afraid I'm going to have to put this dolly in hospital to fully recover. Let's see if I can make you a more suitable one to play with at school out of an old sock."

When Anya went to call on Yelizaveta for dinner she saw, as she was hoping, Boris was still there painting. She said, "You didn't knock. I'll leave these beets here outside my door. Be sure to come get them when you're done." While he was bent over the railing, Anya took the toothbrush from her apron pocket and dipped it into the green paint, turned and went back to her place. Iskra was coloring in a book at the kitchen table. Anya kissed her daughter on the forehead, retrieved the diamonds from the egg basket and walked straight to her bedroom where she brushed paint onto the doll's eyes, thinking they were a bit dark in color. She'd put a dot of white in them tomorrow and cover them with clear varnish if Boris had any. She perched the two loose diamonds against the small lamp, painted and blew on them and closed the light. When they were dry she'd place them into the curtain's false hem. She washed the toothbrush in the kitchen sink, and stowed it underneath.

After dinner when Yelizaveta left, Anya put Iskra to bed and checked to see if the doll's eyes had dried. They had and so had the loose stones. She took the two painted diamonds in her hand, studied them, and a quick decision made her toss them into a cookie tin full of odd buttons. She closed the top and shook it.

So much for hiding them in the curtains.

Chapter Nine

It was near the dinner hour when Grigory saw two *babushki*, bent old grandmothers, enter the pawnshop with bundles like grocery bags. How long would he have to wait for them to conduct their trashy business of pledging one cup, one plate, one odd piece of silverware, perhaps a wedding ring? He walked away and waited in a small café called Beridze, an old Georgian inexpensive bistro that sold cheap *chebureki*, basically street food. The inside was drafty and dusty, but the smell of food frying made his mouth water. He ordered a traditional Tatar dish. He counted and recounted his coins to be sure he could pay for two deep-fried half-moon pies, one filled with meat and the other with cheese. He burned his mouth biting into the flaky, crunchy dough. He blew on it and took another bite, the juicy filling spilling down his chin, the spicy goodness satisfying. He gulped a glass of water and poured another from a chipped liter carafe.

A half hour later he walked back to the pawnshop, situated on a dark street of low-income houses. He was about to knock on the door: five times, three, then once, but changed his mind. He peered inside to see the old man with wire spectacles wearing a yarmulke, his mouth murmuring a silent prayer. Grigory watched Yasha pull off the skullcap and stash it in a drawer. *A religious crook.*

Grigory was long and lanky, dressed in black wool jacket and sports pants he'd stolen. The letters of the Soviet Union, CCCP, were in bold red print down the front calf of the *sharovary* sweat pants that cinched at the ankle. Up by the pocket on the left thigh were the same letters and above it a five-pointed red star with a hammer and sickle inside of it.

He circled around to the back alley and knocked five times, then three, and then once. A curtain was pulled aside and a tall, lean man with stooped shoulders came to the door and unlocked it. The pawnbroker stepped aside to let Grigory enter, swiftly closing and relocking the door.

"At this hour. Why so late?" the older man asked still standing in the dark.

"Have you seen what's coming down from the sky? And the gusts? There was a fallen tree across the road—the wind so strong it almost flattened me."

"Wear something warmer. Must you all the time look stylishly dressed? No one's supposed to see you. You're the invisible man. This—" he swept his hand up and down—"calls attention, you know."

Grigory smirked. "As if I had something better or warmer."

"Come in. I'm just making some tea." The pawnbroker pushed aside the curtain and a small candle burned on a high-standing jeweler's work table, two wooden extensions on each side, where he leaned his arms. Grigory pointed to the candle. "I hope you weren't trying to cut stones in this dim light."

"Don't be foolish. I'm heating water in the samovar. Want a cup of tea? I have some dried mint from Israel."

"Sure. Maybe it'll melt me. I'm an icicle." Grigory sat down in an old kitchen chair built from oak house beams, which still bore the marks of woodworm and nails.

The back part of the shop served as home to the willow-stick man. He had a bed, covered with a knitted woolen blanket, a wood-burning stove, and a low shelf with the samovar near a cracked white porcelain sink, the faucet dripping slowly. A dark woolen coat hung on a coat stand, a moth-eaten astrakhan hat perched on top.

"I won't ask if you want to remove your jacket. You're shaking. Sit near the stove." The old man threw in a few twigs and three broken small branches. The scent of burning resin filled the air along with the smell of damp wool of Grigory's jacket and scarf. He pulled off his knitted hat and held it near the fire.

"Don't put it too close or it'll burn."

Grigory pulled his hand back and hung the cap on the back of his chair.

The pawnbroker poured tea into two glasses and handed one to Grigory. "What's new?"

Waiting for the tea to cool, Grigory thought back to a week ago last Friday, the 14th, a few days before his mother had been killed. He remembered the conversation he had had with Yasha.

"My mother is onto what we've been up to and she isn't stupid. She knows she's not getting her fair share. She's complained about not getting a bigger cut because of Tamara. We can't take a chance of her talking to the working people—accidentally or on purpose."

"What kind of son are you? You're saying she has to be eliminated because she knows her son is a *goniff.*"

"A what?"

"A thief."

"No, I meant her friend, not my mother."

"Isn't she your cousin? The one who sells the dolls—"

"She has a big mouth—talks too much to customers and other stall sellers in the plaza. She needs to be silenced."

"By whom? Me? Never."

"She's not my cousin. No blood relation."

"Let's see what Kolya has to say about this."

"He hates that nickname. Call him Nikolai." Grigory walked over to a display case that held fancy knives. He fingered a porcelain handled red and gold switchblade, pushed the button to release the blade, closed and pocketed it.

"*Ladrón que roba a ladrón tiene cien años de perdón.*"

"What the hell is that?"

"It's an old Spanish expression that means: a thief who robs from a thief has a hundred years of pardon. Perhaps you'll spend less time in hell after all."

"How do you know Spanish?"

"I know several languages, philistine," Yasha said.

"What?"

"Uncultured swine."

"Watch your mouth, old man." Grigory said with menace in his voice.

"Or what? You'll sic Nikolai on me? Leave now. Come back next week. I've got work to do. And if blood ever touches that blade, I don't want the knife back. Understood?"

The retracing memory over, Grigory sipped the tea.

Yasha sat down and put dry mint leaves in Grigory's cooled tea and then in his own glass. He fanned the tea and swirled the mint around with a spoon.

Grigory blew on his glass and with his left hand fingered the knife in his pocket. He was going to put it back but recalled the old man's admonition about blood touching the blade and decided to keep it.

Yasha saw him fingering something in his pocket and pointed to it. "What're you hiding?"

"Your knife, but I'm keeping it in case I need it."

"I never want to see it again. Understood? Now drink up and get going."

Grigory nodded very slowly, his hooded eyes cast down, looking subservient so he wouldn't reveal hate or jealousy.

Chapter Ten

Morning
Thursday, December 20, 1956

Andrei Garin picked up *Pravda,* the newspaper he privately thought of as The Big Lie, but in reality was called, "The Truth." In his office, he read a sketchy piece that there had been a police raid in the market place, but before any arrest took place, an accidental death of a doll-seller occurred. She was identified as Tamara Petrova Blataskya. Why hadn't Nikolai told him about the incident in the Plaza? Andrei put down the paper and left his office to do some investigating. He went to the morgue and received no information, even after dropping names from headquarters. It was like this woman never existed. For some reason he hesitated rather than approach Nikolai. Andrei decided he'd go to the cemetery where her body would be kept in a receiving vault until gravediggers could dig a grave when the ground thawed.

He was surprised there were no family members, however some of the deceased's friends and neighbors were there. Giving his condolences as if he were a friend, Andrei discovered the "accidental death" was really a murder. Andrei gleaned information from a fellow-vendor. In the mayhem and confusion that day with police cars surrounding the plaza, the vendor overheard an unnamed witness state that the doll-seller had been killed by a man who walked and ran with a limp. The vendor repeated the words of the observant bystander: "A man appeared from out of nowhere, attacked her, and disappeared into the crowd. The strike was a vicious assault, a violent slashing of her neck." The description in Andrei's mind fit a contract killing—lacerating the jugular vein. *But why would the killer hazard such daring and in public with the authorities policing the area?*

Andrei picked up a stone and left it on a memorial slab near the receiving vault. There'd be no tossing a handful of dirt on the coffin after it would have been lowered into the ground. He shook with the bitter cold and walked away. Toward the cemetery gate, he picked up a handful of dead leaves and rubbed his hands. He walked to a little niche, recalling the tradition his father taught him. In the wall to the right of the gates, he washed his hands in a trickle of icy water that stung his hands. He shook them off and dried them on his jacket and put on his gloves.

Who was the witness? Why wasn't he brought in for questioning? Why hasn't anyone else come forth to make a statement? Why wasn't Andrei asked to photograph the scene?

Why wasn't he asked to take pictures of the dead woman in the autopsy room? Why was no one willing to talk to him at the morgue? He found it strange, all hushed up and he wasn't privy to any of it. Where had he been? What was he doing? Who was at the crime scene?

Some odd kind of calculation presented an equation and was about to solve itself. *Could the man with the limp be connected to Calina's murder? Could it be Anya's Ex? Anya had said that the doll-seller had foisted three dolls upon her when she got scared because of the policemen approaching. Was there a connection?*

Midday
Thursday, December 20, 1956

Andrei Garin was back in headquarters by noon. As he unpacked his camera and equipment, his mind reviewed and considered his work up until this time. He had worked for the MGB, the Ministry of State Security, the Soviet Secret Police from 1946-1953, and in 1954 when it became the KGB, Committee for State Security. He despised it and then became part of a secret Special Forces unit that was involved in investigating murders but he lacked status. He hated being demoted, but it served his purposes of getting out of the dreaded KGB. He managed somehow to ensconce himself into a position he invented, an investigating photographer, which his friend Sasha helped him secure.

At the Police Commissar's Office at the Police Station, Andrei knocked lightly on the open door.

"Come in, Andrei, I've been waiting for you," Chief Vladislav Sergeyvich Linsky said. "Sit." He motioned to a straight-backed chair. Andrei spotted a box of cigars on the desk.

"Please, help yourself," the chief said, and handed Andrei a box chock full of cigars. In fact the box was overstuffed, and therefore contained the remains of yet another box.

Andrei took one, regarding the brand H. Upmann stamped on it. He sniffed the cigar and handed back the box, wondering if they'd been counted, or if he could filch one for later when perhaps the chief looked the other way. Yeah, sure.

The chief closed the box and extended his hand toward Andrei, who reached for the clipper, a double bladed guillotine, and then cut the tip off the cap of the cigar head about 0.3175 centimeters. "Thank you, sir. You live well, Comrade Commissar and are much appreciated."

The chief shook his head.

Did that mean, 'Not really?' Andrei doubted it. *Had he overstepped his bounds?*

The chief shifted in his chair. "I saw the pictures of the dead woman Nikolai showed me in the apartment. A tragedy—a break-in for nothing."

Andrei nodded and put the cigar in his mouth so he wouldn't have to answer. He took hold of a box of matches from the desk and lit the other end with a wooden match. He puffed several times, wishing he had a good cognac to accompany the cigar. He took a long drag on the cigar, held the smoke in his mouth, and then puff-puffed it out in round ringlets into the stale air that hung in the office like the scent of a moldy shower curtain. He looked up at the ceiling. The brown water marks reminded him of a map of countries he'd never visited but would like to.

"I'm waiting, Andrei."

"Beg pardon, sir?"

"I want to hear why you think there was possibly something more to this—something overlooked. Nikolai and Sasha assure me it was nothing more than a delinquent, malicious theft."

"Maybe," he said, trying to stall and cover his tracks, "it was perhaps what the child mentioned."

"Which was?"

He thought before implicating policemen. "She kept indicating heavy shoes. Like a workman's perhaps."

How Andrei would like to be anywhere but here this minute talking to this son-of-a-bitch-cocky-bastard. The chief, out of uniform, wore an imported tweed coat, silk tie, and starched white-collared shirt, freshly laundered by a maid he never tipped.

The last time he smoked a cigar he was heading home. He'd stolen it from a busy train station store in the Moscow terminal. Then it dawned on Andrei he should've pretended not to have known how to smoke one so the chief could have shown him. A missed opportunity. Wasn't his whole career fucked-up anyway?

The phone rang, which startled the chief, and with an abrupt dismissal and wave of the hand, he sent Andrei on his way, oddly, without having been questioned further. And what was the reason for the chief's magnanimous behavior with the cigar? Was that to put Andrei at ease and throw him off guard?

Walking down the corridor to his office, Andrei thought how he'd rather be playing a game of marbles on the tattered carpet with the little girl, Iskra, toying with the cat's eye beauty she had in her measly collection. He'd like to be making breakfast for that girl's sweet-smelling mother. He pictured Anya stepping out of the old-fashioned copper bathtub with her wet hair dripping onto freckled shoulders. He'd followed her down the small hall of her apartment and watched her through the crack of the door she'd neglected to close all the way, because the painted door had swollen with humidity and no longer fit the frame. He'd moved away quickly as she started to towel off. He'd like to be making love, which is what he should have done instead of talk to her all that night long. Anya. He whispered her name in between the trails of smoke issuing from his mouth. In his office, he put out the cigar and wrapped it in a piece of paper, and put it in his camera case to enjoy later.

A knock on his so-called office door. Nikolai— a mouth he'd like to sew shut. How Andrei didn't want to speak to this *sookin syn*, son of a bitch, in front of him, occupying the space behind the perimeter of the scarred pine desk, the warm walnut stain wearing off.

Andrei decided to wait till flowers started sprouting from the mold on the walls, but he certainly wasn't going to initiate a conversation. What did this guy want from him?

"Nice of you to take the woman and child home from the crime scene," Nikolai said.

Was Nikolai his friend? He sure had a big mouth and rumors were he'd spoken ill of Andrei in front of the chief.

"Let's hear what happened with the little girl and what the mother had to say."

"Well," Andrei began, coughed, thinking of how not to implicate Anya, or make it sound as if he were involved with her in any way. "At first the child's mother said the dead woman was—she didn't know the woman was dead—but she did say, the woman in the apartment of the crime scene was her mother. Later, she changed her story and said the woman was her mother-in-law. She must have thought that by saying it was her mother, she'd have quicker access."

"No conjectures, please, let's just hear the story. Tell me what happened." Nikolai leaned his bulk against the door jamb.

Andrei repeated almost verbatim what the little girl had said about being hidden under the bed when her grandmother was attacked.

Nikolai's expression changed from confident to anxious. "But she didn't see the actual crime committed, right? The body was found in the living-room."

Andrei shook his head. "She said she saw only pants and shoes and heard the drawers of a piece of furniture being smashed. That's it. Nothing concrete or important."

Ten minutes later, Andrei was once again summoned to the chief's office and sat opposite him. There was a knock on the door. "Ah, Nikolai, I'm not ready for you yet," the chief said from behind the antique desk. "I'll send for you when I'm done with Andrei," he barked.

"By all means, sir," Nikolai said, and winked. *Sincere or not?*

Andrei smiled a crooked little smile and saluted, but all he could think was, Nikolai, ever the fawner—he practically genuflected and kissed the chief's putrid feet. *If that what's expected of me I'll never make the force.*

"Oh, and close the door," the chief said.

Nikolai hunched his shoulders a bit, the way a hunting dog does when assimilating a command he was just given.

The office chatter became louder and people were shouting orders for coffee and tea to an office boy.

Chief Linsky moved aside the blind on his left, then moved it back and pushed down one of the slats and peered out to see if anyone was not manning a desk.

Andrei had a feeling of revulsion as if this man would stab you in the back instead of getting you back-up in a hot crime scene. He was a snake—hard to distinguish his colors he was so camouflaged and didn't know himself who's side he really was on, but certainly not Andrei's.

"I knew your father," the Chief said. "*Politseyskiy.* An excellent policeman, a top investigator, who never ranked high in the force because he wouldn't bend to circumstances."

Andrei thought about his adopted father, how he had quit teaching at the university to become a policeman to show loyalty to the party. "And those circumstances, sir, what would they have been?" What was Andrei thinking? What had emboldened him to ask? He knew some of them—the ones that Aleksandr Ivanovich Garin hadn't used—coercion by torture. But Andrei never knew what had made him become an enemy of the state. Andrei Aleksandrovich Garin was sure he wouldn't be hearing that.

Instead the chief said, "Those, I'm afraid I'm not at liberty to speak of, however—he had to answer to his chief in command and lieutenant."

"And at the time, sir, you were the lieutenant?"

"In fact, I was." The chief shifted in his seat and there was a loud creaking noise as if the chair objected to the weight being moved around.

Andrei had ventured too far. The chief was perspiring, so Andrei changed tactics. "My father was my father and what little I knew of him in his position, I respected. I know nothing of his service record because he was sent to Siberia before I understood exactly what kind of job he held." How smoothly the lie rolled off his tongue, it was so practiced.

Andrei lit a cigarette and puffed on it, playing dumb and wondering if his two fathers had ever met up in Siberia. *Two wonderful fathers lost to the Gulag.* He wanted to blow smoke in this asshole's face, but he, unlike his adopted father, did bend to the circumstances. He was young and wanted to continue living. He wanted to live to see Anya's face in the moonlight of a summer evening, or in the miserable hall light of her dingy apartment. He wanted to see her with the street light falling on those dark eyes and wavy hair, or all in a tangle on the unwashed sheets of her bed after he'd made love to her all night long.

Light from the window toward the street played upon the chief's desk. In the striped lines of light, he watched a profusion of dust motes. How he wished to be as quasi-invisible as these are right now. He would hop into the air and just be. Right along with all the other insignificant motes. But reality came crashing in on his fantasy daydream when the chief broke his reverie with yet another unreasonable demand. "You will go to Vladivostok. Nikolai and you leave tomorrow."

Andrei thought, Why me? but asked instead, "Can you spare him, sir? What has this to do with the case of the woman being murdered?"

"What? Don't be insolent." The chief abruptly rose from his chair.

"I was hoping, sir, for some information concerning the investigation."

"Confer with Nikolai about it. This has to do with the conflict near the Chinese border." The chief sat back down and flicked his wrist toward the door. Andrei had been dismissed. He stood to leave.

"Wait one moment. Sit down. I've never divulged this to anyone. Your father once did me a great service and his brave actions saved my career. You're probably wondering why I'm sending you with Nikolai. I," he hesitated, "want you to pay attention to him." He leaned forward. "Do you get my meaning?"

Garin nodded and lowered his voice. "You want me to shadow him, sir?"

"This could get you lost in a proverbial deep forest you're unfamiliar with. You may have difficulty extricating yourself. What's more serious—your life may depend on it. I want you to remember this phrase and to be able to say it to any senior officer of any of our many Soviet divisions." Linsky rose from his chair and walked to the front of the desk. "In case something untoward occurs and you're hundreds of kilometers away and unable to contact me." He leaned in and whispered in Garin's ear: "*Cave idus Martias.*" Linsky straightened and tapped his heart.

Controlling his emotion, Garin looked into Linsky's eyes. "I studied both Latin and Shakespeare, sir."

Linsky nodded and raised his hand.

Garin stood, opened the door quietly and walked into the hallway, thinking about the expression Linsky murmured: *Beware the Ides of March.* The chief distrusts his next in line. Andrei's thoughts darted to the Sino-Soviet clashes at the border. He'd have to do some digging around. All he knew was Vladivostok was the administrative center of the Far Eastern Federal District and Primorsky Krai, Russia, which was located somewhere around Golden Horn Bay, not far from Russia's borders with China. Maybe they wanted him because he was not privy to what was really going on there. So concentrated was he as he walked down the hallway, he almost tripped Nikolai.

"Garin. In my office. Now." Nikolai motioned toward his office with a thumb.

Stepping inside the office, Andrei remained standing while Nikolai lambasted Garin because he'd gone missing for a day.

Finally, Nikolai calmed down and took a breath. "Where were you the day after the apartment murder?"

"I had car trouble and there was heavy snow." Andrei covered his mouth and cheeks and drew his hand slowly down. He wanted to look as ashen as he felt. "That and I was sick. I'd eaten some of the dead woman's soup. Cramps, the shits." He put his hand on his stomach and pulled a face.

"There's no time for you to be ill. You knew you were supposed to be on call to bring the child and her mother in. Yet we won't get to talk with them until later today." He stood up from his desk and walked around. He thrust his face close to Andrei. "And I needed you to take photographs of yet another murdered woman in autopsy." He stood and slammed his fist down on the desk. "A murder committed the day before the one in the apartment. But about the same time."

"Bizarre, isn't it? Two women."

Nikolai nodded. "This old crone was a vendor in the plaza."

"What did she sell?"

"What the hell does it matter?" Nikolai said in a gruff voice.

"It's just that—is there a possibility there's a connection to Afghan drug smuggling?" Andrei tried to look disinterested, but the best he could manage was lowering his eyes and rubbing his hands on his thighs.

"She sold trinkets, those touristy nesting dolls."

Andrei was struck by the thought, could it be? Oh shit, *vot govno!* Anya's doll-seller was killed. A mere transient thought of Anya brought to mind: supple and eloquent, like flowing satin draperies. *Pay attention, a voice within warned.*

"The chief said you'd arrange our travel plans," Andrei said.

"Don't change the subject. What else did the chief want from you? Sit down. I can't stand you towering over me. Remember, it was Sasha and me who got you this job of photographer—I'm responsible for you, you idiot."

"Since I wasn't there, can you tell me what happened?"

Nikolai handed him the report and after Andrei finished reading, he handed it back.

"The plaza literally crawled with our colleagues, yet someone reached the vendor before our men could pick her up. It happened about the same time only a day before the other murder in the apartment. Some witnesses. No precise visuals. A man, with a loping gate, strolled up to her, seemingly to ask for a light for a cigarette and slashed open her jugular—casual as a Sunday morning stroll. My men sealed off the plaza and left the corpse and everything else cordoned off. You, fuck-off, were supposed to be there to photograph the scene. Where were you? No bad soup, no shits excuse—"

"I was in the office till noon and then I was sent to take photos of a tank driver who'd been in the Hungarian conflict." *So it wasn't anything surreptitious and I wasn't left out.*

"Now we have shit morgue shots from that incompetent snot-nose kid—what's his name?"

"Brodsky."

"You've taught him nothing. What do you do when you're supposed to be instructing him—a pair of jerk-offs."

"Not my fault if he's a no-talent kid. So your men went to the plaza to bring the vendor in for interrogation—in connection with a smuggling ring. Drugs? Or something else?"

"Yes. On a tip."

"Which?"

"Doesn't matter now. Too late because she was slain in broad daylight, surrounded by Leningrad's finest. And the assailant got away. Limp and all. And where was our photographer that day? In the toilet where he belongs? No, he was taking la-di-da photos of a ten-day war hero. Who sent you on that job?"

Andrei got up and closed the door, knowing it wouldn't help much to muffle Nikolai's angry yelling. Andrei sat back down. "The chief."

Nikolai punched his chest and cleared his throat, meaning he'd make a far better chief.

"Any connection between the two women?" Already knowing the answer, Andrei coughed into his sleeve.

"Probably not. None we can establish." Nikolai lit a cigarette and tossed the pack of Belomorkavals on the desk.

Andrei moved his chair so he wouldn't get the brunt of the awful smell. What was he smoking, shit?

"Do you know something more about the apartment murder?"

"Me? No. How would I with my head in the sink of the crapper?"

"Brodsky called you. Three times. You never answered the phone." Andrei shook his head. "If you were as sick as I was, Nikolai, you wouldn't have either."

"But were you home?"

"Where else would I be messing my pants every hour?"

"Brodsky tailed you after you brought the girl and her mother home. You stayed late."

"Car trouble." *But why did he tail me?*

"But then you left."

"Got the car to start."

"You've got every kind of excuse. You stay up late practicing these?"

Andrei shook his head.

"Vladivostok," Nikolai practically spat out the word. "I'm taking you along. We'll need photographs. It's supposed to be a covert operation, but they make it so clandestine, we don't even know what on earth we're supposed to be on the lookout for. The chief doesn't let his right hand know what the left is doing, and mostly he's just jerking off."

Andrei didn't know what to say. "Is it possible there's a smuggling racket going on that has nothing to do with these murders?" he asked, knowing it was a disingenuous question.

"I doubt there's a connection—these murders and drug smuggling. Completely random. Nobody with a motive. No ties to a possible trafficking case—" Nikolai gave Andrei a look that cut off all possible dialogue, making him feel as if he'd stepped in a pile of dog dirt.

After they'd gone their separate ways, Andrei realized he'd never heard Nikolai disparage the chief before. Was this supposed to ingratiate Andrei, make him speak more freely? Andrei had a feeling it was something that had nothing whatsoever to do with the border clashes and had more to do with him being tested. *What furtive crap could they be after now?* Nikolai'd said I'm taking you along, but Linsky had made it clear he was sending Andrei to keep an eye on Nikolai.

All that day Andrei Garin had tried to find out more about the case involving Anya's dead "mother-in-law" and Tamara, the doll vendor who had been Calina's friend. His search was to no avail. Either nobody could piece together what had happened or there was no link between Calina and the doll-seller. Calina's case had conveniently been dismissed as breaking and entering by a street hood. The vendor's case got smothered as some kind of grudge killing—shelved under more important files. But something kept nagging at Andrei. What had Iskra said about her father? Something about the way he dragged his foot. A club foot? An injured foot? Something he didn't always do—only when he was tired or was nervous? Andrei's intuition told him there might be an association, a relationship, not only between the two women but also to their murders.

Chapter Eleven

Friday, December 21, 1956

The next day Anya stood in front of the pawnshop and looked up to see the familiar three gold balls dangling from a straight rod. She recalled Calina saying that you address all pawnbrokers as "uncle." At least she wouldn't appear ignorant and inexperienced. Upon entering the shop she heard the tinkle of a bell. Surprisingly the man who greeted her wasn't old. He inclined his head and said, "Good day."

Anya looked around. "Good day to you, Uncle." She stood in front of a jewelry case and took off her gloves. The ticket fell out onto the glass top. "I'd like to redeem this." She handed him the stub.

He gazed at it for a few seconds. "One moment, please." He stepped to a desk, retrieved a book and looked up the number. He then went to a cabinet and brought out a doll. Anya was surprised to see another *matroyshaka*, but tried to keep her face neutral.

"You didn't leave this here," he said, a note of accusation in his voice.

She shook her head. "My mother did, but she's too ill, and asked me to get the doll for her."

"You'll have to sign next to her name. It will be one thousand."

"Of course," she said, trying to hide the fact that she expected it to cost far less.

"She said it was antique and a family treasure, but it doesn't look so old to me." He pushed the book toward her to sign, dipped a pen in ink, and handed it to her.

Anya saw that Calina had used Rada's name, so instinctively she used Yelizaveta's first name, and invented a patronymic and finished the signature with Rada's surname. Anya took hold of the doll. The eyes were not jewels. She wanted to open the nesting dolls within, but would do it at home. *Could the man have switched out the stones and repaired the painted eyes?*

She dug into her pocket and paid the man, thanked him as she watched him wrap the doll in brown paper and tie it with a string. He accompanied her to the door, which tinkled once again as she left.

At home, once more, Anya undid the package and opened the nesting dolls, seeing that the outermost doll did not have diamond eyes, but every one of them within had smaller, painted diamonds in the eyes. *Had Calina been killed because this doll with ten sets of smaller stones had not been found in her apartment?*

Chapter Twelve

Friday, December 21, 1956

Andrei overheard the chief's ideas which were more concerned about a smuggling ring involving Interpol than any of the recent murders. The latest communique—a teletype and a brief dispatch—Andrei only got a glimpse of the compromised words: jewels, drugs, illegal imports, Middle East, and ....

The chief's stamps of "Top Priority," conveyed a message that Andrei interpreted as meaning: Russia is worried about what China thinks, and now wants friendly relations.

China? How did that figure? Hadn't Anya told him the pawnbroker was also a hidden Jew? Wouldn't that involve Israel? Andrei sat at a small desk in a partially secluded shared office, an array of photos covering his desktop. His office "partner," the kid Brodsky, was infirm and on hospital leave.

As he sorted the photos, he noticed the victim's right hand was tightly closed in a fist. The autopsy would be held today, and he intended to be present.

He gathered all the photo prints, shoved them into a manila envelope and pushed them under the blotter.

He needed much more information if he were to solve the puzzle of Calina's murder—he'd wait till after the autopsy, hoping for more. But what was happening in two other countries? An impossibility. Israel had been mentioned last week in a meeting, and now this sudden upcoming trip to China. What about the other things? What kind of drugs? And jewels? What little Andrei knew of goods-for-trade, he understood they were popping up suddenly as bribes. To whom? Other than department heads and *shkvorni* kingpins? From where and to where? Retrieved in which country? His own? Smuggled or trafficked out, but how? China? Israel? Finland to Alaska? Or brought in as contraband?

Andrei made no sense of it, so made a pretense of reading the newspaper. His mind bustled with private thoughts of the geopolitical situation in which the Soviets found themselves. There was nothing in the paper except the usual Communist rhetoric—nothing substantial as to what the Western Bloc was up to of late. Hearing approaching footsteps, he ditched the newspaper under his desk and shuffled around some papers.

His chief interrupted with barely a knock on the open door. "Quit daydreaming. Screw the dead woman—start concentrating on more important things. She's not getting any deader by you going to the Chinese border where all of the unrest and clashes are occurring. Chinese soldiers murdering our patrols—Mao Tse-Tung thinks he should be called the world leader of Communism now that Stalin is gone. Besides you're not going to solve this case—you're not even on the force. People get killed all the time. Turn up missing. All the time. You'll leave tomorrow with Nikolai. Now get down to the morgue."

After the harangue from the chief, Andrei sauntered out of his office. On his way down the staircase into the bowels of the building, he kept thinking of all of the medical examiners, coroners, pathologists, detectives, mortuary workers, and cops that worked in the morgue. Did they ever get used to it? He laid his camera down carefully on a small outside desk and sat in the folding chair next to it to put the coverings over his feet. He picked up a smock, a pair of rubber gloves, a mask, and then read a sign on the door.

не вводите процедуру
Ne vvodite protseduru

He read: **DO NOT ENTER PROCEDURE ONGOING**, donned the smock, took a small vial out of his pocket and put two drops of essential oil of lavender on the mask, put the vial back, and popped a peppermint in his mouth hoping he wouldn't vomit. He put on the mask, pulled on the gloves, picked up the camera and pushed the door open with his shoulder. The doctor in charge, Viktor, was a studious, mousy little fellow with wire-rimmed spectacles always sliding down his nose. He looked up. "Just in the nick of time, dear comrade," the *vrach* said, buttoning his white doctor's coat.

Andrei nodded to everyone and noticed that Nikolai stood back of the little gathering. The naked body was prone on her abdomen. "Homicide, that's certain. But look here," Doktor Viktor said, and pried open the corpse's clenched right hand. "Interesting. A charm of some sort. I want to take a sample of what's under her fingernails."

Andrei snapped a close-up of what at first looked like a small gold trinket, but on closer inspection, he saw it was a small earring mounting with a screw back. The doctor picked up the object with a long tweezer to examine it and confirmed Andrei's evaluation. "Seems to be an unset earring," he said, and dropped it in a kidney-shaped, white porcelain-covered metallic bowl on a rolling table.

"Looks like a child's earring," Andrei said, and snapped another photo.

The doctor inspected the wounds on the woman's head and shoulders. He described the blows and the possible instruments used. "I make the judgement, discerning from the majority of gashes, position and angle of the truncheon-type marks, that the assailant was most-likely left-handed." He looked at Andrei, whose camera seemed to be a rapid snapping turtle, shooting one after another of several photos of the lacerations, bruises, and injuries of the blood-matted head and upper back torso. "But that's speculation. I'd never swear in front of a judge, or for that matter," he said, pausing, and pointed to Nikolai, "anyone upstairs."

"The weapon of assault was indeed a fireiron from the hearth, located at the scene." He pointed to it leaning in a corner. "Must be a very old building if it still had a wall fireplace oven—haven't seen one of those since I was a boy. And before any of you even ask the answer is no—forensics won't get any fingerprints off—either a glove was worn or the prints were smudged and wiped clean." *Did that mean the assassin was a professional?*

With the aid of an assistant technician, the doctor turned the body over to a supine position.

Andrei Garin wasn't going to stay for the rest of the autopsy. He'd seen plenty of them and didn't care for the gruesome dissection when the doctor would make a Y-incision, starting at the tip of each shoulder, running under the breasts to join at the sternum, around the solar plexus, behind the stomach below the diaphragm, extending downward, terminating at the pubis. Garin didn't care if the doctor was able to determine what the woman had eaten, or the time of death, or any other pertinent information the police required. He'd gotten what he needed.

Garin made a little salute to the group with his camera and leaned his shoulder to the door and pushed it open. He tossed the autopsy gear in a large garbage bin.

He trudged up two flights of stairs, his camera case swinging from his shoulder. Sasha from fingerprinting was on his way down. His full name was Alexandr Abramovich Sokolov, an underground brother Jew, who sometimes acted in an arrogant manner towards Andrei in front of other officers. He wore an Orthodox cross on a silver chain around his neck. Sometimes, he'd accidentally allow it to fall out of his shirt so he could make a show of placing it under his shirt. They'd met by chance at a hidden Kaddish service when a distant relative of Andrei's father died.

Sasha and Andrei became close as brothers, but anyone working in their department would think they were antagonistic toward each other.

Andrei nudged his head toward the exit door to the backside of the building to a fire escape. "I need a breath of fresh air."

"Oh, mind if I join you for a smoke?"

"Not at all," Andrei said a bit too loudly.

Once out of doors, they moved quickly down a flight of rickety stairs to a ledge away from the offices. Sasha took out a cigarette. Andrei bent down as if to tie his shoe. "*Azoy, bruder, vi'zenen di tingz mit ir?*"

"How are things with me, brother? Not bad," Sasha whispered.

"Still think there's some conspiracy underway?" Andrei cupped his hands as Sasha's lit match touched his cigarette.

Sasha shook his head so slowly the move was almost imperceptible and barely moving his mouth muttered, "I wouldn't trust anyone. Especially The Bear."

Andrei knew the reference was to Nikolai. Both men looked away from the building and continued to speak in hushed tones.

"It's dangerous to speak Yiddish," Sasha whispered.

Andrei agreed, nodding and switched to Russian. "I remember so little of it anyway."

"Can you write Hebrew?"

Andrei shook his head slightly. "I read it."

"That means I can write you, but you can't answer. Better never to use it anyway. Do you know the Torah?" Sasha took a drag of his cigarette.

"Not well enough to decipher and write a response."

"Didn't think you could, so I brought this." Sasha unbuttoned his shirt, reached inside, faced away from the building, pulled out a children's fairytale book and handed the book to a surprised Andrei.

"I think I read this as a child," Andrei said.

"Numbers." Sasha buttoned his shirt quickly.

Andrei looked at him. A question creased his brow.

"First number is the chapter, the next is the page, next the line, next number count the words in the line and so on until a break and the next chapter number. I have an exact copy. Don't use the system too often and always typed—even numbers can give a person's handwriting away."

Andrei's first thought was, And so can a typewriter.

Sasha began to shake, and as if he'd heard Andrei's thought, said, "Use someone else's typewriter." He ground out the nib of his cigarette under his shoe and, without another word, walked up the stairs and inside.

While still facing away from the building, Andrei put the book as surreptitiously as he could into his camera case. He crossed his arms over his chest and stuck his hands beneath them. He waited until he felt his feet numbing with cold before he, too, re-entered the building, noticing the book sticking out from his case. He stopped, shoved it deeper into the case and tried to zip it closed. No luck. He shoved the case under his arm.

When he got back to his office, Andrei took the book out and put it in his satchel, considering the lie he'd tell if someone saw the book. But of course. Iskra. He'd read to her from the book.

He grinned to himself, and then started cleaning his police camera, remembering the first one his father had given him to shoot pictures of nature. He still had the photograph of the family's dacha hidden in between the layer of cardboard and fake leather of his desk blotter. If the picture were ever discovered, he had ready a perfect explanation—a gift from Sasha, who'd seen it.

As he loaded film, he whistled in admiration. The police camera was a beauty, the Leningrad, 35 mm rangefinder manufactured by GOMZ or Gosularstvennyi Optiko-Mekhanicheskii Zavod, the State Optical-Mechanical Factory.

Nikolai popped his head around the corner. "Stop making love to the camera—you'll never own one."

"Never say never. This baby was conceived by Shapiro and has a spring motor advance, and takes 39 mm screw lenses."

"Hooray for Shapiro and yay for you—get it together and fast. You're on loan to the KGB, Big Uncle Danilov has requested you to take pictures of a downed aircraft. There'll be a car waiting for you at the Bolshoi Dam. I don't know anything more."

"Uncle Danilov, eh? How come the chief is so connected to him?"

Nikolai gave him the snake eye. "Don't ask, and you'll never have to worry or cover up anything, and don't slip and call him uncle. It's Comrade Commisar Oscar Petrov Danilov, but don't use his patronymic, or it's your ass. It's Comrade Commisar to you. Got it?"

Andrei stood, nodded, and thought: you and him both. Out of earshot, but under his breath said, "Comrade—*tovarishch*, my ass."

When he arrived at the Bolshoi Dam, he could feel the bracing wind blowing off the Neva a block away. He looked up at the sky—clotted cloud cover—distant thunder, and not a bird singing. *Would it ever be spring again in this godforsaken mottled gray city? Spring is just late winter. Will I ever see the White Nights again? Will I ever be able to shed coat, boots, and gloves—be free to walk with Anya on my arm and buy her an ice cream?*

A car was waiting and drove Andrei to *Shosseynaya* Airport, named after the nearby railway station.

On the scene of the downed aircraft, Andrei snapped pictures of everything he was told to and more. He asked the lower echelons any questions he had without trying to sound inquisitive. It seemed to him the lower ranking officers were always willing to talk more and give out with intelligence they didn't think was top secret.

Andrei singled out a young officer who was reading over his notes at the edge of a potato field.

"Do they know what kind of plane it was?" Andrei asked innocently enough.

"A single pilot plane—of extremely high technology. It must have been flying very fast and high."

"A spy plane? Did we blow him out of the sky?"

The youth shook his head. "*Niet, niet,*" he said, his tone serious. The wreckage indicates no weapons, but it was loaded with cameras and equipment."

"So it was a spy plane—to gather information."

The boy realized his mistake. "Da," he said almost in a whisper.

Three hours later, Andrei delivered the developed film to Nikolai, who would get it to the proper sources.

He couldn't wait to see Anya again to tell her what Calina had held in her hand and news that Tamara, the doll-seller, had been killed, but that was an excuse—what he wanted was to see her dark flashing eyes, and with that thought, the song *Óči čjórnyje* came into his mind. *Dark Eyes.* It struck him he didn't remember the exact words to the song, but felt there was a line that went something like: *we had a chance encounter on a luckless day!* He recalled his Gypsy friend Omar had sung the song on many occasions—surely he'd know the lyrics; Andrei would ask him.

Chapter Thirteen

Morning
Saturday, December 22, 1956

Andrei walked into the train station, looking at every kiosk to find Nikolai who should've been purchasing train tickets to Moscow, seven-hundred and five kilometers away. Andrei bought the tickets for the second leg—the connect with the Trans-Siberian railway system from Moscow to Vladivostok. That way they would both be out some money, but neither one would have to sport the entire price. Supposedly they'd be reimbursed immediately but with red tape that could be a month from now.

Andrei found Nikolai seated in a cold waiting-room sipping hot tea with honey and eating what looked like a stale brioche.

"Breakfast and lunch," Nikolai said. He took a big bite of his pastry and while chewing, reached into his coat pocket and pulled out the two tickets for the first leg of the trip, waving them theatrically at Andrei. "Cash them in for me. We're in luck. The KGB godfather to the chief, our dear uncle, said we can hop on a transport plane and be there in no time. Do you have the tickets for the connection in Moscow to the Trans-Siberian?"

Ah, my fat man, you're not the only one to obey orders. "Look, my dear *tolstyak*," he said, patting Nikolai's girth. With a smile as big as the trip from Leningrad to Moscow, Andrei fanned his face with the two tickets from Moscow to Vladivostok.

After cashing in the tickets, Andrei handed the money to Nikolai, who pointed to a beer house. "One drink and then you're free to go until later."

The last thing on earth Andrei wanted to do was sit drinking this early in the day in the company of one of his least-liked human beings on the planet. Yet, he had no choice. It was like being asked to fraternize with one of the demoted princes of the royal house of Romanov. What was worse was that Nikolai would conveniently get up to use the WC when the bill arrived.

Afternoon
Saturday, December 22, 1956

Andrei dashed from the beer hall to the turnstile, noting the time, 12:22. There'd be time enough to see Anya and then go to his apartment to grab an extra sweater to stick in his duffle bag before he had to leave.

Nikolai had said they'd catch the transport at twenty-three hundred hours. Almost midnight. Andrei rethought his plan, decided to go home first, pack, and then see Anya. He could leave from her place for the air transport.

At the hovel he called home, Andrei tossed the sweater into his duffel, and at the last minute wrapped a bottle of Zubroŭka in newspaper and put it in between his clothes inside one of his boots. Zubroŭka. Andrei was quite fond of the Belarusian dry, herb-flavored vodka distilled from rye, better known as Bison Grass.

He went to Anya's flat and banged on the door. There was no answer and inside there was no movement, but he could swear he'd seen lights on when he stood out in the street looking up at her window, picturing her long legs encircling him.

He banged again. "Who—" Anya didn't have time to finish because the door opened and Andrei strode in like she was expecting him.

"How did you get in? What are you doing here?"

"Here's your key back. I made a copy," he said, his boyish look coy as if saying I stole a cookie from the jar.

"Aren't you just a slight bit presumptuous? What makes you think I want you to be able to have access to my—" One look at him told her the time for questions was over. He grabbed her by her sweater and pulled her into him. He kissed her hard and then harder and slammed the door in back of him with a solid kick. Reaching behind him, he locked it without looking, never taking his mouth from hers.

She staggered backward, put a finger on her mouth.

"Iskra?"

"Sleeping. I put her to bed early. She wasn't feeling well."

He went into the bedroom, picked up the child and put her on the couch and covered her with his jacket. Then he took Anya by the hand and brought her into her own room and closed the door.

"Will she wake?"

Anya shook her head. "She's a sound sleeper."

After they made hurried love, she shook her finger in front of his face, crooked it, opened the door and he followed her back to the kitchen.

She opened a cabinet and reached in back of some china, took out the small flask he'd left behind, and two glasses. She poured. They drank.

"Have you eaten? I have some borscht, but no dill or sour cream."

"Beets were made in Heaven. My mother never put sour cream in it because she'd sometimes add meat."

After he downed a bowl of hot soup, he asked for another shot of vodka.

She poured some into his glass. "What makes you so sure I'm interested in you, *ment?*"

"I'm not a cop. Only a photographer. Let's get that clear."

"Perhaps. For now, but it's what you want, isn't it?"

"Sorry, but I don't have time for a discussion of what I'd like to do for my life's vocation."

He drank the shot, got up and cleared off the table. As he washed the dishes, he told her about his day.

While Anya watched him, she pictured Grigory flinging the dinner off the table, smashing the dishes and cursing because she'd forgotten the sour cream.

When he finished he sat with her at the table, caressed her hands and told her why he found her to be an enchantress. She almost choked on her drink. He gently pulled Anya to her feet, patted her behind, and ushered her back to the bedroom. They undressed each other with slow determination that had been omitted in their hasty first performance.

When they were naked and trembling with expectation, cold, and delight, she stared down at him.

"What?"

"That." She pointed at his erect member.

"And? Serviceable, no?"

"Quite." She hesitated. "Only I didn't realize—you're enormous—a miracle you didn't rip me apart. And, and," she stuttered, "it's circumcised. I've never seen one of those before." She giggled.

He yanked her into an embrace. "Not so funny when you're trying to hide it while taking a piss with other men in the lavatory. Men— who could have you arrested for being a Jew."

"Oh, now I feel as small as that word," she said, but with so much emotion packed into it—it seemed like an explanation.

"No regrets—we don't have time for explanations for every misstep of spoken words."

In that instant she flung her arms tighter around his neck, both making a dive for the bed. He kissed her gently and petted her all over as if she were a soft toy. He took her again, more slowly and determined to pleasure her.

After they made love, they sat smoking on the bed. He told her what happened to Tamara, Calina's friend. The shock on her face told him she knew nothing about it. Andrei mentioned the assailant limped. She looked startled and whispered, "Impossible. Not Grigory."

"Would you know why Calina clutched a gold unmounted earring in her hand when she was killed?"

This brought a flash flood of tears to her eyes. "I've no idea. Maybe she found it in a guest's room at the hotel."

He shook his head. "That won't fly with the police. Little Gypsy girls wear gold earrings. Do you think—"

"Perhaps, she was going to have a pair mounted for Iskra."

"How did you know they were unmounted studs?"

"I didn't. Are you accusing me?"

He shook his head.

"Calina mentioned Grigory working with her pawnbroker friend, buying and selling stuff—I don't know. Then one day last week, she said she wanted to give Iskra something to remember her by—at the time, I didn't give it much importance—another crazy one of Calina's ideas. Just talk."

"Ah! Speaking of your little girl, I've brought her something. He got up and walked over to his satchel on a chair. He took out the book Sasha had given him and handed it to Anya.

"*Narodnye Russkie Skazki*. Such a beautiful collection of Russian fairytales by Alexander Nikolayevich Afanayev. I'm speechless."

"Then maybe you should show your appreciation in another way, Anushka."

The way he said the sweet, diminutive form of her name, had the effect he'd wanted to make her melt into him once more.

Anya went to the WC to wash and when she came back, walked over to him, took the cigarette from his hand and snuffed it out in the overloaded ashtray on the makeshift night table.

She backed up three paces and looked at him. It was all he needed. He pulled off the green sweater he was wearing, yanking it over his head, the undershirt coming off with it. His skin puckered with the cold. She dropped the raincoat she used as a bathrobe and sauntered over to him naked. She sat on the edge of the bed, bent and kissed his chest, his neck, his cheeks, and finally her mouth found his. He flipped her over and this time he was even more patient, warm and considerate.

"I'm afraid. I want to pull away from you, but here I am a willing captive to your gentle persuasion." She arched her back and head, her hair cascaded down, spilling around her like a curtain.

He kissed her neck and his mind reached an echoing pleasure before he actually brought her to the state of physical satisfaction. He sensed her skin felt every pulsation as if her body could somehow talk and spoke in reverberated tones into a microphone.

Of all the times for it to hit him. *Why now, when he thought it was a mere feeling of momentary elation he was after and nothing serious? Some are lucky to be touched by true love, that all-encompassing, myriad-marvelous gossamer, inexplicable thing. Am I falling for her? So soon? Impossible.*

"I must tell you this affair between us is going to be short-lived. It's going nowhere," she said.

He brought her face toward him. "If you don't care for me, why did you give me your body?"

She made a face, pursing her lips.

"I always wanted to be able to do that," he said and pointed to her face.

"What?"

"Make one eyebrow go up in distaste the way yours did now."

"I didn't give you my body," she said with emphasis. "Let's say it was a mistaken loan. Hunger. Desire." What she didn't say but he intrinsically knew was she felt an appalling loneliness. Overwhelming, enough to envision she could never be a woman satisfied, not even by a man she'd come to love.

"Call it whatever you want. I know what I felt. You felt it, too." Andrei yanked on his green sweater.

"Oh, you have a tear on the seam." She touched his left shoulder. "Come to the kitchen. I'll sew it for you."

"Ah, a domesticated lady."

"Sit. You're too tall for me to reach up. And don't tease. You must know all ballerinas are proficient with needle and thread. We sew elastic and satin ribbons on pointe shoes." From under the sink she pulled out a wooden box with crossed handles.

"Looks like a tool box."

"In a sense it is." She placed it on the table, opened the chest, threaded a needle with some green cotton, and sewed up the tear.

He reached with his opposite hand and ran his fingers along the seam. "Good job. It lays flat."

"Don't you carry a kit with you for emergencies?"

"I did in the Army, but I don't know what happened to it."

"Here, I'll fashion a quick one for you. This was supposedly my grandmother's and my mother's so there's double of everything." She sat next to him.

"Supposedly?"

"*Da.* My uncle told me it was theirs and gave it to me before he died. The only thing I have left of them."

She took out a square felt envelope, undid the button, removed a tape measure and laid it aside. On a four-finger size piece of cardboard, she wrapped around white thread, above it, some navy blue, triple the amount in black, and then brown. "Handy colors." She took out a silver instrument.

"What's that pretty thing with the engraved handle—looks like a piece of silverware for a fancy table?"

"An antique seam ripper so you don't cut material with scissors and only cut stitches."

"You don't want to trust me with that. What if I lose it?"

"You won't. Just don't hock it at a pawn shop. You can either give me a coin because it has a sharp point or give it back after your trip."

"What's the coin for?"

"For a sharp object. As if you're paying me or buying it so we don't break our friendship."

"I'm shocked."

"About what?"

"You're superstitious and you consider us friends."

She put a thimble on her finger and showed him how to use it. Anya gathered the supplies and put them in the felt kit, handing it to him. "There. A traveling gift for Andrei Garin." She held out her hand. "The coin?"

He shrugged on his jacket and put the kit in his breast pocket and patted it. He dug into his pants pocket and gave her a coin. "From your," he hesitated, "friend?"

"For now."

She didn't kiss him goodbye. He merely held her in a soft embrace. "Rest. Sleep. Dream of me." He kissed the top of her head and closed the door.

Chapter Fourteen

Saturday night
December 22, 1956

After Andrei left to meet up with Nikolai, Anya carried a groggy Iskra to bed. But Anya couldn't sleep and didn't even care to. In her cover-tossed bed, she told herself she must be careful with this man. Was Andrei a fox in sheep's clothing? Would he come to her as soon as he returned, or was this it? Hadn't she told him as much—that this was a brief affair. Nothing more. A transient convenience. But the key?

She folded an arm across her eyes and was somehow hurled back in time. She pictured herself seven years ago as the girl on the dock. She had left Grigory and infant Iskra stayed with Calina. She was going away with a married man she'd met in a temp job in an office. It was a crazy, impromptu thing, and she knew she didn't even care for him. What she needed, she'd convinced herself was to get away. Alone. Not feel the weight of responsibility for her child.

Sunday, April 24, 1949

On the pier she had waited in stormy weather. She watched the rain, marveling how the blown water sheeted above the slanted trees, the leaves silvering as they gusted. A fog horn sounded. She turned and walked away from the wharf, back to a small dingy café. She opened the door and went inside, sat down at a table and ordered a Russian coffee. The hot drink arrived made of a base of coffee with coffee liqueur, hazelnut liqueur and vodka. She thanked and paid the waiter, who also brought a glass of water, although she hadn't asked for any. She wanted to leave a tip, but she couldn't as she had no more money in her purse. Before she sipped, she made a big fuss about blowing on the hot liquid and fanning it with her hand, when in reality she was dumping in three lumps of sugar. Four more of which, she slipped into her pocket. She sipped the coffee, inhaling as she did, slightly burning her mouth and throat so that she had to take a sip of water to quench the fire.

She stared out the grimy window into the rain. She hoped he'd come for her. Come to take her away from all this misery. He'd said that he couldn't live without her, could not live if he knew he was never going to see her again. He told her to wait for him. If he didn't come, she should return again the next day, and then the day after that. He would surely come for her. Just as soon as he could.

She finished her coffee and looked at the big round-faced old clock on the far wall. Many people had boarded a boat, and she was almost alone in the café.

The ticket vendor closed the window of his booth and pulled down the shade on the inside. She knew she must leave. But where would she go? She picked up her battered suitcase borrowed from Calina and walked out into the night. It had stopped raining, but the wind had picked up and the temperature had turned bitter—much colder now than when she'd arrived. Street lamps were on, and she was tired from waiting almost all afternoon and now she was hungry and had no money, the last of it spent on that coffee that only warmed her temporarily.

She needed a place to sleep and was afraid the temperature would turn glacial. She couldn't face going to Calina's and telling her that she'd been ditched by yet another man. Where could she go? A woman alone with no means. She walked several blocks away from the pier and thought about a park she'd seen not far from here. She would go there and hide in the bushes and cover herself as best she could. Maybe if she could sleep she wouldn't feel so hungry. Maybe if she put on every article of clothing mashed inside the valise, she would warm up.

However, she got turned around somehow and knew she was lost and nowhere near the park. She entered a bad area of ramshackle buildings and derelict stores. She passed a grungy neighborhood she intuited wasn't in the direction she'd wanted to go, but it was late now. Anya saw a light at the end of a long dark alley, a black lane, and at the end of it three old men huddled around a fire. If the cops saw them, they'd haul them away and throw them in prison. Why weren't these men at home or at a job or doing something useful for the community? What was she doing here? Bait for these migrants?

She smelled something heating on their makeshift fire. She approached, though she told herself how unsafe this was, how dangerous and stupid. But like a body attached to a falling parachute from out of a plane, she either pulled the chute or fall to earth and crash.

She decided to give the chute a tug.

"Greetings," she said in a chipper voice as if this were broad daylight in the middle of Krasnaya Ploschad, Red Square. Krasnaya, the word meant both beautiful and red, and it was the farthest thing that her mind would let her dwell on. The only thing here was the middle of that open pit flame—one that could consume and burn her and her meager things to total oblivion. "Good evening," she said, because her salutation had fallen on deaf ears, "may I warm my hands by your fire?"

The men shifted and eyed her cautiously. They were as afraid of her as she was of them. "I only mean to warm my hands a bit, they're numb. She fumbled with her gloves and the man noting her gestures and the loss of feeling in her fingers, grabbed her hands as she was about to place them near the flames. "No," he screamed.

"Why won't you let me warm myself? I'm harmless," she wailed. "I swear to you."

"Your fingers," the man with a scarf tied around his hat pointed to her hands. "Your fingers could fall off if they're frostbitten. Here, let me look at them."

She was glad then, she had placed the small ring in her skirt pocket.

He took her by the hands to a nearby rain barrel full of frigid water under a drainpipe near a dilapidated wall. He dunked her hands into the ice water and they stung as if she'd just placed them in hot coals. "Ay!" she yelled.

"Hush up. Want to get us arrested?"

"So sorry—of course not. It's just," she tried to twist her hands from his grip. "My hands hurt. Please let go of them. Let me take them out of the water. You're wetting my sleeves. It's so cold now."

"Wait," the man said kindly. "A little while longer until they've thawed out with the cold water."

"Ivan, that'll do," said the man by the fire. "Let her come and warm herself now."

Shaking, uncaring of her suitcase and her few valuables, she approached the fire.

The man who had held her hands in the water tossed her gloves to the man closest to the fire. "Soaked and frozen. No wonder she couldn't feel her fingers."

She looked from one man to the other as she stood with them, her palms outstretched toward the flames. The man who caught her gloves went and got two pieces of wire and put them inside the gloves. He attached the wires to a grate of some kind and leaned the gloves high over the spit—like two shriveled baby chicks.

Ivan handed her a bottle of vodka and said, "*Nastrovya.* Drink. Don't worry. The alcohol in this would kill any germs from my mouth, if that's what you're wondering."

"It'll warm your heart, my pet," said the man who'd dunked her hands in the frigid water.

"I've got something for you too," she said, and pulled from her pocket three of the four lumps of sugar she'd taken from the café.

"Aha!" Ivan cried. "Where did you make such a big heist?"

The three men laughed, and she laughed with them.

When they sucked on their sugar cubes and drunk more vodka, Ivan said, "What have you got in that case there?"

"Clothes," she said.

"Don't be modest. Put them on, unless you'd like to freeze to death this night. Or," said the jolly man with the reddish whiskers, "unless you want someone to come and steal your case, you'd best open it and sleep on it."

Ivan pointed to an open doorway. "Go there, now, and do what Grandpa says."

There was uproarious laughter from the other two men.

The man labelled Grandpa called after her, "When you're in your nightie, and all of those other pretty frocks, come join us for this tasty soup we've made from the fish heads off the dock."

Hot soup. Nothing in this world sounded more wonderful to her ears. And her mind was a swirl—why did she always make such poor choices? Grigory. The suave man from the office. Would she ever get it right?

To be alone. Isn't that what she had craved? Aloneness? But in a doorway of a ramshackle, derelict building? She stepped as far back as possible, opened her case, took off her coat and put on two sweaters and a pair of wool gabardine pants Calina had given her under her skirt. Back in her coat, she wrapped a shawl around her shoulders.

Grandpa came to her, pointed out a place under the stairs where she could bed down. He placed cardboard from boxes on the ground, three layers thick. "Use your case for a pillow. You couldn't get better accommodations in a hotel," he said, wheezed and laughed. "Come now, supper's ready."

At dawn, she awoke next to a brazier, the coals still hot. When had the old man brought it to her during the night? No wonder she didn't freeze to death. The old man was standing over her. He told her the way to go. She thanked him and gave him a box of tea and the last sugar cube.

He gave her a glance that was all too knowing. "You could have been raped last night, or not woken up this morning with your throat slit. Promise you'll never run away again."

Anya nodded and touched the coarse sleeve of his coat. "*Ya obesh-chayu.* I promise."

Chapter Fifteen

Leningrad
Midnight
Saturday, December 22, 1956

Andrei and Nikolai embarked for the Ilyushin 11-14 twin engine passenger cargo minutes before takeoff. They had spent the rest of the night playing cards in army barracks located near the airport.

~*~

Moscow
Sunday, December 23, 1956

The next morning the two men boarded the Trans-Siberian train in Moscow for a seven day trip going through seven time zones. The majority of the trip would be on Moscow time, a bit confusing, but nevertheless, on to the border, and Andrei wondered how cold it was there. He hoped for sunnier and warmer days. Next to them, there was a train pulling out of the station, vomiting smoke and pulsating as though it had a spirit, then stopped.

A few hours outside of the station, Andrei felt hunger pangs as a hand on his shoulder directed him toward the doorway. "Let's go eat, Garin," Nikolai said in his huge baritone voice.

They passed yet another long panel before an open door that exposed an elegant boudoir.

Andrei pointed and said barely above a whisper, "Looks like a forbidden den, a rich man's upholstered seducing bedchamber?"

"Damn. Another stuffed and padded sleeper. Will we ever find the dining car? Ah, here's the conductor."

"Nikolai, please pipe down. You've had too much to drink," Andrei said in a hushed voice.

"Nonsense, when we get to the dining car we'll order a nice French wine. The meals are cheap enough." Nikolai burped, and staggered through the narrow passageway, the train rolling smoothly along, while he was bouncing off the closed doors to people's berths.

Andrei said, "I'm looking forward to the Chinese dining car being attached when we get to China. I love the food."

"What's wrong with our food?"

"Nothing, nothing at all." Andrei certainly didn't want to start an argument with his companion, who could get rather boisterous when provoked. All Andrei could think was what a terrible partner they gave him at headquarters. Nikolai was the worst undercover cop in the entire downtown station. Andrei couldn't help thinking that this was a set up to make him fail so he'd be demoted before ever being promoted and making the police force. The more he thought on it, the more it seemed as though it was the truth.

At the next town, Andrei must lose this guy and get to a phone. There was one person in the office he could trust. One. Now that was a sickening thought. And then he had a more terrible one—what if he really couldn't even trust Sasha?

They finally entered the dining car, saw that the waiter had lit two candles and the table was covered with a dainty pink cloth and matching napkins. It was set with a small vase of rosebuds, as if for lovers.

Throughout dinner, Andrei made sure he kept pouring healthy glasses of wine for Nikolai. He merely sipped his own. On occasion, when Nikolai had his chops buried in his plate, Andrei added water to his wine.

They dined sumptuously on *pel'meni*, a doughy dumpling, blini and caviar, patties, *varenki*, little cheese pockets. The dinner was costly and Andrei thought it strange that Nikolai kept ordering the most expensive items on the menu and to accompany these foods, he ordered a bottle of Moet et Chandon. Nikolai touched the bottle to see if it had been chilled properly, and then he even criticized the waiter when he poured out the French champagne. Nikolai actually took the bottle from the waiter's hand and showed him how to tip the glass, then to wait until the bubbles settled and then to top off the glass. He was an expert. Andrei was baffled. How did this seemingly uncouth cop know all about such delicate things as the correct way to serve champagne?

When the men had finished the blini and caviar, Nikolai switched to Chateauneuf du Pape, a rouge wine that Andrei had never tasted. It seemed to be as familiar a choice to Nikolai as a comfortable pair of old slippers.

The man was insatiable. Not only did he eat and drink for a regiment, he seemed polished enough to know all about expensive imports as if he'd attended thousands of state dinners. Who had shown or taught him these elegant things? How does he know about fine dining and refined drinks? And when had he learned about them?

Nikolai ordered Napoleon cake to finish the meal. Andrei waved a hand in front of him to refuse the sweet. After dinner, Andrei left his partner snoring soundly in their compartment. At the next train station rounding the city of Perm, Andrei hopped off the train to find a telephone. Using caution, he decided to walk two blocks from the station rather than calling from the phone booth that was right there.

Perm
Monday, December 24, 1956

Andrei placed a reverse call to the office and luckily Sasha answered and accepted the charges.

"Are you mad, Andrei?"

"Listen I'm in a phone booth near the train station and I've got some information about Nikolai. Is this guy a fop or a fool or is he going to be my downfall on this trip to get the—"

"What're you talking about? He's okay. Maybe involved in something on the side—"

"He guzzles wine and champagne like a Frenchman. *Der'mo.* Crap. I left him sleeping it off—thought he'd be out cold. He must have followed me. Sasha, something's screwy—he's walking right toward me and he looks like an angry bear." Andrei waved and smiled at the approaching man, and in a soft voice into the phone said, "Leave a telegraph message in Vladivostok to say my Aunt Lada died if he's—"

"Not kosher?" Sasha said.

Andrei realized Sasha would never have used that word if someone had been in the office with him. Andrei heard Sasha still talking, but cradled the receiver.

"Nikolai, I thought you were sleeping. Come. I just wanted to stretch my legs and had some excellent vodka in the train station. Let me offer you a drink."

"Who were you on the phone with?" Nikolai asked in a sober voice.

"Are you spying on me? Why that's the love of my life, but she won't give me a turn. Won't even look at me. I've been after her for a year now. *Nichego.* Nothing."

"You don't have a girlfriend."

"You don't know everything about me," Andrei said in a sly, cajoling tone. "A man has to have some romantic secrets, neh? Let's head back. There's still time for that drink." Andrei took Nikolai under the arm and started walking.

Nikolai stopped short and roughly pulled his arm away from Andrei. "I don't want a drink. Who were you talking to?"

Andrei stood under a street-lamp and lit a cigarette. "What's it any of your business?"

The light cast a sallow color on the man's bruin-like face.

Nikolai scrutinized Andrei, as if seeing him for the first time. "You're part of my business. I'm here to keep an eye on you. That's why Sasha didn't come with us. Are you that dense?"

"Keep an eye on me? Whatever for?"

"You're suspected of anti-communist leanings. You're—"

"Because I was sick the other day?"

"You weren't sick. I've already said too much."

"Come back to the train with me now. I have something to show you. Thought we were friends." He flicked the end of the cigarette and stepped on it.

"You're trying to get me drunk so I won't pay attention to your sneaky actions."

"Hey, you were pouring the drinks at dinner, not me."

The train whistle sounded and both men began to run. Andrei, lean and athletic, pushed and pumped his legs into high gear. He saw the heavier Nikolai struggling to catch up. He huffed and puffed till it seemed his lungs would burst and his legs would topple under him like two bowling pins just hit by a powerhouse rolled ball.

Andrei tossed back over his shoulder, "Slow down. You'll have a heart attack. Don't worry, I'll get the train conductor to stop."

"If you don't, I'll kill you," Nikolai yelled.

Andrei shouted back, "Is that anyway to talk to a fleet-footed broth-er?"

Nikolai screeched something into the wind, but Andrei was already out of range for him to hear and darted out past the train station and grabbed onto a handrail, hopping onto the bottom stair of the moving train. He looked back, smiled, and waved. Under his breath he said, "Drop dead, you fuck."

As Andrei walked back to the compartment he shared with Nikolai, his foreboding over what he'd just done began to prey on him, a worm eating through his small intestines. Why would Nikolai be spying on him? He opened the door to their shared berth and walked inside and closed the door behind him. The couchette was freezing. The window was open, the curtains fluttering and an odd feeling came over Andrei that someone else had been in the room before he got there. He sniffed the air. Nothing. He closed the window. Nikolai had probably opened it and that's how he saw Andrei by the telephone.

As Andrei began to move around searching in luggage, briefcase, and toiletries, a familiar smell came to him. *Aha, a man has been looking into our things.* He looked at himself in the mirror. "You complete ass, that's Nikolai's scent. He was riffling through your things, you moron." Thoughts of Chief Linsky came to him. Was Andrei the hunter or the hunted?

What could Nikolai have found that was incriminating to Andrei? He couldn't think of a single thing.

Maybe Nikolai wasn't looking, but hiding something in Andrei's belongings. Absurd, or was it? When passing the border, Nikolai would be safe from concealing something he wanted to transport illegally. Andrei wouldn't know about it so he'd act calmly and not be suspected of anything surreptitious. Andrei went through his duffel bag, but found nothing suspicious. He dumped everything out on the lower sleeper bunk, turned the bag inside out and searched the lining. A new narrow pocket had been sewn into the side lining. He pulled out his knife to slit the stitches, but was afraid he'd rip the material. Instead, he took out the seam ripper with the ornate silver handle like a tiny piece of cutlery Anya had put in the sewing kit she'd fashioned for him. He used it to cut the seam partially and extracted a cut-off straw-sized cardboard cylinder filled with white powder that Andrei identified as pure cocaine. His eye fell upon the opposite side of the duffel with the same new long pocket seam. He slit it open part-way and took out a screw-capped aluminum cigar travel tube, like the one he'd seen on the Chief's desk, only this one was brushed silver. He unscrewed the top and pulled out a small wadded–up bundle of cotton wool. He shook the cigar case and gently poured into his palm a handful of gleaming white diamonds.

Sasha had mentioned an "ant trade" which referred to small smuggling operations, and also carrying Paschal Eggs, minor scale ventures. Was he being set up or merely being used as a courier mule to smuggle the goods into China? And now what to do with them? Andrei sat on the bed and made a hasty decision. He rolled up stiff toilet paper and filled the thin pockets. He re-sewed the seams. *Army sewing skills come in handy. Bless Anya for the gift of the small kit.*

He opened Nikolai's luggage and to his dismay found two brand new blue uniforms—one large and one a size that would fit him. He never saw this kind of livery before. An enigma he'd worry about later. He took the two short cylinders, made tiny slits in the hems of two different pair of Nikolai's pants and shoved them in. He sewed the slits on the cuffs and inspected his work.

If Andrei was meant to be caught, Nikolai would be surprised, but if he wants this stuff, he'll be shocked not to find it in Andrei's duffel bag.

Andrei summoned the porter, showed him his identification and told him he needed to get to the conductor and engineer.

The porter accompanied Andrei rushing through the cars to the first car motor unit where the engineer's cabin was located. After a difficult entry to the cabin, there was a verbal scuffle between Andrei and the conductor. Andrei assured the conductor that he needed to speak to the train engineer because Nikolai, who had missed the boarding whistle, was doing a serious undercover investigation and somehow had to get back on the train. Like he did as a child, he crossed his fingers behind his back hoping to be believed.

The train engineer swiped his brow with his gray handkerchief. "I don't care if he's First Secretary of the Central Committee in the Communist Party of our Soviet Union, Nikita Khrushchev, or Premier Georgi Malenkov—he's not stopping my train."

Andrei looked at him as if the man had sprouted a third eye. "Not exactly that high up, but I guarantee the first Secretary would want him back on this train as soon as possible."

Fifteen minutes of haggling went by.

"Would your man have the brains to get to the next station? It's not a designated stop—only a milk town, but—"

"I guarantee he'll be there."

"Impossible. We'll make the next scheduled stop at Omsk. If he has brains, your man will be there."

Finally, Andrei gave the engineer and the conductor a military salute which left them baffled. Andrei went back to his compartment, made another quick search, and ambled to the dining car. He ordered vodka and blini. If Nikolai were picking up the tab, or if someone were hefting it for him, Andrei was going to enjoy his elegant meal. What had Nikolai meant? What stupid mistake had Andrei made to be suspected of conduct unbecoming?

The waiter brought a stack of thin *blini*, golden brown pancakes on a warmed platter, and another platter of caviar, crème fraîche, chives, smoked salmon, and minced onion.

~*~

Omsk
Tuesday, December 25, 1956

The following night, an hour after he finished dinner, Andrei saw ahead intermittent fires glowing beside the tracks, and then he saw red signal flashings, indicating stop markers.

Squealing brakes and the slowing motion of the train. Andrei looked out the window. The conductor was making the unscheduled stop. Was it possible that dear comrade Nikolai would be picked up here?

Andrei went to the dining car exit and watched as Nikolai alighted from the first of two unmarked NKVD vehicles parked on the tracks. So not only had he gotten a ride from the last station, he'd been in touch with NKVD. Nikolai was more entrenched and higher affiliated than Andrei imagined. He knew Chief Linsky was in bed with them, but this was surprising. Andrei hadn't realized the power Nikolai wielded. Men in trench coats and shiny knee high boots, as black as the night, stopped the train, two of them waving submachine guns. Nikolai wore a coat, too, made of expensive cloth with a karakul collar and a hat to match. Andrei considered the clout Nikolai possessed in order for this extravagant outerwear he donned. *He can crush me. I can end up in Siberia like both of my fathers.*

The locomotive engineer and the train conductor were outside shaking hands with Nikolai, pointing back at the train. Andrei hoped they would tell Nikolai that Andrei had made an effort to stop the train.

Andrei stuck his head out and watched them. Feeling anxious, yet having the gut instinct that these NKVD officers would board the train at Nikolai's command, he threw on a dirty motorman's cloak hanging on a nail and exited. He was all smiles—a Shakespearean actor who had memorized his lines to perfection. But would he get the chance to speak them? Supposedly thrilled to see Nikolai, he clapped him on the back. "You made it, old man. Wonderful to see you."

Nikolai recoiled and jumped back. He sneered at Andrei, turned to the senior officer and said, "Arrest this man."

Two guards seized Andrei by the arms. "On what charge? Running faster than you, Nikolai?"

"For trying to sabotage and abort my mission." He slapped Andrei across the face.

The senior officer stepped in front of Nikolai. "Prisoner, shut your mouth." The officer held his pistol and clubbed Andrei in the crook of his neck with the muzzle, thrust his revolver deep into Andrei's gut, and then pistol whipped his head and shoulders. Next, the edge of the gun barrel punched circular lesions making skin flaps on Andrei's face to the conforming firearm's bore.

Another two guards, each carrying an AK 47 moved to flank Andrei in back of the two restraining guards.

"Sir, a word, please." Andrei yelped when he caught his breath. "I've a message from a head officer in my district."

The NKVD officer kicked some pebbles on the ground and walked away. Andrei raised his voice. "It concerns Caesar."

"Take him away. He's an enemy of the state," shrieked Nikolai.

"No, wait," the senior officer in charge said. The officer stopped dead in his tracks, did an about face, and moved closer to the confined prisoner.

Andrei pushed his head up and spat out the words: *Cave idus Martias.*

"What's this gibberish?" Nikolai said.

The senior officer nodded, comprehending. "Release him," he said to the soldiers. Turning to Nikolai, he said, "I cannot arrest him. He is also on a secret mission."

"What nonsense. Who would trust him?"

"Apparently your Chief Linsky isn't quite in your back pocket as you stated earlier. You're going to have to take this up with him. But for now. This man goes free. We've held up the train long enough." He gave Nikolai a half-hearted salute.

He turned to Andrei. "I hope your face heals well and you'll not hold the brutality against me if in the future our paths cross."

Garin nodded his head, several drops of blood falling onto the ragged cloak.

The Officer clicked his heels and snapped a formal salute.

Once back on the train Andrei returned the soiled coat to the motor-man, apologizing for the blood, and followed Nikolai back to their stateroom. *How much power did Linksy wield if he can afford all of these amenities?*

Nikolai removed his coat and began a row browbeating Andrei all the way back to their cabin.

"You know me, Nikolai. How could you or they," he pointed toward the window, meaning the NKVD, "suspect me of anything but loyalty?"

"The Chief said you were too interested in getting details of the case and trying to go above his head. You're here to take photographs of a meeting. I'm the killer dog he sent to pick up your scent along this voyage."

Following closely behind Nikolai's bulk, Andrei said, "Ludicrous. He's delirious. I was merely interested in helping that girl find out who killed her mother."

"Mother-in-law."

"Not even. Apparently the woman's son abused Anya and she never married him, but he fathered her child, and Calina, the dead woman in the apartment, loved the little one as only a *babushka* can."

Nikolai opened the cabin door, tossed his hat and coat on the lower berth and sat down.

Andrei closed the door, stepped in front of a tiny sink, soaped his hands and rinsed them. He washed and dried his cheeks, and hung up a small linen towel. He turned, but remained standing.

Nikolai passed him a bottle of vodka. Andrei poured some of the alcohol into his palms and patted his cheeks, wincing a little. He faced Nikolai, seeing him sweep a hand over his face.

Andrei interpreted the hand gesture as an unintended giveaway—a signal Nikolai's brain was trying subconsciously to suppress deceit.

"So it's Anya now—this is your love interest?"

"Maybe. Although, I don't think I'm capable of love—perhaps only lust." He handed back the vodka.

"She's easy, this Anya? You cheated on your girlfriend with her?"

"*Niet*. She's difficult—stand-offish, like she's special. She was a ballerina, but that boyfriend of hers ended her career with a beating."

"Kirillov—the son of the dead woman—the ex-boyfriend of the ballet dancer. I'll bring him in for questioning."

"You know him?"

No answer. After a minute, Nikolai looked up. "This Anya—she's fair game, then?"

Andrei sat down and raked his hands through his hair. *What hornet's nest have I gotten her into?* He looked up and shook his head. "She's not interested in men," he said as convincingly as he could, drawing an hour-glass figure in air.

"Forget that case now. What babble did you speak to Barek Vladimirovich Stepanov?"

"The senior officer?"

"He recognized you."

"Never saw him before."

There was a knock on the door.

Garin opened it.

"Would you like the bed pulled down now?" the sleeping car porter asked.

Nikolai called from behind Andrei. "Not now, but bring us tea. Make sure you use the *savarka* method—not the piss water you serve the foreigners. Lemon and honey. And sandwiches."

"Which bread, sir?" the server asked.

"Lithuanian wheat. Thick slices of kielbasa, soft yogurt cheese and cucumbers. Bring four. With *Mayonaise Maheev Provensal*." Nikolai patted his stomach.

The server inclined his head as if to go, and Nikolai said, "Make that two orders."

Andrei shook his head. "Thanks, but I'm not a bit hungry. I ate sumptuously earlier."

The server closed the door.

"Stepanov. What did you say to him?" Nikolai asked.

"Exactly what Chief Linsky told me to say if I found myself in a prickly situation."

"What does it mean?"

"I've no idea. It's not a Russian dialect I recognize."

"It's not Russian. Why did he tell you this?"

"He said you might become too ardent and confuse me with someone who's out to get you?"

~*~

Irkutsk
Wednesday, December 26, 1956

Andrei evaded Nikolai by reading and sleeping most of the day, ticking off how many more days he'd have to be chugging along on the blasted train. He barely spoke to Nikolai all day and after dinner was lucky to find some businessmen in a card game and asked to join them in order to entertain himself.

China
Sunday, December 30, 1956

After they crossed the border and stopped, Andrei acted nonchalant, tossing his duffel bag on the metal table to be opened and inspected. Andrei was surprised to see Ethnic Russian guards, and held his breath, but they didn't check the seams. All the while, Nikolai feigned disinterest. Then Nikolai's case was opened, his clothes patted, and his pants cuffs felt, slit open to reveal the items Andrei had switched into them.

Andrei shrugged his shoulders, wondering how Nikolai was going to get out of this predicament without the NKVD to back him up. Andrei asked the guards if he could be seated.

Nikolai started arguing fiercely, yelling at the Russian Chinese inspectors something about diplomatic immunity and for his personal use. He said he had an appointment to see some headman named Kan. He even used the Mandarin, *tóu rén,* that Andrei gathered meant to emphasize headman.

Nikolai pulled out a concealed pouch he'd tethered around his neck with a leather lanyard. From it, he withdrew a paper and smirked, asking for diplomatic immunity.

Andrei stared at the extracted paper. *Very cool, Nikolai.* Silent danger flares exploded in Andrei's head. Doomed.

At the hotel, Nikolai unpacked and sent the two odd uniforms to be pressed and told them to repair the cuffs. Shortly after, a Russian Chinese knocked and Nikolai let him in. The business transaction was swift and after Nikolai passed off the diamonds and the dope, he said farewell to one of the border guards Andrei recognized from the entry point. Nikolai turned and congratulated Andrei on his astute performance of switching out the goods.

"I didn't think you had it in you. Very clever." Nikolai tapped his temple, and then ran his index finger in front of his eyes. "All is not forgiven. I've got you now forever sighted in my finder-scope—but perhaps you can be useful to me. You owe me now. Why are you chasing me? Is Linsky siccing you on me?"

"He trusts you implicitly, I'm sure, but the Chief wanted me protected from your over-zealousness."

"But why are you tailing me? Linsky owes you nothing, but we are in the same league. Am I set to be a sacrificial lamb?"

"To tell you the truth, I think he liked my father and couldn't stop his arrest or being sent to Siberia."

"Do you know what my mission here is?"

"A bunch of cloak and dagger that I can't figure. Whatever it is, you're traveling unarmed and unescorted—how dangerous a mission could this be?"

"First off, I don't really have diplomatic status."

"Falsified documents for your own protection?"

"I do a little dealing on the side."

"Smuggling."

"Semantics. Call it what you will. Anyway, I'm what's known as a trade delegate. You understand?"

"You're going to spy for China? How does one operate as a spy? You're a cop."

"I'm a test case. They should've sent a member of the intelligence service. Believe it or not they operate openly. But as a trade delegate I'd be accepted in some other capacity—work undercover in another invented official position— functioning covertly. The trouble is I'm meeting with the head of the Intelligence Service Yàlìshāndà Kan who has already intimated—"

"Who even knew there are Russian Chinese?"

"They've been here since the Seventeenth Century, sons of Cossacks. Kan wants someone in the higher echelon."

"Not a mere policeman."

"I told the committee to send Stepanov."

"But he's not expendable. You are."

"The Chinese consider NKVD top priority for the job."

"So you're a guinea pig? And I'm your swineherd?"

"Kan is coming to the hotel. As soon as the uniforms get here, we'll dress for the occasion. You'll refer to me as *Direktor komanii*."

"Chief Executive Officer of what company?"

"Kan has been informed of this cover-up, guzzling it like kvass, as the directive came from the office of our First Secretary Nikita Krushchev." Nikolai poured himself a shot of vodka. "You'll not speak except to position us for photographs, using a respectful tone when asking me. Make sure to call me by my now official title. Take many pictures of us together, especially shaking hands, so I've got proof the meeting took place."

Chapter Sixteen

The Epiphany
Sunday, January 6, 1957

The meeting situation, known as a "Dangle," Andrei learned, between Nikolai and the head of Chinese Intelligence Kan, went off without a hitch. It transpired exactly as it had been explained to an astonished Andrei. The thing that perplexed Andrei the most was why Kan allowed the meeting to be photographed—a conundrum Andrei didn't think he'd ever figure out for a long time to come. What Andrei did know for certain was that Nikolai was unacceptable and refused for the position and sent back to Russia with his tail between his legs, as he knew he would be.

Once back in Leningrad, Andrei wasted no time going to his own place, and instead, climbed the stairs of Anya's building so fast, his heart pumped like a fire truck's hose. He stopped and put his ear to the door. Classical music. A bit of static from a radio. He knocked gently.

Anya called out. "I'm practicing, Yelizaveta. Please keep Iskra. Come back tomorrow morning. You have the key."

Andrei tapped again lightly, unlocked the door and entered what had been a kitchen now transformed into a dance practice hall. No table, a rounded wooden bar, balanced, extending from one chair top at the window to another one placed cater-cornered at the entrance to the living room.

Anya's mouth dropped at the sight of him. His eyes took in the form of a lean dancer in black leotards and tights, her hair bunched up on her head, tied with a headband, sweat on her face and arms, and coursing down the cleavage in front.

"When's the recital? Don't stop. Please. I'll stay here. I won't move. He placed a package on the floor, took off his hat and jacket, and dropped them where he stood.

Anya pointed to the floor. "What's in the package?"

"A Chinese fan for Iskra, and a surprise for you, but you can't look now. Please dance for me."

"Oh, she'll love it. She's next door. What makes you think I'll dance for you when you haven't even paid admission?"

"Oh but I will. Whatever your asking price."

She whirled on him, extending her arms and pirouetting around the room with grace and speed that was intoxicating. She leaned on his shoulders, and pointed her right leg out, swung it around into an ara-besque position, letting her hands slip down his body until she touched his toes extending her back leg above her head into a needle. Her hands swooshed up his leg until she stood in front of him.

"What did you just do?"

"The first part—the turns are *fouetté* turns, meaning "whipped turns."

"How do you do it?"

"Are you serious? You are, aren't you? It's a full turn in *passe* or a pirouette, like this." She stopped. "It's followed by a *plié* on the standing leg, like this." She demonstrated the move, saying, "While the *retiré* leg extends to *croise* front and *rond de jambes* to the side or *a la seconde*. Here it is again." She broke down the steps as she exhibited them for him as slowly as she could. Then she repeated the moves.

She stood in front of him again and reached once more for his shoul-ders.

"And the rest—when you used my body for balance?"

"You mean this?" She performed the move. "This is an arabesque, and then—" she slipped into the position with one foot on the floor and the other above her head in a straight line. She held it a few seconds, then brought her leg down and stood smack up against him. "That was a needle."

"Yes," he said, "I see," his voice breathy with desire.

She turned, held onto the barre. "This" she said, jumping up and over sideward, "is a glissade. Do you want more?"

He caught her in his arms and covered her with kisses, pulling off her headband, shaking out her hair, ruffling and tousling it, covering her face with fluffed hair while continuing to kiss her. He picked her up as she threw her head back laughing while knocking down the ballet barre.

He stepped over it. "I've never heard you laugh before—it's a magnificent throaty sound. I want to make you happy so you'll always laugh for me."

"You can't."

"Why?"

"I'm a damaged soul," she murmured into his chest.

"I'll heal you." He kicked the door to her bedroom closed. He embraced her.

"What's wrong?" she asked.

"I'm starving." He kissed her neck.

"I have brown bread. Shall I fix you an open-faced sandwich of *salo* with black pepper?"

He shook his head. "Too fattening. I want to taste—"

She pulled her face back from him.

"What?"

"You in every single solitary sense."

~*~

Anya fell into a fitful sleep. A shadow crossed her face and she glanced over to the wall where she saw a towering shape. She turned and looked up quickly—his body loomed larger than it was—he was tented in a rug. "I'm freezing—would you like to cuddle?"

She smiled. "Sure. If that's all you want."

He dropped the rug over her and crawled in beside her, chilling her to every sinew and the marrow of her bones. She started to rub his arms briskly and soon they were ensnared around her. She rubbed his shoulders vigorously. He reached up and grabbed her hands and then kissed her slowly at first and then with unbridled passion she never knew he possessed—this calm, unknown man.

After they made love again, she fell asleep. When she woke he was not beside her. He stood by the window, smoking. She called in a hushed voice. "Andrei. Come here."

He didn't answer her, so instead she went to the window where he stood looking out.

"Look. What do you see?" he asked.

"A universe of stars," she said.

"We're here alone in a world they don't know. Behind them—beyond those stars—what is there really? I don't know, but I understand there's a world beyond this one, looking into your dark eyes—I see light like a starry sky."

"Can I trust you not to crash my heart to smithereens? Your voice in my ears says yes, but I've fallen into trusting mode before."

"Your heart has been smashed? Can anyone repair that? Can I or anyone promise anything on this planet on which we live? What is our reality?"

She peered out at the sky where stars wheeled and spiraled in a cyclonic tempest. Were they reeling this fast or was it only that Anya had begun to care for someone other than herself or Iskra? She felt she couldn't afford to fall for him because she'd made bad judgements about men before. Yet . . . Unbalanced by this new sensation, she leaned her body against him, a buoyed feeling of levity overcoming her despite her gravid situation. Was this, then, what love is supposed to feel like?

He lifted her chin and brushed her lips with his.

Unhurriedly, she moved away from him.

He followed. "I stood there too long." He shivered.

"I'll light the kitchen stove," she said.

He shook his head. He looked at her sheepishly.

There was nothing for it, but for her to take action. "Take off the sweater. I'll massage you."

He stripped off the sweater, dropped his pants and got beneath the covers with her. He was shaking.

"How long have you been ill?"

"I'm not sick."

"Of course not, but you're trembling like an earthquake."

"My spirit's cold and I need you to infuse me with your warmth."

"What happened to you on that trip?"

He confessed most of what occurred on the train ride. "I'm beginning to wonder if Nikolai is somehow involved in more serious drug and diamond trafficking."

"Wonder all you want. I have other things on my mind. We don't have the luxury for this."

"What?"

"Our lives don't permit us time to become a couple—"

He drew her close and silenced her with his lips. He held her for a long time.

Gradually when he felt his manhood would burst if he didn't move, he kissed her neck and shoulders. They rocked in each other's arms and the warmth seeped into his muscles—the muscles of his forearms and upper arms bulging under his t-shirt. He untangled himself from her embrace and took off his t-shirt. The air in the room was gelid—frigid beyond belief—he might as well have been standing outside in the snowstorm. He reached again finding her under the covers. He no longer shook. He parted her lips with his and kissed her long and hard as if the world around him could come tumbling down upon his head. But he would never let go of the suction of her lips and the feeling of vertigo as if he were being pulled down into a vortex of swirling water. An undertow claimed him. His tongue slipped inside her mouth. It was warm and moist and when he felt her tongue move against his, he felt like he'd just come home from a long struggle at the front. He knew without a doubt this was his first love. Perhaps his only love, but surely a great love.

"Draw the curtain," she said, in a timid voice.

"Do you think anyone can see us? Even if they could, do you think they care?"

"I care. Please."

"It's freezing. You've got to be kidding?"

She shook her head. He dashed from the warmth of her body and the covers into the bitter cold, hostile air of the bedroom. It felt like invisible icicles dangerously teetered above on the ceiling about to fall, hurling downward to impale his back.

"Brrrrrr," he said, rubbing his arms furiously.

"Come to me, I'll roast you like a chestnut."

They made love again and fell asleep in each other's arms.

When she awoke she knew in her dream that she'd been at the ballet school. Her thoughts, unheeded, galloped toward a memory field. She couldn't stop them, like she couldn't stop a runaway train.

"Hello?" Andrei said, waving his hand in front of her eyes. "Are you there? You've been staring at the wall as if in a trance."

"Thinking of old times."

He handed her a cup of tea.

"Me, too."

"A strange thing happened to me before I came here."

"What's that?"

"Standing by my car, a solitary feather fell to earth and lay upon the snow—and I wondered if it signified something."

"Flight. Feathers. Air currents. Wind. Breath. Dreams of winged creatures. The freshly fallen snow."

"I think it's a token of memory found. Last night I dreamt of when I was a boy and used to play in the woods surrounding my great-grandfather's dacha. I don't remember him, only stories about him from my grandfather."

"Is the dacha still standing?"

"Probably. It may exist, but I don't know in what condition or if someone else lives there now. I never went back—not since my grandfather died. There was a young priest—Vadim, a friend of my grandfather—and also my friend Omar, a Gypsy. The priest hid many Gypsies during the Great Purge."

"I'd be so curious to know if the dacha still stands. Why don't you try to go there—to see?"

"Mmm. I remember a pantry filled with jars of honey, goose-fat, and dried mushrooms—jams made of handpicked lingonberries, wild strawberries, and my favorite, cloudberries. On the verandah we strung ropes of onions and braided garlic, and sometimes I helped heft heavy pots of red cabbages being primed for pickling. For how long have I romanced the plundering time that has ransacked and pillaged my youth?"

"Very poetic. I take it you were fond of it. You must have happy memories?" She blew on her tea, the smoke rising eerily, gauzing her face. "Want to tell me about it?"

"Not now. But I will."

"A matter of trust?" she said, and smiled coyly.

He took the cup from her and sipped the tea. "Needs more honey."

"Like me," she said.

They got up and went to the kitchen, repositioned the table, and sat on chairs near to the lit open oven.

"I remember a bitter fermented drink made of birch bark my father made me to cure my wheezing. It must have worked, because I don't wheeze anymore," Andrei said.

"You look pensive. What else are you thinking about?"

"Iskra."

"What about her?"

"I'm not saying this to be cruel, but you probably wouldn't have named her 'Spark' if you'd known—" his voice trailed off.

"That she would be backward? You're right," she said, and hesitated. "She would have been normal, you know."

Andrei waited.

"Look at this drawing she did." Anya reached under a pile of papers on the opposite side of the table and handed the depiction to him. The picture was a large printed letter "A" and a little letter "a" inside of it with tiny asterisks surrounding the bigger letter.

"Know what this is?" Anya asked.

"The big letter is me, the smaller one is you, and these are stars," he fingered the circle. "Iskra has adopted me as her father and made us a family."

"I think you're right. I can't see her hurt, Andrei."

"There's always a danger we cannot fulfill the destiny we want to complete."

"You mustn't hurt or delude her."

"Not on purpose. Never."

"If that lout Grigory hadn't beaten me with a metal pipe while I was pregnant . . ." She shook her head.

A look of anguish passed across Andrei's face. Anya noticed he'd actually hunched his shoulders as if he were about to receive the blows.

"You appear so tough but have suffered." She touched his shoulder gently. "I'm sorry," she said.

"For what? You took the beating."

"For whatever happened to you that made you wince. Tell me a story from that time you were happy."

"Whenever we speak of our youth, we reveal much of our soul."

"And you believe we have," she hesitated and took the cigarette from him, puffed and coughed, "souls?"

Andrei patted her back with gentleness used for a baby. "That's what separates us from beasts, does it not?"

"Perhaps. But you're stalling. I want to hear something about you. Shall I say, please?" She turned off the oven and they moved back to the bed where she fluffed up her pillow, pushed it against the headboard, and sat leaning on it.

He gave her that lopsided grin that was beginning to beguile her.

"I'm listening. Begin," she said.

"You sound like a school teacher."

"You're stalling, Garin. Giving yourself time to think. I want the spontaneous version."

"All right, then. When I was young and would look at the Heavens in the night from the closed-in porch at the back of the dacha, it seemed to me the entire world was pitched into darkness, but the stars fascinated me. If my father found me star-gazing he'd often say some profound thing that would startle me and make it difficult for me to fall asleep. One night he said to me, "I think for every grain of sand a star shines brightly somewhere in the Universe. If you dwell on it—it'll drive you mad. But if you write about it, you could become a sage for time immemorial. I think sometimes stars dispatch not only brilliance but intelligence for us to capture if we are open to receive it."

"That's profound thinking," she said in a quiet voice. "Like melodies and music I hear in eventide breezes. Sometimes I dance to them."

"Where? When?"

"I've been to a Gypsy camp—they move around a great deal, but I've found them twice and danced with the women whirling around a fire." She placed three fingers over his mouth before he could ask her more. "But now more about you. Your father—he was an astronomer?"

Garin shook his head. "A maths professor at Moscow State University."

"At Lomonosov University?"

Garin nodded.

"Very prestigious."

"Yes, until the Great Purge—Comrade Stalin purged not only Jews, but political enemies of the state, intelligentsia, and—"

"*Yezhovshchina.* "

"Ah, yes. Under the head of Secret Police Nikolai Yezhov. Our beloved NKVD," he said, sarcasm dripping with every letter. "Yezhov was later killed, too little, too late, I'm afraid."

"Is it true?" Anya asked.

"That they also killed him? That they did, and also used gas trucks to slaughter, without trial, a million souls. Some were sent to Siberia. At the trials the supposed number was reportedly only six hundred thousand."

She scooted down in the bed and covered herself to her shoulders. "What happened to your father?"

"Stalin promised Hitler he'd get rid of the 'Jewish domination,' especially among the intelligentsia—most were dispersed throughout Siberia, my father included."

"What happened to you? Was your mother deported as well?"

"She was Jewish but had papers to prove that she was baptized Russian Orthodox, so I was able to stay with her—almost a year. Then she took sick. They say it isn't true you can die of a broken heart, but that's precisely what happened to her within a year."

"And you?"

"The orphan children, the homeless, were taken to *"Danilovskii detiperviemnik."*

"For adoption?"

"Their thumb prints were taken, and they were tagged with a sign and number and photographed. The younger ones were sent to orphanages. I think the older ones still under sixteen were "re-educated" from their parents' Bolshevik ideologies."

"But you escaped somehow?"

"Fingerprints can be altered or destroyed by acid burning or deep cutting. I didn't want to have to face that in my adult life so I paid a kid to substitute for me the day of thumb printing. His were taken twice under his name and mine and right under the nose of the authorities—I guess they figured all us Jews look alike."

"Clever. How did you have the money to pay him?"

"I didn't. I beat up a bigger kid who was ridiculing him because he was effeminate, but that wasn't enough to seal the deal. He blackmailed me into giving him my father's watch."

"So there was no escape?"

He shook his head. "I was one of the lucky ones, taken in by my father's university colleague, who dropped out to join the police. I became Andrei Garin—the name he gave me. I have a wonderfully forged birth certificate and papers to prove it."

"But how? Do I dare ask your real name?" She sat up straighter. "How?"

"As an imported relative from Poland. Of course, my darling Anushka, you may dare to ask me anything." He kissed her nose. "But you won't get a response. Not now."

"You can't let me possess knowledge that may harm us both, right?"

"But I already possess knowledge that may." He looked at her for a long time without speaking.

"What is it?" she asked.

"There's an expression you might have heard."

"Tell me."

"I'm unsure if it's from Hebrew or Arabic, but it holds a limitless truth for me. You're the light of my eyes."

"Oh. That's exquisite."

"*Ohr* in Hebrew means "light" and I believe it's a central Kabbalistic term in the Jewish mystical tradition. The analogy of physical light used as a means of describing metaphysical Divine emanations." He was quiet for a moment and then looked at her inquiringly. "Anya?"

She blinked. "What?"

"You were staring at me. Why?"

"That was so reflective, philosophical even, but did you mean it?"

"Without a doubt. You're the light of my eyes."

"That's more beautiful than saying you love me, but you do, don't you?"

"Shall I sign a paper in blood to prove it?" He scripted in air. "There. Now you have it. Or do you really want my blood?"

"I don't think I can love like you—your intensity overwhelms me," she said, and cried. When she stopped, she beheld him for a moment. "How can I invest my affections in someone I know nothing about? Tell me something of your youth. Give me something to hang an angel's faith on—I'm begging you."

"I can't begin to tell you, but I do have an old hidden diary I kept and in it I have a brief remembrance story—would you like to read it?"

She shook her head and smiled. "With pleasure."

"I'll mail it to you," he said, looking pensive.

"Is that safe?"

"Yes. But then you're to burn it."

"Seriously?" She saw his brow crease. "Of course you are."

Chapter Seventeen

Tuesday, January 8, 1957

Anya hardly ever got mail, and when Yelizaveta handed her the stamped package, Anya's hands began to tremble. Andrei's story remembrance came to her in the form of a posted letter.

"Open it!" Yelizaveta said. "Read it to me."

"I can't. It's private. And it could be dangerous."

"Dangerous? How could it be?"

"It's Andrei's story of how things were back then and might have his real name in it. I promise you, if it's not, I'll read it to you after dinner."

"Such hugger-mugger over a letter."

But Anya knew it was more than a letter, it was his diary.

"Come over later, Mistress of Mystery."

Anya went back to her apartment and kissed her daughter's bent head as she sat drawing at the kitchen table.

Anya went to her room and tore open the envelope. There was no cover, only several folio sheets folded into what could be made into a chapbook.

It was so long ago and I remember how I felt then in the body of a boy, and was just now reminded of what Gogol had written about a troika in *Dead Souls.* I can almost hear the bells on the horses pulling the troika. The first sound is that of silence surrounded by woodlands. And then the faraway swoosh of wind in the trees, the pull of three horses tramping over snow, bells breaking the quiet falling of snowflakes. Then twelve hooves roar over hard packed dirt and ice as if they were only one gigantic, heraldic horse.

I picture the troika, its distinct component was the shaft bow—the *duga,* a brightly painted centerpiece arc above the middle horse, which straddles the two side horses as a spring-like function to ease the strain of the animal's shoulders. Our *duga* was a work of art imprinted with hand carvings of stars, trees, and pinecones. Leather tassels, Valdai copper bells, and chains hung from metal rosettes. The clinking bells and the clanking chains were a cacophony and all part of the musicality effected dashing over snowy fields.

Later, I learned what dear old *dedushka,* Ilya Ivanovich, cried out: "Here they come rounding the curve by the frozen pond—let's pray they don't tip it over. Look there! No control, that boy never listens. This isn't the same as horseback riding. He has no experience—he should have asked the coachman to drive the troika. Wild boy!"

Afterward, Feodora told me she'd given him that look that said, You want him to be brave and daring and then you worry he'll kill himself in a troika accident!

The troika went flying by the back road leading to the dacha and the snow whirled in eddies as though trombones of snow were hurtling skyward in an attempt to defy nature.

"Good grief," Feodora, the servant called out, "they're going onto the pond. Do you think the ice can hold them?"

"Of course it can, woman!" Illya said with authority that belied his apprehension. "It's been below freezing for days, hasn't it?"

Feodora told me our voices and peals of laughter from the troika faded but she said she could swear she heard them still.

Her fear was that the sun was so bright reflecting onto the snow that it would melt and she asked Ilya, "Do you think the ice will crack with the weight of the sled, three horses and the girls?"

He scoffed at her and shook his head.

After the ride, I entered the porch solarium and laughed. I cleared my voice, then spoke in a derisive way. "Ninotchka took the troika. Now if she falls through the ice, we'll finally see if she can really swim like she said she could last summer—though no one witnessed her feat."

"I can't believe you're always so skeptical of your cousin," Illya said.

"She is not my cousin," I said.

"Your grandson is just a little jealous, my lord, Illya," Feodora said.

Illya continued as if she hadn't spoken. "Ninotchka can and will surpass him in every physical endeavor and sport she attempts. The girl is a natural. My grandson must try harder to succeed."

"Why don't you say it? You hate me! And besides, she has you to coach her—you've never helped me."

"What an outburst. I'm surprised at you, my dear boy. It's only because you must stand on your own and be able to face the future and all that will come to you unbidden—alone. You must be strong. You must invent, adjust, and surmount difficulties. Go now and have a nice cup of hot tea. Hate! Indeed!"

"The samovar is ready," Feodora said. She took me by the arm and led me away. "We'll have a nice *zakuska.* Then she called out. "You come too, my lord, when you've had enough watching the antics of your neighbor's child."

"Here she comes again. She has her father's shotgun and it looks like she's chasing a fox!" Illya shouted.

In the dining room, the huge round chestnut table was draped in a fine white embroidered cloth. Candles were lit in the candelabrum, and the finest plates and cutlery of the house were laid like so many soldiers in a line, shot glasses for vodka, and tea cups abounded.

There were so many covered dishes to feast upon, and so many uncovered serving trays of toasts and open-faced sandwiches. There was always liver paté. Usually the cold piquant dishes such as a sharp-tasting fish were meant for starters, and then so many other platters containing different foods, such as eggs, salads, and all leading to the finale of tastes which were the hot meat dishes. This *zakuska* table was a Russian smorgasbord, hors d'oeuvres conceived by the numerous French chefs living and working in Russia in the 19th Century and consisting of European and Russian delicacies. We were not a kosher family, but we were Jewish in every other way as much as possible.

When it was intended that this *zakuska* should replace the dinner meal, then coffees and teas and dessert platters of petit fours and cakes, pies, and fruits of the season were also present.

Feodora said, "*Zarkusit*—take a small bite—no one's looking and I won't tell."

She loved me like a son.

In a sullen voice I said to Feodora, "I'll mess the appearance."

"For pity's sake, I'm here to fix it—no one shall know. Don't you credit me with anything? I'm mistress of this house and the kitchen details are always left to me. Even hiding in your textbooks, you must know that."

The sun came in huge swathes across the shiny dark forest wood parquet floor.

Feodora went over to the curtains and drew them slightly across the windows, blocking out the sunlight and giving a somber and formal air to the room.

"Here now, let me make you a small plate," she said returning to the table.

"No. Just give me some little thing in a napkin."

"What then?"

"A trifle."

If I continue to think about how things were back then, I shall make a complete ass of myself and cry. Ninotchka, such a muscle-bound farm girl. She wasn't really my cousin but a neighbor—a big, strong country girl. She and her family moved to Samara.

Feodora, Grandpa. All perished.

There was a note on a separate piece of paper instructing Anya to burn the sheets. She read: "Don't feel badly—I need to destroy these pages, and anyway, I have these memoirs written on my heart and impressed forever in my mind's eye." She pressed the sheets to her chest, read the pages again, and then once more, but hesitated. *How damning would it be to keep this?* Then with determination to comply with his wishes, set them on fire in the kitchen sink, watching the bottom of the note take flames.

Andrei had asked for an encounter with her at three o'clock the next day, an hour before evening would set in. Andrei had written for her to meet him in Decembrist's square by the statue of Peter the Great, the Bronze Horseman, situated on the left bank of the Bolshaya Neva, in front of Saint Isaac's Cathedral.

Anya hadn't been there in such a long while she'd forgotten how far it was to travel across the city to get there. It was situated on the Moyka River about a half mile west of the Nevsky Prospekt and a bit further from the Neva River. What came to mind was not so much the gorgeous equestrian statue Catherine II had sculptured by Frenchmen to ingratiate herself into the hearts of Russians, but the monolith upon which it was situated—the "Thunder Stone" that served as a pedestal for the Tsar on horseback. It was magnificent and weighed an incredible amount—the legend says it was the largest stone to ever have been moved by man.

With remorse invading her, Anya held the note over the flames of Andrei's written remembrances, inhaling the smoke, like his youth.

Chapter Eighteen

Wednesday, January 9, 1957

Anya walked around the statue, which was truly magnificent—not just a work of spectacular artistry, but of might and power. It embodied Leningrad itself, and Anya thought back on to the stories, the mystery, and the legend that surrounded it during the war. Calina had said, Don't believe Russians aren't superstitious because they believed as long as the statue of Peter the Great went unharmed, the city would preserve and even thrive. She told a tale—a 19th century legend that as long as the Bronze Horseman stood, the enemy would never conquer the city. During WWII the statue was covered in sandbags and a wooden protective barrier that saved it from enemy aircraft shelling. In fact after the nine-hundred day siege of Leningrad, the statue still stood. Safeguarded, encapsulated, and protected from bombing and artillery, it went unscathed, and so the myth persisted and Leningrad withstood enemy invasion.

The day was frigid and the sky clear except for fast–moving white and puffy clouds that signaled snow. It was only when Anya finally arrived at the meeting place that she realized she was unsure of the time as she had no watch. Late afternoon. She thought back to Andrei's message. The weak sun raced behind clouds to make sure afternoon would be orphaned of any sunlight or warmth. She looked off to the left. The five lamps on top of the street lantern flickered on and off, but doggedly refused to stay lit.

Why had he chosen such an open yet desolate place so close to evening? Anya heard muffled footfalls approaching and turned, knowing it was him. His face glowed with joy and radiated a smile that could melt the very snow beneath her.

Without preamble or prelude, he started speaking as if she'd seen him mere minutes ago. "So glad you waited for me. Couldn't help being late." He glanced about, took her arm, and ushered her to the other side of the statue. "I might have been followed."

"By whom?"

He ignored her question, dropped her arm, and undid three breast buttons. He reached into his three-quarter jacket. Anya wondered if his legs were as cold as hers and did a short run in place.

"You're freezing. I'm sorry. Here," he said handing her a rolled paper. "Keep this for me. I'm afraid if my dwelling gets searched it'll be found. It's of no value but precious to me and all I have left of my parents." He handed me a parchment tied with an intense sky blue silk ribbon. She started to fuss with the ribbon, untying it. He put his hands on top of hers. "Not here. Not now. Put it in your purse. Look at it later."

"Let's move to a warmer place." Anya pointed in the direction of St. Isaac's Cathedral, now a museum. They started walking at a brisk pace. He hooked his arm underneath hers and practically whisked her off her feet. Anya was surprised by the open display of physical attention, and his strength of all but carrying her to the entranceway of St. Isaac's.

"The museum will be closed but we can stand where it's more protected. This wind's chilling my bones." She pulled her arms away. They stood huddled together by the side of the church. He said, "Now if you want to know what the scroll is, I'll tell you."

She nodded and reached to take it out of her handbag.

"Don't," he said, putting his huge hand over hers.

"The scroll is written in Hebrew. It's called a *Ketubah* or marriage certificate. It belonged to my parents. I have to be careful, even though

I'm trying to gain entrance into the Communist Party—they're investigating me."

"But why?"

"Why are they scrutinizing me? A paradox. They want you to be a member in the party, but then don't trust you enough when you want to join."

"The party?" Anya's look and slight head nod answered his statement.

"I don't really want to—I'm forced to if I want to get into the police department and be promoted from a photographer to a detective. You understand?"

She patted her purse. "This evidence against you cannot be found."

He brightened and tapped her shoulder. "Good girl."

"But why must you join them?"

"I don't want to, but it's a requisite to enter the police."

"Why do you even care about being in the police when they've shunned you before?"

"You mean so many times already? Need to gain entry to be able to move about freely. I want to solve this smuggling crime and crack the ring. It involves Jews, I'm sure. We're hated and hunted enough."

"So you want to know who's behind it and tell them politely to quit it?"

"Not quite, my little sarcastic Anushka. I've a feeling there's someone dirty in the ranks who's involved somehow."

She stamped her feet. "Your truthful Anushka says mind your own damn business before they do something more drastic than shunning you from joining the party—you know what I'm saying?" She shuddered.

"We must move—we need to walk fast to warm you. There's an old Gypsy tea room in the basement of one of the semi-abandoned buildings on a street nearby on the other side of the Moyka River. We have to cross Krasnoflotskiy Bridge and then go right about a twenty minute walk—less than two kilometers. Let's go, but walk behind me by twenty paces at least. If you see someone following me, start coughing."

"Will you hear a cough?"

He lit out faster than a fleeing cat released from bondage. Anya waited and then, shaking with cold, started to follow at a distance.

She couldn't believe how fast Andrei's long legs carried him toward the bridge. She'd fallen thirty paces behind, when a man bolted past her, seemingly from out of nowhere. He looked like a ghost dressed up in someone's fancy black short coat with an Astrakhan hat, and wore a balaclava to hide his face. He was tall, moved fast with long strides, and was gaining on Andrei.

Anya gauged how her cough might not even reach his ears, but she strangled out cough after cough as loudly as possible. Then she rooted herself in place and screamed, but not Andrei's name, afraid to give him away to the person tracking him. She yelled, "Iskra!" over and over until he turned slightly. He must have realized what her shouting meant and had seen the man shadowing him, for he quickened his pace to a jog and then a flat out run. She started to run towards him, when she saw the person tailing Andrei had reached and attacked him. They scuffled. The assailant's hat went flying. She slowed her pace, arrested by the spectacle of the two men, not just fist-fighting, but involved in some arrhythmic, macabre dance of progressive wrestling with leg kicks and arm thrusts. She gasped watching Andrei grab at the man's mask, exposing his neck. Then she saw a flash from the overhead street lamp. The assailant had a knife. As soon as she realized that Andrei might have been stabbed, the lights dimmed and then flickered and continued to waver. Two figures struggled. Someone was pushed or hurtled over the bridge railing into the water below. She froze in place not believing what she'd just observed. She started to move when she heard a huge splash.

A body hit the frigid water. By the time she arrived at the scene, the man who'd attacked Andrei had run across and reached the other side of the bridge.

Her thoughts jumbled together. This meant Andrei had either jumped or been thrown into the murky, swirling water below. Anya leaned over the railing. Still afraid to use his name, she looked to see if his pursuer had disappeared. Gone. She leaned out as far as possible, calling, now screaming, "Andrei! Andrei!" She screeched his name in a voice loud enough to awaken the mythic sea-creature Meluzina. After a few minutes of scanning the water, she ran to the opposite side of the bridge. Nothing. Then she ran the gauntlet length of the bridge to the other side looking for signs of him in the water. In frustration and grief, she crumbled to the ground, buried her head in her arms, and wailed in exhaustive disbelief. An old man walking his pet dog stopped to ask if she was all right.

"I'm fine," she said looking at the man holding a leash. "I've, I've lost my pet dog. He's drowned in the river." The old man, stronger than he appeared, yanked her to her feet. She brushed the tears from her face. "You're very kind."

"You must drink something strong," he said.

"I will," she said, gazing into his Asian face. *A minority. What was he doing in Leningrad?*

"There's an old Gypsy tea room, more of a tavern, a short way from here. Shall I accompany you?"

She shook her head. "Where? Where is it? I can go by myself. Really. I'm quite all right."

"I'm not so sure, my child."

"Honest. Please."

He gave her the directions holding his hat, his profile shadowed by light coming from below the bridge as a boat streamed by with a lantern.

The man put his hat back on, and tapped his fingers in a fake salute, and continued with a spry step that belied his age. On his way to the opposite side of the bridge, he stopped, and called to her. "Be safe, Miss."

Anya turned and waved.

Of a sudden she felt uprooted, in the middle of nowhere familiar, she was breathless, lost, and had only taken a few steps. "Move!" she commanded, and her feet obeyed. She walked several blocks toward the place Andrei had mentioned. As she strode in a semi-dazed state, her mind bustled with muddled thoughts as murky as the water she'd just passed over. *How was this possible? How could he come into her life for such a short time, become so endearing and be gone forever? Who was the assailant? Andrei had been followed for certain.*

In the near distance she spotted a dilapidated building with a boarded-up railing and partially concealed staircase, which she hoped was the place she sought. She stumbled along until she reached the tavern the old man had indicated. Anya teetered down a flight of narrow stairs, entered a cheerless passageway that led to a wooden door, dark moss green paint peeling. Should she knock? She struggled with the latch, leaned her shoulder in and pushed it open. Inside, it took a moment for her eyes to adjust to the dim lighting. A tall man in a black shirt and pants covered with a white apron approached her. He asked if she'd like to sit at a table near the stage. "It's cozier there," he said.

"Please," she said as he escorted her. When she was seated, she judged the room was warm enough for her to remove her hat, gloves and coat. The waiter showed her a menu.

She pushed it aside. "Hot tea and vodka."

She realized the effects of all that she'd just witnessed had her on edge and she began to shake.

The waiter returned within minutes, placed a squat glass and a bottle of dark-ruby red wine on the table. "Kindzmarauli," he said. "From

Georgia. It'll warm you quicker. A favorite wine of our former leader Joseph Stalin. Too sweet for my taste, but for you, now, good."

Anya looked up into his strong, chiseled face and steel gray mustache. Bewildered, she simply nodded. He opened the wine and poured. She took hold of the glass with a trembling hand and sniffed. The strong bouquet was enough to knock her over.

"Drink," he said.

She tentatively sipped, swallowed and then took a bigger sip. "*Spasibo.*"

"I'll bring *pirozhki* and *pel'meni.*"

"I haven't enough to pay—"

"You must eat. You've had a terrible fright," he said and disappeared behind a curtain to the left of the stage.

Anya rubbed her arms, poured a second glass of wine, and took a big sip. She kept it in her mouth for a few seconds before swallowing, welcoming its richness to warm her. She touched her cheek with the back of her hand. It felt inflamed. *How did the waiter know I'd had a fright?*

A shadow appeared to her right side, she turned so quickly, some of the wine spilled onto the table.

A man dressed in a white Cossack shirt, a colorful waistcoat and *tsyganskiye shirokiye shtany* billowing black pants tucked into soft boots, stood beside her. He wore a yellow and red silk *diklo*, a scarf, at his neck and a maroon bandanna around his head in the outfit of a Ruska Romani. Her eyes played a devilish trick—for this Gypsy was the identical twin of Andrei.

"Close your mouth, my little one. I lived."

"Andrei," she cried. He was kneeling by her chair engulfing her in his arms. "Andrei," she muffled into his shoulder.

170

He grimaced and pulled back from her. A red bloom flowered the pearl-colored shirt above his heart at shoulder level. "Lucky for me he missed the jugular. My friend Omar," he indicated the waiter, "disinfected it with hydrogen peroxide but it looks like he didn't patch me up good enough." He got up from the kneeling position and went to where the waiter stood. "It seems, my friend, we need to wash the shirt."

The waiter laughed and escorted Andrei behind the curtain. A woman with long black hair swooped up and gold hoop earrings greeted Anya with a nod and a smile. "Omar will tend your man. No worries."

Fascinated, Anya remembered the colorful dress of the Gypsies she'd danced with by their campfires. Anya studied the dancer/singer from head to toe. The woman, dressed in a long skirt and a puff-sleeved peasant blouse with a "V" neck, showing a great deal of cleavage, used her bra as a pocketbook. Anya saw her pull out a pack of cigarettes and matches. Her coal black hair tied in a chignon offset the gold earrings that jiggled when she moved.

Andrei returned in a clean shirt and sat opposite Anya. After she'd eaten and drunk more wine, he blanched almost as white as his shirt. "They're very particular about washing their clothes." He lifted his chin to indicate a group of musicians and the woman who'd greeted Anya. They consider the top of the body clean but below the waist is unclean and so they wash their garments separately."

"Oh," she exclaimed. "You seem to understand their language."

"A few words perhaps. Our Ruska Romani use certain German, Polish, and Russian words—somewhat bastardized and similar to Yiddish, but not really. To them we're *Gadje,* non-Roma. Omar is older than me, but we've known each other since we were boys. His father and grandfather were horse traders and knew my grandfather. When they travelled with a caravan near his dacha, they'd do business. The women would read fortunes for the superstitious peasants who were descendants of serf or unfree farmhands."

"I don't know much about them—*tsigane*, but Calina knew some. I think *tsigane* tend to be regarded as suspect and have been marginalized—"

"Unfairly—they have an interesting culture." Andrei flinched.

"Maybe we should have this discussion when you are healed."

"You're right. I feel a bit weak." He sipped her wine. "I'd like you to know this though—Romany Law is the heart of the traditional, spiritual and moral fiber of Roma—the precise source from which the genuine ancestries initiate are in perfect harmony with the ancient Israelite Law and with pre-Talmudic Judaism."

"What religion are they?"

"Here, they're Orthodox. I seem to think they take on the most popular religions of whatever country they're in. Perhaps seeking to fit in better."

"I only know some of their old Shishkin songs Calina used to sing to Iskra."

"You yelled Iskra's name. To warn me, right?" He didn't wait for an answer and asked, "She's all right, though, yes? Who did you leave her with?"

Anya patted Andrei's hand to reassure him. "She's with my caring but nosey neighbor. I told her I had a date and wanted to get laid."

"What better time than the present?"

She leaned forward. "Oh, Andrei, how can you be so cavalier after what's happened?"

"What? Tell her we ate. We drank."

"You were almost killed!"

"I'm a strong swimmer, and I know martial arts, thanks to my friends here." He made an expansive gesture with his hand. "What was that you said about getting laid? A truly humane gift to cheer a wounded lover, my Anushka."

Anya bristled. "I'm not your anything. I've been scared out of my wits. My emotion upended—"

"Not yet, but soon, my *dorogaya.*"

"I'm not yours, and certainly not your darling. Do you mean there's worse to come than today?"

"I intend to have you vaulting between elation, ecstasy, and nights of sleeplessness, merely conjuring thoughts of me." Andrei leaned forward almost slumping. All at once he paled again, looking like he'd seen a specter or at least had had a night of sleepless exhaustion.

"Look at you! Quivering. And now my heart is racing and my breathing accelerated, as well as having heightened anxiety. It's not from feelings of affection, I assure you—it's from fear, seeing you attacked and thinking you dead. You're a maniac who's bleeding." She pointed to his wound. "We must get it stopped. Did you recognize the man with the knife?"

He shook his head.

She looked toward the curtain. Omar approached, reached under Andrei's good arm, heaved him up and said, "I need to look at that gash again and change the bandage to staunch the bleeding." Omar held the glass of wine up to Andrei's mouth. "Drink."

Anya tracked them with her eyes, wanting to follow, but distressed at what she might see. She felt the trepidation of being chastised for not minding her own business.

"Eat!" Omar said to her and disappeared behind the curtain with Andrei.

Anya looked at the food, her stomach rumbled. She forked a *pel'meni,* dipped it into sour cream and took a bite. She sipped the liquid out and then ate the meat. The doughy part that was left, she popped in her mouth. She hadn't realized how hungry she was until that taste burst into flavor.

Time seemed to float away, and she became a spectator observing a recent walk on a nearby street, seeing a Gypsy and stepping aside, fearing the evil eye. How long ago was that? From that time and when she'd danced with them until now, Anya couldn't shake the feeling she'd been destined to meet and get to know *tsiganes*. Somehow she understood the need to override past prejudices and learn more about them.

She'd finished the plate of dumplings when Omar came back. "He passed out. He'll stay here tonight. Do you want to stay or shall I have my brother Vadim take you home?"

"Oh. You're so kind. I'm sorry I can't stay. My little girl waits with a neighbor. They'll fret if I don't go home."

Omar introduced her to a thin young man dressed in a black sweater and wool slacks, shrugging into a black raincoat. Even his scarf was gray and black. *Was this attire a uniform? He certainly wouldn't stand out in a crowd.* Even his eyes were black under tar-colored eyebrows. But he smiled at her and when he did his eyes took on a bright gentleness that seeped into them. He could be trusted, this brother of Omar. He patted his chest as if he'd forgotten his cigarettes, but it was to make sure he had two revolvers holstered. Trusted and safe.

Omar handed Anya a package wrapped in butcher paper. "For later. You need to eat. The shock is great, no?"

"How can I thank you for all you've done for Andrei, and also for feeding me?"

"Life has a way of adjusting debts," Omar said, and helped her into her coat. "I'm sure we'll meet again."

A shiver travelled the length of her spine to the base of her neck and she knew Omar saw them together in the future.

Outside, the wind howled. Anya and Vadim, her bodyguard, walked three blocks. She pulled her hat down and double knotted the kerchief under her chin before climbing on the motor scooter—a Vyatka—named for an endangered breed of horse. This model was a VP-150, an unlicensed ripped-off copy of the Vespa, built of thicker steel and tyres to cope with poor road conditions. Another feature that differed from the Vespa was it had an adjustable headlight and a glovebox under the front seat. Grigory had owned one once.

"You're not afraid, are you?" he shouted back to her.

She cupped her hand against his ear. "Anything is better than walking!"

When they arrived at her building, he asked if he should accompany her inside.

She got down off the scooter and leaned forward and hugged him. "*Spasibo*. I'll manage, squashed package and all."

His smile was a torch-light in the dark.

Chapter Nineteen

Late Evening
Wednesday, January 9, 1957

Anya walked up the stairs and before she'd reached the top, Yelizaveta's door flung open and she yelled a greeting. She leaned over with another small face next to hers.

"Mama!" Iskra said, excitement in her tone.

"My girl. How are you? Did you have fun with Yelizaveta?"

Iskra babbled about her time while, under her breath, the neighbor woman said, "You look as if you've seen a spirit. Are you well?"

"Later, dear," Anya said to her neighbor, unbuttoning her coat. "I need to sit by the stove and give Iskra supper."

"You have food?" Iskra asked with a smidgeon of surprise in her question.

"Something special for you and for our Yelizaveta as well."

"What?" The neighbor asked almost salivating.

"Ukrainian *pel'meni*." Anya slipped the key in the old lock and opened the door with a shove of her shoulder.

Anya laid the package on the table, unwrapping it quickly.

Yelizaveta scrutinized the food with ravenous eyes. "How'd you come upon such bounty?" and under her breath, she added, "And with no money in your pockets."

Anya's eyes shot up. "Later," she mouthed and closed the door. With weariness overtaking her, she said, "Sour cream, too. Come. Help me get settled. Eat with Iskra."

She placed a medium-sized sky blue tin of Russian Caravan tea next to the food. Yelizaveta picked it up, and read the contents aloud: "A blend of oolong, keemun, and lapsang souchong teas, produced from *Camellia sinensis,* a Chinese tea plant." She looked up. "This is a wonder of wonders," she said, and continued to read the label: "An aromatic and full-bodied tea with a sweet, malty, and smoky taste."

Anya shook her head. "I can't wait to taste it now that we've had our health lesson. I'll get the plates and cups. Sit." She shed her coat and draped it across the back of her chair, and pulled up a little stool for Iskra. She handed the mismatched dinnerware to Yelizaveta, who set the table.

Anya put the kettle on to boil water, and placed an individual tea purse in two cups. "I've had this tea before, Iskra. I'll let you taste mine. The smoky taste was said to come from tea being close to the camel caravans' camp fires as it travelled across the Mongolian Steppes to Russia."

"What's a camel?" Iskra asked.

"A beast of burden—one who carries supplies between its two humps."

"Two humps?" the child asked.

"I'll draw you a picture tomorrow. Now eat."

An hour later, Iskra was asleep. Before Yelizaveta left, Anya told her some of what transpired that afternoon. Her fright, meeting the Gypsy, and finding Andrei had survived the ordeal.

Yelizaveta patted Anya's hand. "Be wary, girl. This man is trouble. He carries peril with him like a shadow. Dangerous," she repeated. "Break with him now before it's too late and you get involved in something unsafe."

Anya shook her head, and then was quiet for some minutes. "I'm drawn to him. Like a moth to flame. He's magnetic—I'm a piece of scrap metal."

"He's a rake who's going to break your heart and hurt you in more ways than one, even if he doesn't do it himself. He fetches trouble." Yelizaveta said as she left.

As soon as the door shut, Anya rifled through the shoulder bag she'd worn like a bandolier across her chest. She extracted the rolled paper. She uncoiled the silk ribbon and pulled open the scroll, setting a weight of varying sorts, a cup, a bowl, a tin of tea, and a plate at each corner so she could examine it. On top of the paper above the heads of four angels, she placed a candlestick, deciding not to light the candle, afraid hot wax might drip onto the exquisite parchment.

The vivid paintings were startling yet vaguely familiar. Could they be representational of biblical works? The sides held several different tableaux. In one, a tree, a woman and man—Adam and Eve in Paradise before the fall? A delicate fawn was painted in another oval. Two large peacocks faced each other to frame a centered section of decorative writing in a script she didn't recognize. She knew the symbolism of peacocks. They were noted for their qualities of human traits, and a peacock, she remembered from somewhere, was a symbol of integrity and beauty attained when we strive to display our true colors. Had she studied this in history? Literature? "Myth, fable and folktale," she said out loud. "Ah, yes, the peacock—its mesmeric colors and thousand eyes, symbols of beauty and attraction, like falling in love. What's the allegory? A portent of virtues. What are they?" On each of her fingers she snapped out and said, "Dignity, Piety, Guidance, Safety, Vigilance." Christianity comes from Jewish heritage. "We're not so different after all."

She brushed her hand lightly over the manuscript, thinking, *Andrei has entrusted me with something important.* "He trusts me implicitly," she whispered. "How is this possible?"

She would think on this later, but now she knew she must safeguard the paper. She rolled it up again, tied it with the ribbon, and paced the kitchen, searching for a hiding place. If someone found this it would be hazardous, damning for him. The thought, *Thanks be no one is interested in me,* ran through her head. "I could probably stick it anywhere," she mumbled. With that, her thoughts fell back upon what Yelizaveta said about Andrei being escorted by danger. She spoke her next thoughts. "Perhaps better if I hide it outside of here. Safer." She wrapped it in an old but clean dish towel, left the door ajar, and went to the end of the hall to the WC with the parchment held to her side out of sight.

Yelizaveta opened her door a crack. "Are you all right?"

"Fine. Going to use the *tualet.* Go to bed."

Yelizaveta closed the door. Anya waited for her to lock it, and then opened and closed the door with gentleness and put the rusty hook from the door into the loop on the wall. She reached up behind the water tank, and secured the scroll over two metal hooks. Hoping it would hold, she used the toilet, yanking hard on the chain to see if it would fall. Success. Tightly wedged. She washed quickly and went back to her apartment.

Shocked to see a man at her door, she jumped and cried out, "Oh."

"You left your door open," he said.

She looked him over. His face and build were familiar. Where had she seen him before?

Then, recognizing him as the beefy cop she met at Calina's apartment, she answered slowly, "It's open so I can hear my little girl if she wakes."

He opened the door all the way. As if he could read her thought, he said, "We met briefly at your mother-in-law's murder scene."

She kept her face placid as if recognition apparently didn't register, although she knew he was the gruff policeman.

Without an invitation to enter, he stepped in after her and closed the door.

In an instant the skin beneath the hair on the back of her head prickled and she became wary. *Was this man a friend or foe of Andrei's? Wasn't he the one on the train?*

"I have a few questions for you."

"Concerning Calina?" she asked, her brain alerting her to something—*they come late at night to catch you unaware.*

"Actually—"

"I know nothing about her murder," she said.

"Actually it's about my comrade."

"Which one? I saw many at the apartment where Calina—"

"Andrei Garin."

There it was. She took a minute to compose herself, decided to be pleasant.

"Which one is he? Such confusion that day."

"I want to hear what you know about Garin."

"I don't quite understand," she said, but feigned a pleasantness she didn't feel. "I haven't much, but would you like tea?"

He nodded.

"Who is this other policemen?"

"The photographer who drove you home."

"Oh him. He's not a *ment*?"

"No. Not a policeman, not a copper as you put it so rudely."

"All the same to me. Thought he was. He ordered me to the police station to make a statement. I assumed he was a person of authority." She set two chipped cups on the table.

"I can question you here, or make this more official and take you to headquarters."

"What is it you want? About what? Calina's murder?"

"Garin seems to have disappeared. I thought you might know where to—"

She looked at him quizzically, internal dialogue made her wary, warning her not to resist too much. She turned her head this way and that, as if she had a crick in her neck.

"Me? Hardly." She moved to the sink, glad she'd put away the tin of good tea. She filled the pot and placed it on the stove to boil. She struck a match under the kettle and turned to light the candle on the table, the candle she'd left unlit on top of the scroll.

As pleasantly as she could, she said, "Please, you're so tall, it hurts my neck to look up. Please, sit." Hadn't she said that very thing to Grigory so long ago? "The tea won't take but a minute."

The man took off his coat and tossed it on Iskra's stool, adjusted his bulk into the chair, took off his hat and tossed it on the table. "You know him."

"He was kind to my little girl and helped me with the packages."

"We've been watching him. You're under suspicion of corroborating with an enemy of the state."

"The cop who gave me a lift home?"

"Photographer."

"What for?" Anya tried to act nonchalant as she poured boiling water into the teapot and into the cups and then poured it all out. She filled the teapot with more water, bringing it once again to a boil. Anya sprinkled in loose black tea, making sure the tiny sieve spout was free to catch the leaves.

While it steeped, she said, "I've no sugar, but a bit of honey one of the sellers in the market gave me with a honeycomb for my daughter. Care for some?"

"Generous, but we won't be staying long enough," his tone menacing.

"Please," she said, ignoring his intent to unsettle her. "It's steeped enough," and with that poured the tea through a strainer to catch the smaller leaves that the sieve didn't. She took the honeycomb from a jar and dripped a few precious drops into his cup and replaced it screwing on the lid with sticky fingers she licked and then ran under the cold faucet. No dish towel, she dried them on her skirt.

He looked at her as if he might swallow her whole and placed his cup next to hers. "You'd better drink this one, too, it'll be the last liquid you'll have for quite some time."

Fear clawed up her back, a troll with sharp talons, but she knew she couldn't lose resolve. "Don't care for sweetened tea?" she asked, blew on the hot liquid, and sipped.

"Finish it. Call on the neighbor lady to watch your girl. Get your coat."

"I never call on her this late." *How did he know Yelizaveta watched the child?*

"Put your coat on," he said, almost a growl, punctuating the air with his forefinger to the back of the chair where she'd left it.

She sipped more tea, stood, put on her coat, and smoothed down the collar, the hiding place for a handful of rubles she'd sewn underneath it.

"You won't need anything else where you're going." He stood, his huge frame shadowing her, a recall of the feeling of having been followed for some time—perhaps as long as she'd known Andrei.

Now realizing she'd been tracked, she quickly recapped how often Andrei and she had been together. Could this cop know how involved they were? Their romantic liaison? She drank both cups of tea. Her sight disturbed by the presence of tears she refused to let fall, she picked up the cups and put them in the sink. She started to wash them.

"Leave it," Nikolai said.

His voice was a taunt that made her jump and drop one of the cups, smashing it. The sound of the break stressed the bleak situation she was in. "Of course," she said, "drying her hands again on her skirt. I'll get my daughter and bring her next door."

Thinking of a beating and torture, as soon as Anya reached the bedroom she grabbed three pain killers she kept in the nightstand. Rada had given her these to use in case of an emergency. She popped them in her mouth, swallowed, and picked up the child.

Yelizaveta came sleepily to answer the door. About to protest, her eyes seared Anya's, and she immediately took the child into her arms. Not a word passed between the women, barely an imperceptible eyebrow lift—Anya's indication to look at the man who was taking her away in the night. She saw Yelizaveta study him, memorizing his features and bully stance. She leaned forward to kiss Anya three times on alternating cheeks, whispering, "Be brave."

Deep night had fallen too soon, like her plunging spirits. As she stepped on the frost-sprinkled ground, her leaky felt boots were no protection for her sore feet. A brusque hand was thrust under her arm leading her as if she would dare to run away.

The car jerked to a halt, the driver parked it at a wrong angle taking two spots. The big policemen took Anya by the arm, almost carrying her to the gate they passed through to the entrance of what she now knew was a prison. Not any prison, but Kvetsky.

"I don't understand," she repeated over and over. "What do I have to do with your photographer?" her question a whimper in her own ears.

She was pulled, dragged and then lifted through a doorway and into a gray cement hallway. Anya knew she'd never withstand whatever torment they prepared for her.

She'd be mistreated she knew, but how badly she couldn't possibly imagine, and so made a conscious decision to admit to any lie they'd throw at her.

Fear immediately accosted her as she passed through a gated door that slammed. Another prison door opened and clanged to lock shut. Imprisonment was the mindful thought, along with the dawning sensation of hopelessness that gripped her, generating a bustling tenseness in her abdominal cavity.

Abruptly, she was dragged into a sterile hospital-type room, stripped and searched by a short, strong, fat woman. Anya intuited at first glance this woman enjoyed her work. Anya had seen her type before—a bull dyke for sure.

Splayed naked on a cold table, Anya was searched in every orifice. Then still in a state of undress, taken by two guards and thrown into a tiny dank, damp but brightly lit cubicle, loud military music piped in. She sat on the floor, drew her knees up to her chest and cuddled and cradled herself. The same woman guard entered the cell, yanked her to her feet. Abdominal and facial slaps—a nightmarish existence had begun, yet she wondered if it would end with her still breathing and on this earth. In a flash, she grasped this was merely the beginning. At least the pills would get her through this first night.

She was left alone. Hurt and shivering. What seemed like hours passed, but in reality was a matter of minutes. Anya was wrenched to her feet once more, but her knees caved and she slumped to the ground. She guessed the reaction was from the effect of the pills, but hoped would be attributed to fright. Raised up again. More pummeling. Her sides, stomach, back. Anya screamed, knowing she couldn't withstand more ferocious torture they'd submit her to, she yelled over and over, "What do you want? I'll tell you anything. I know nothing but will admit to anything. Everything." Her head was pulled back by her hair. Sputtering and slurring her words, she murmured, "Sign whatever you want. Call me a traitor. Kill me, but let me sleep."

More blows rendered her unconscious.

Doused with ice water, she screamed as she was lifted by two different colossal male guards and dragged into what she knew was a basement interrogation room. Terror seized her. Alarm and dread of the unknown made her urinate, shame accompanying it. She was nauseous, yet had the temerity to sarcastically say, "Sorry. It was the second cup of tea he made me drink."

The guard on the right whacked her with a nightstick across the backs of her legs. They dragged and shoved her into a chair, arms tied behind her. She shook with iced panic.

A bright light shone in her face. Blinded, she couldn't see the face of her interrogator, but the minute he spoke, she recognized the voice of the man who'd brought her to this circle of hell.

He questioned her. The same thing over and over. "How long have you been corroborating with Garin?"

"Who?"

"The photographer."

"I barely know him."

"How many times have you slept with him?"

"Never."

"How long have you been lovers?"

"He's not my type."

"Did you know him before the day of your so called mother-in-law's murder?"

"No." Her fogged-over brain relived their time together. No, he'd been careful and stealthy, even said they might be tailing him. He'd taken precautions. Maybe they hadn't been sufficient.

"You never saw him before that day?"

She shook her head.

"Answer me!"

Without lifting her head from her chest, she murmured, "Never. But tell me who murdered Calina?"

"You tell me. Who're you covering up for?"

She shook her head.

"Who told you she was murdered?"

"He did. You did."

"Who?"

Careful not to use his name, she whispered, "The photographer."

"What's his name?"

"I don't know."

"You don't know the man you're fucking? Admit you set a sex trap for him," he said coming closer, and repeated, "*medovaja lovushka,*" sticking out his tongue and then licking his lips.

She shook her head.

"No?"

"We're not lovers."

Pacing in front of her, he asked, "What's his name?"

"Who?"

"The photographer?

"Garov?"

"Garin."

"Yes."

"Say his name." Nikolai blew smoke in her face and she glowered, but wouldn't raise her head. He pulled her chin up. She didn't open her eyes. More smoke.

She shook her head, her breath shallow. "Photographer Garin," she spat out along with saliva and blood, making his name formal with the title of his occupation.

"What was on the paper he gave you?"

No answer.

"What's Garin's first name and patronymic?"

"I don't know."

"What was the information he gave you in the park by the Bronze Horseman?"

"Information? The paper?"

"I'll ask the questions. You were seen. He handed you a paper."

No reply.

"Answer me!" He slapped her one way and then backhanded her.

Anya thought surely he'd broken her jaw. Her head whipped back and then again slumped to her chest. "Paper. Paper." She repeated, nodding, pretending to recall giving herself time to come up with something. Maybe they hadn't followed her into the Gypsy café, so she could've gotten rid of it. "An article."

"What article? What was it? Anti-communist propaganda?"

"No."

"The paper! What was on it? Let's not be coy, comrade," he said as he wrenched her chin upward. Wincing with pain, she grumbled, "Ay!"

He raised his hand to hit her again.

She tucked in her face and hunched her shoulder away. "About backward children—my Iskra—my daughter—" and playacted falling into a stupor. Her head drooped to her shoulder, her arms and legs went slack. A voice in her head told her she could bear this treatment, that she was stronger than he knew. She'd kept up with exercises and ballet training to the best of her ability, despite her injured leg.

He jerked up her head, squeezing her jaw tightly.

There was an odor of mold, smoke, and sweat. The fat man perspired profusely.

She struggled to open her eyes. "Children like her can be taught."

"What?"

"A skill."

"A skill? Like ballet?"

She tried to shake her head, but it hurt too much. "A craft."

"Answer." He slapped her face hard forward and back.

She cried out. "Wood-carving. Painting."

"Where did this article come from?"

"I don't know."

"Think. What did it look like?'

"A typed page."

"From a typewriter?"

She shook her head slowly. "A textbook."

"You're lying. It was a tube. A rolled government document, wasn't it?"

She shook her head again. The woman guard tossed a bucket of ice water at Anya, and she shivered.

"Ay!" She shook like a wet dog, her hair flying left and right. "Ripped paper from a book."

"What book?" Nikolai paced. He stopped at a desk, picked up a pack of cigarettes, shook one out and lit it, inhaling deeply.

She gazed at the pack. It was the same brand as the one from Calina's apartment the day she was killed.

Again he screamed, "What book?"

"Don't know. A library book. Maybe a magazine. I only saw it for a minute."

He blew smoke in her face. "What did you do with the paper?" Her stomach grumbled with hunger and nausea. She spit up and then heaved bile all over herself.

"Take her," he said, turning to the matron who had first stripped her and another burly male guard in a drab green uniform, a holstered gun at his hip.

How she wished she'd had strength enough to grab the gun and fire it under her chin. End the nightmare.

She looked up from a crouch on the ground to see a hose being dragged into her cell. She was pulled to her feet and water whipped against the wall. *What day and time was this?* The stream and pressure knocked her to the floor, arms flailing, trying to cover her face, her torso: breasts and belly. She thrashed her head from side to side but wouldn't scream, afraid of opening her mouth and being drowned. Where had she read about such vile treatment? How long will it go on? She turned around, and the whipping water assailed her back, buttocks and legs.

Abruptly, the hosing stopped. She keeled forward. Someone turned her around, yanked her by the hair so that her head flew up and smacked against the wall. Mercifully, she passed out.

Anya lay unconscious, but didn't know how long she'd been out. *Rvota.* She lay near vomit. It was like they'd given her an emetic. The smell of it sickening, making her want to heave again. She squinted one eye open a slit, tried not to blink or move, or in any way make it known she'd come to. Then, she shook with anxiety and from cold. The next thing she knew, she was dragged to another room and forced onto a chair. Instinctively, she pulled up her knees, crossed her ankles and put her arms around her legs.

"You wish to confess?" A deep voice asked.

She could barely focus on the man addressing her because her eyes were swollen.

"Anything you say," her words slurred. It was difficult to form a thought or phrase. Her puffed lips were bloodied.

"Not what I say. What are you confessing to?"

She peered with one eye because the other wouldn't open, trying to focus on his face. "Anything you want."

"You conspired with Andrei Garin against the State."

"Who?" she asked, knowing the answer was a lie but hoping it sounded ingenuous.

"Take her back to the cell. Use the hose to clean out her lies."

Oh, God, no, her mind screeched.

The guard who'd first stripped and searched her gripped her under the arms and hauled her back in the direction of her cell, but she never reached it. Anya couldn't stave off the blows from the guard, as much as she tried. She was tied down on what looked like a conveyor belt. Her legs and feet were beaten and then a nozzle was fitted into her rectum and as water gushed inside her fast and furiously, she thought her insides would come spurting out with the force of the water. She was so weak that blessed unconsciousness once again overcame her.

Soaked and freezing when she once again regained consciousness, the smell of her own feces assaulted her, but she forced herself to feign the blackout state. She was savagely prodded until she tried to defend herself with snaky arms of rubber.

Left on the cold cement floor, all sounds were hushed for quite some time before she pulled herself into the fetal position. If there's a waiting room for death, that's where Anya felt she was—bolted down and shivering, remaining expectantly for mortality.

Inside her head, she hummed a lullaby for Iskra, cancelling the present, refusing to focus on her condition by removing the recent past violence. Her mind drew landscapes—pastoral scenes of the countryside, envisioning the dacha Andrei had described. Anya internalized a mur-

muration of starlings moving in black swirls falling into a pattern, whirling in twists and spins to change shape. Hundreds of birds moved fluidly as coursing water only above in the sky, falling together in opaque patterns, stretching, extending, and retreating with the clouds above the trees like billowing smoke. She imagined and imagined and imagined until dizziness overwhelmed her and she was pitched into a dank well of complete darkness.

Her cell was hosed out and she was left to sit on the wet floor. After another day of interrogation, but without physical torture, and dressed in a gray smock, she was left in the cell. She was given a cup of water and a cup of what was supposed to be broth, she guessed, but smelled like dirty socks. She drank it anyway. At the end of an hour or so, she underwent another interrogation. She was then given her clothes, told to dress and escorted to the exit. She was allowed to leave. Why? Had she signed something? No. There'd been no pen or confession. But she'd told an audacious lie. She'd said she'd been so upset when the photographer was assaulted, killed, and thrown in the river that she went to a café and had several shots of vodka. It was either there or afterward she lost the paper he'd given her, because she no longer had it when she searched her bag at home.

~*~

11 P.M.
Saturday, January 12, 1957

Weak, without sustenance, a purse, money or a tram ticket, she made it back to her apartment building with the small stash in her coat collar. She literally crawled up the stairs and sank to the floor in front of Yelizaveta's apartment, and banged on the door with her elbow.

"Oh Sacred Blood of the Savior!" Yelizaveta shouted when she saw Anya on the floor. She hoisted her up, dragged her inside, took off her coat and boots, and laid her on the bed, next to Iskra, sleeping soundly.

~*~

Sunday, January 13, 1957

Ten hours later, Anya felt the bed next to her for Iskra. Yelizaveta sat on the bed and said the child was downstairs playing with her friend. Anya told her neighbor everything that had occurred since the last time she saw her. Yelizaveta's face changed from shock to horror and back again. The women talked, until, exhausted, Anya drifted back to sleep after a cup of tea and honey. Sometime later, she stumbled into the kitchen where Yelizaveta sat at the table, peeling beets. She put a shawl around Anya's shaking shoulders and set some hot broth and tea in front of her.

"Do you think you could swallow something solid?"

Anya shook her head. "I'd throw up. Haven't eaten in days. Perhaps later."

"He came back."

"Who?"

"The *ment* who arrested you. He was with another man and they searched your apartment the afternoon after he took you away. Then they went to look in the WC at the end of the hall."

Anya's hand holding the spoon froze midway to her mouth. She dropped it. "Oh my God."

"Relax. Don't worry. They didn't get your paper."

Anya's head snapped up. "What do you mean? How do you know about the paper?"

"The morning after you were arrested, I led Iskra to the WC to wash. I stood her on the toilet seat so I could give her a good sponge bathing. Curious little minx that she is, she saw the paper. I took it down. I had seen you trying to conceal something the night when you went to use the toilet. I told Iskra it was our secret and the paper was mine."

Anya didn't even know she'd been holding her breath, and let it out, followed by a sigh. A wave of disbelief yet relief washed over her.

"Drink."

"I will. What did you do with the paper?"

"I hid it. Naturally. But some niggling fear—an odd instinct told me they'd come sniffing around your place again. I said to myself—and if they come to look there—they'll come to my place, too, knowing we're friends and you leave the child with me. So I wrapped a piece of oilcloth around it and put it in one of the old dysfunctional drainpipes in the back of the building that had been sealed for years. I made sure to push it back far enough past where those druggies hide their stash. Next morning I tell Boris to seal it off with a round piece of plywood he cut to size and covered with wire mesh. Me saying rats were getting in and I needed him to stopper it good. That makes it appear the pipe is blocked."

"Genius! Maybe you should be working for the good old boys at Kvetsky."

Yelizaveta smiled. Then her face morphed into a stern and serious expression, the corners of her mouth turned down. "They came later that day. The one who took you away and another skinny one. Sure enough, they went down the hall. On my knees, I thanked the icon of Holy Mary. Next, they bang on my door. And as is their proper, polite manner, shoved me aside and rummaged through everything—"

"What did you do?'

"Me protesting all the while: who are you hooligans? What do you want? Anya is missing. What have you done with her? Her daughter is

193

frantic. The child isn't well. When everything was thrown inside out, *shivorot-navyvorot* topsy-turvy, they left. And here you are."

Anya embraced herself, nodding. "Finding nothing here, and my saying it was an article about backward children—worked. Unbelievable. How could it? I must find Andrei and tell him they are after him and what he should say."

"He's been here, too. Maybe now's time you told me about this man. Your Iskra says he's going to be her papa."

"Did they question you? Ask if we were a couple?"

"*Niet.* Even if they had asked, do you think I'd have told them anything? Especially when you keep me in the dark." She folded her arms across her chest and lifted her chin.

Anya put down her spoon, lifted the bowl, and drank the rest of the broth. She put down the bowl. "I'm famished. Have you something solid?"

"Bread and cheese. I'll toast the bread and you can dunk it in more broth. No cheese now. Tomorrow. After such beatings, you'll be sick and lose it. Drink the tea. Are you still in pain?"

Anya nodded. "Only when I breathe or move."

"Ah! Those bastards." Yelizaveta reached into a cabinet, took out a bottle of vodka and poured. She placed a tiny glass in front of Anya. "To rid the soul of misery."

Anya smiled and shook her head. "If only."

"I'll make you a boiled potato and smash it with sour cream."

Anya downed the shot of vodka, winced, and shivered. She sipped the hot tea.

"Now. Go rest on the bed. I'll get you when I'm done preparing your elegant dinner. Time enough later to tell me about this Romeo."

Well into the night, Anya found Iskra asleep next to her and Yeliza-veta wrapped in a blanket and huddled in a well-worn easy chair, her feet slippered in wool socks propped up on a table.

Yelizaveta's eyes flew open. "Come. You need to eat."

Anya took hold of the blanket.

Yelizaveta stood.

Anya draped the coverlet over the chair. Yelizaveta ushered Anya to the kitchen.

On the stove was the mashed potato. A dish with some sour cream was on the table, a fork next to it. Yelizaveta lit a match and heated the potato pot on the lowest flame. When it was warmed through, she scraped in the cream, stirred and gave it to Anya, who ate it straight from the pot. After a minute standing, Anya sat and slowed down, savoring every bite.

As she ate more slowly, Anya told her friend some things about An-drei, but not everything she knew about him.

"This is no time for a love story. Tell him you can't see him any-more. Especially after what they did to you." Yelizaveta turned, fetched the vodka and poured a shot. "I forget so much of late." She scribbled a note to buy more liquor on a piece of butcher's paper with a carpenter's lead pencil. Anya looked at it, realizing Boris and her neighbor were sharing more than the vodka.

When Anya had finished, she looked up.

"Don't worry today is Sunday. I'll keep the child for the next few days," Yelizaveta said.

Anya hugged the stout woman, grabbed coat, boots, hat, and scarf.

"Where do you think you're going?"

Anya opened the door, turned and asked, "Will they be watching me every minute now?"

"Be alert and careful. You'll probably be followed in daytime. I doubt they'll think you'd go out now. But you'd better warn this Andrei of yours. Do you know where he lives?"

"No. Keep Iskra also tomorrow night after you pick her up from school, will you?"

"I told you I would. Don't concern yourself."

"Bless you. I know where I can leave word for him."

"You can't go out in daylight, and you're weak now. Wait until tomorrow evening."

"That may be too late. I must go tonight."

"How will you go? Walk—there are no trams."

"Bicycle. You must let me borrow Boris'."

"Never. It's a German Diamant from the war. He keeps it in pristine shape, chained in the cellar, but it's got a bent green metal plate. Stolen."

"I've seen it. Four big numbers on top and OR 1956 below that."

Yelizaveta nodded.

"He must have tools there, too. Where else would he keep them? I need a bolt cutter to cut through the chain."

Yelizaveta looked sheepish and tugged at her apron. "Come back in and lock the door."

"What? You know where he stores them? You keep them for him, yes?"

When they were back inside, Yelizaveta said, "He'll beat me."

"Not if you replace the cutters after I use them. And play dumb to the theft. Besides, I'll return the bike. If I can."

"You must dress in his work clothes—pants and jacket. Even a hat. I have them. Do you think if you leave late you can get back by morning to give me back the clothes?"

"I can only try."

~*~

Monday, January 14, 1957

Past midnight, Anya grabbed some rags and pushed them underneath the shackle. She didn't want the chink of the heavy chain to make noise as it fell to the ground. As soon as the two women secured a link in the cutter, they both squeezed on the tool, knowing the strength of one wouldn't be sufficient to cut through. On the third try, they succeeded slicing, and Anya handed over the cutter.

With a torch light, Yelizaveta pointed out the way to an old underground passage that led to the twin building next door. "Make your exit from there. Get away from the building as soon as you can. Take the torch. I can feel my way back."

Anya took hold of the torch, smiled and nodded her thanks. They embraced.

Not a soul would be on the streets unless someone had followed her. Dressed in men's work clothes, still sore and with a well-padded crotch, she walked the bicycle along the underground passage until she reached the next building. She used the torch to determine the side door to the left—the furthest point from her own building. She unlocked the door, closing but leaving it unlocked. She pulled the bicycle up a short flight of stairs with great effort and breathing heavily. Outside, she stopped momentarily to catch her breath and swept the area with her eyes. Then once more. Nobody. Before making her way, she stowed the torch in her rucksack. Hugging the building whenever possible, she made a path around back to a side street. She mounted and began pedaling fast. It was cold, but the exercise warmed her. She was thankful that it was a little like *rasputitsa,* ice had thawed to muddy conditions, and where there was snow it was slushy, but manageable. One thought only: she must get to the Gypsy café to warn Andrei.

Chapter Twenty

Soft violin music drifted toward her as she walked down the stairs, the bicycle bouncing on each step. Anya entered the underground passage-way to the door. She knocked quietly. The door was opened and she was pulled inside. Blessed warmth. Her hands and feet were numb with cold.

It was Omar, the Gypsy man she'd met with Andrei. She didn't even have to ask. He shook his head. Andrei wasn't there. She approached him, stood on tiptoe and whispered in his ear, "I must get a message to him. Now."

Could she trust him? Hadn't Andrei? The man led her through the beaded curtains to the back and she told him she'd been arrested and all about the paper.

"You're a block of ice." His eyes didn't betray the shock of seeing her swollen face and dressed in men's clothing. "Follow me." Behind a purple curtain at the back of the café, he motioned for her to sit.

She did and he covered her with a blanket and went to a samovar to get her hot tea.

Anya watched as he poured it into the cup and stirred it with a piece of cinnamon. He held a large spoonful of honey above the tea. "Take this. Don't stir it in the tea."

She took the spoon and licked it clean, and ran her tongue over her lips, savoring the sweetness. She gave it back to him.

He handed her a glass of amber liquid. She sniffed it. "Drink this and wash it down with the hot tea."

"Cognac?"

"It'll heat you up faster than vodka and you'll stay warm longer."

"No wine?"

"Not tonight."

Anya knew not everyone could afford it, but many Russians drank cheap brandy as well as vodka, for its warming properties. She sipped the tea and put her cup down.

"Tell me," he said.

She recounted everything she could remember about Nikolai coming to her apartment, the arrest and torture. "Most especially you must tell Andrei if they question him to say the paper he gave me was from a text book—an article about slow children being able to learn a craft, such as wood-carving. Tell him to invent a story where he found it in a magazine or something. I told them I lost it."

"They believed you?"

"They saw Andrei give me the paper, but I don't think they followed me here, knowing they'd catch this little mouse at home."

"What makes you think they didn't follow you here?"

"I had stopped to speak to an old man with a dog. There was nobody around when I set off after talking with him."

"Did they ask you what you did with the paper?"

"I said I didn't know. I think I dropped it. Lost it. They ransacked my place, the WC, and my neighbor's—thoroughly."

"And?"

"No paper."

"Who has it?"

"It's well hidden now."

"I don't want to know where. You may have to destroy it, if it isn't totally safe and secure. It means his life."

"I understand."

"Do you know what the paper is?"

"I opened it and guessed."

"What?"

"A paper in Hebrew."

"Then you know." He was pensive for a minute.

"Is he a spy?"

Omar shook his head. "However, I've told him to leave Russia."

"Will he?"

Again, he shook his head. "Not now."

Anya wondered if that 'Not now' was because of her and the child.

"It's very late and unsafe for you to leave. Will you be missed? How did you get here?"

"I took the handyman's bicycle. Poor Boris. I left it in your passageway."

"I'll have someone get and hide it. It'll be secure."

"Too dangerous for you to leave. Sleep here. I'll accompany you home tomorrow on the trolleybus. They should be working."

Anya shook her head. "My neighbor will worry if I stay out the whole night, but will understand I couldn't make it back because of the exertion. She has my little girl with her. I have to get the bike back. And these clothes."

"You can return the clothes, but for now, the bicycle—well, she'll have to consider it stolen. We'll get it back to the owner in due time."

"Will you see Andrei?"

"I'll make sure he gets your message. Sleep on the cot. There's an extra cover in the trunk." He pointed to a hallway. "The WC is down that corridor. I'll send a boy around shortly with something to relax you."

"A sleeping draught?"

"Pethidine—an opioid analgesic."

"Your internal organs are inflamed—your body needs healing and rest."

As Anya started to thank him, Omar made a slicing motion out in front of his chest and left.

Anya stretched out beneath the heavy blanket, thoughts crowding in on her. *How will I ever sleep?* A silent mantra, over and over, until a boy brought her the opioid with some kind of fragrant herb tea. Wearily, she drifted into a dreamless sleep. The smell of coffee woke her. Bleary-eyed she sat up to see a painted red and black lacquer tray hosting coffee and a brioche, a linen napkin, and impossible to believe dried yellow flowers in a vase. A fleeting thought that yellow flowers symbolize sadness, but any flowers made this a wonderland dream. She stretched, yawned, and then reached for the carafe of coffee, inhaling the perfume as she poured it into a porcelain cup.

The Gypsy knocked and entered. Anya looked up. "How in the world is this bit of heaven possible? How can there be rich coffee and wild cress flowers to greet me?"

"They say we are magicians as well as fortune-tellers."

"I'd never heard that—only that you steal babies."

Omar smiled. "Andrei is safe. Somehow he got a surgeon friend in the hospital to fake paperwork, saying he had a concussion when he accidentally fell into the river. He's back on the job at the police station. So you won't be bothered by anyone for a while. I told Andrei again to leave Leningrad."

"Leave Leningrad?" Anya placed the cup on the tray.

"Maybe even the USSR, which to me is still the Russia of my forefathers."

"Oh," she said.

"Of course he won't now."

"You said that last night. Why not?"

"The reason sits before me, sipping coffee and enjoying a bouquet of *zheltyy kress-salat*," he said, pointing to the tray.

"Me?"

"Surprised? Don't be. Men do stupid things when they're in love."

"He's in love with me?"

"Love or lust—you tell me which?"

"But he's in danger."

"He put you in harm's way and feels responsible. He could leave— one person alone can get out—not that difficult. Far more complicated to plan an escape for another two persons, one of whom is a child."

"You're angry. It's not my fault. How could I know I'd be a detriment to him?"

He shook his head. "Not angry. I know how he thinks—and apparently now all he thinks about is to thieve moments to be with you. Finish your repast. I'll see you home." He placed a bundle of women's clothes next to her. "Change into these."

"When will I see him?"

"He'll find a way."

"If he can't get to me, make sure you tell him what I said about the paper."

"Done. *Fait accompli*. Take the flowers for your little one."

~*~

Early morning
Monday, January 14, 1957

The trolleybuses were crowded, and although there was no heat, it seemed that steam was rising from the woolen garments of the passengers. The cold from outside appeared combustible with the heat of the passengers all pressed together like canned sprats.

Anya couldn't wait to get back outside in the cold and walk the two blocks to her building.

Omar, who was standing three feet from her, raised his chin and moved his head toward the doors in salute. She understood he'd get off with her.

Although when she alighted from the trolleybus, he hadn't gotten off. She looked about, only to understand something was amiss. Anya did a complete about face when she saw three black cars parked adjacent to her building. She ducked behind a small almost bell covering—a cloche of students—walking in the opposite direction, until she saw that the men who had gathered in front of her apartment complex were now all getting into their cars and driving away.

She broke from the pack of students and all but ran flat out and dashed to her building, and up the stairs.

She banged on Yelizaveta's door, calling out Iskra's name.

The child opened the door, and Yelizaveta berated her for not obeying because she was told to never, under any circumstance, open the door. That was completely in Yelizaveta's jurisdiction and domain.

"It's all right. She heard me calling out to her. Thank you for caring for my darling."

Iskra all but crushed her mother who was squatting to make herself smaller.

"Come in. I need to tell you something. I'll give the child a collation. I'll make cookies and give her milk from the neighbor downstairs who loves Iskra. Do you want some, too?"

Iskra went to the table and sat down. Yelizaveta served her a mug of warmed milk and honey and gave her two "cookies," pieces of stale bread toasted on the gas range with a sprinkle of cinnamon and splash of honey added when the bread turned golden.

Anya stood, shook her head, and said, "I'm sorry I couldn't make it home last night. Were you worried?" Not waiting for an answer, she continued, "Here are the clothes for Boris and I have something for you." She reached into the borrowed coat pocket and pulled out a glass flask. The amber liquid shone in the kitchen light as she set it on the table. She sat next to her daughter, stroking her hair, whispering how pretty she looked and how good it was to see her. "Were you a good girl for Yelizaveta?"

Iskra nodded.

"Brandy?" Yelizaveta asked, eagerness in her voice.

"French Cognac."

"Impossible. Maybe I should taste it to see this isn't a mirage." She reached for a jelly glass, poured herself two fingers and sniffed. She gulped down the drink, coughing and sputtering. Finally, she sighed contentedly, poured a second glass of only one finger, and downed it. "The real stuff of kings."

"Also of princesses in a housedress—you're one."

Yelizaveta blushed.

"I shall cherish you forever for watching Iskra as if she were your own."

"I pray this isn't a farewell. No trouble at all to care for our Iskra." She started to hand back the flask, hesitantly. "Do you mind if I pour myself a bit more?"

Anya smiled, pushed the flask back to her. "The stuff of princesses. Keep it. It's for you."

"They came back."

"I saw the fuss, commotion and cars downstairs. At first I thought maybe it was for someone else, but waited on the side of caution. My place again?"

Yelizeveta shook her head. "Four men this time. They wanted to know where you were. I said the child has been with me for days. They scoured my place. Again. I put on a good, innocent show. That's why I couldn't take her to school. They left, but the little one was upset until you arrived. She kept pointing to shoes."

"My *malen'kiy*. Here, little one." Anya handed Iskra the dried yellow cress bouquet and the child smiled. "Cop's shoes?"

"The child whispered in my ear they could be gangsters. She's calm now."

Over Iskra's head, Anya tapped her ear and mouthed: "Overhear anything?"

"You know I have keen ears."

"Were they looking for the same thing?"

Slowly nodding, Yelizaveta picked up the bottle and put it in the cupboard with her meager glassware. "They were puzzled as to how they could have missed you leaving the premises. And in your beat-up condition."

Before dawn
Tuesday, January 15, 1957

Morning had not yet broken when there was a loud banging on the door. Anya's heart leaped from her chest to her throat, knowing it could only be a portent of bad tidings.

Before answering the door, she dressed in her street clothes, not wanting to be found in her nightdress. Anya closed the door to the bedroom, leaving Iskra sleeping.

She dragged herself forward. "Coming. You'll wake the dead. Please stop banging."

Upon opening the door, she feigned surprise. "Oh, I thought it was my neighbor. My daughter wanted to spend the night with her but I brought her home—"

"Where is it?" Nikolai demanded.

"What?"

He burst through the door. "The paper."

She stopped, thought to say *what paper*, but instead said, "Again? I told you I must have lost it."

"You've hid it in a safe place. Where? Show me."

She waved her arm. "Safer than this, I can't even imagine. Please don't wake my baby, but have a look."

"I already did. Where have you put it?" He slapped her and shoved her back. She tripped, knocking over a chair, falling on her side.

Struggling to get up, she wiped her mouth of the trickle of blood from her bitten lip. She moved aside and tried to stand. He knuckled her. She went down again.

"Let's get to the more crucial issue—what did you do with the old lady's goods?"

"You mean Calina? What goods? She had nothing."

"The stones?"

Anya got up, shielding her face with her hands. "I know you're angry—"

She put up her hands. "Believe me, I'm not playing dumb. I've no idea what you mean."

"The diamonds," he spat out.

"Calina had no jewelry." Anya backed away from him, but not fast enough as she watched his frustration gather into another punch that connected with her abdomen. Doubled over in pain, she knew he'd pound and thrash her or worse. She made a flash decision not to scream, but to absorb the pain so as not to wake Iskra. And she wouldn't fight him either or it'd cause her more harm.

Anya clung to the table. He pushed her to the floor, pulled up her skirt, and ripped off her panties. *No more beating then, mere forced violence.* She averted looking in his face. Courtesy of Grigory, she'd been raped before and knew what to expect. He held her arms with one strong hand above her head as he unzipped his pants and savagely plunged into her. She kept her thoughts trained on how she'd sew the panties. He kept repeating, "*Ty glupaya chertova vlagalishche,* you stupid fucking cunt," until he pulled out and ejaculated on her stomach.

Anya almost laughed in his face at the gesture of his not taking a chance of procreating with her. He stood over her, wiped himself with her ripped panties and threw them at her. *So much for sewing them.*

After Nikolai left, Anya sat on the floor. The entire weight and significance of what that dirty copper had been after hit her. He'd been one of Calina's attackers searching for valuables. She must have resisted and was killed because of it. Who was the other assailant?

Anya shivered. She stood, picked up her undies and whispered. "Not if I have to go naked for a lifetime," and tossed them in the garbage. She went to the WC and washed herself. Looking into the broken mirror, she twisted her face left and right observing the new blossoming bruises. Back in her kitchen, she rummaged around for a container of sorts. She went upstairs. Out on the roof, she gathered icicles from a low pigeon coop into a bowl and took it down to her apartment. Applying the ice wrapped in a dishrag to her face, she was about to close her door, when

Yelizaveta pushed it and came inside. "I heard, but you didn't yell or cry out. That was wise."

A look at Anya and Yelizaveta muttered, "Do they learn that as a childhood skill, how to knock a woman about? I have an opiate. Boris stole some from the hospital where he was painting. He gave it to me for a tumble in a real bed. At least he was gentle. I'll fetch it."

"Will you bring Iskra to school and retrieve her? I don't want to frighten her in front of her schoolmates."

Yelizaveta inclined her head. "You needn't have asked."

When her neighbor left, Anya sipped some hot tea. A tumult of thoughts made her tremble. Nikolai had searched her apartment several times and could've done it again today. She jumped up, flung open the kitchen window despite the subzero temperature. Leaning out, she reached around and down an outer side wall to the right where she'd affixed a canvas clothespin bag—the "doll hospital" for Iskra's *matroyshka*. After she felt its bulk, she closed the window and drank the rest of her now tepid tea.

~*~

Mid-morning
Tuesday, January 15, 1957

A few hours later, Anya went to look for Grigory. She found him smoking hash in the pawnbroker's.

"I need some rubles to pay for the doctor's bill."

"What happened?"

"Tripped on the stairs."

"Looks like one of your boyfriends beat the hell out of you." He inhaled and slowly blew the smoke in her face.

"I had bundles of trash, Iskra's books and missed a step," she said, wondering if he'd swallow it.

She turned her face sideward, and then faced him. "You've got money for drugs—you can give me something, can't you, my love?"

"I don't have energy enough to fuck you, is that what you want?"

She pursed her mouth and raised her eyebrows, shook her head imperceptibly, wanting to spit in his face.

Grigory dug into his pocket. "You're one lucky bitch. I've had a windfall. Here." He pushed a few bills into her open palm.

Without a thanks or goodbye, she eased past him and toward the back door.

At the rear of the shop there was a small alcove with an antique glass-fronted library, the kind that opened into a desk. The bottom part of the bookcase was made up of wooden doors, closed and locked. *Any thief worth his salt could get into that easy enough.* She traced the wood around the glass and noticed several old-style *matryoshka* dolls and antique, worn leather books with strange lettering on the spines. Probably Hebrew. *Didn't Grigory refer to the pawnbroker as the old Jew? Wasn't he the same old man they met when they were younger? Had he changed so much?*

She wondered where the old man was—he wouldn't have left Grigory alone to snoop around.

"Good day, Anya, isn't it?" the pawnbroker asked.

Anya jumped as if a ghost had tapped her on the shoulder. "It is. How are you keeping, sir?"

He stepped forward appearing in a cloud of cigarette smoke. "Manners from the ex-wife of a rapscallion," he said inhaling deeply, and then began a coughing fit.

"I have nothing to do with him."

He managed to stop hacking. "Please drop the formalities." He squashed the lit end of the cigarette between his fingers and placed the butt in an ashtray on a small round table.

"Grigory told me you're a scholar," she said.

"I read, I've studied, not quite qualifying me as learned."

"Still I'd like to ask you a question, if I may." She didn't wait for an answer. "I've been thinking of a story. David and Bathsheba. Would you enlighten me as to its origin?"

"Part of the Torah, our holy book, much like the Bible. I'm not a *zaddik*—not righteous or a saint—but I know that King David spied beautiful Bathsheba as she bathed. She was the wife of another, but he desired her, lusted after her and took her."

"Did he love her?"

"Ah! The eternal question. Is there such a thing?"

She turned toward the case. "The books?" she said, indicating with a bob of her head. They're very old. Are they Bibles?"

"That one," he said, pointing, "is the *Haggadah*. Next is the *Midrash*. The larger text of the three is the *Talmud*? Are you interested in Jewish teachings?" He relit the cigarette he'd put out.

"Heavens no," she lied. She heard footfalls coming toward them, and knowing it was Grigory, said goodbye to the pawnbroker and scurried out the back door.

She went straight to the *pekarnya* and bought a loaf of bread and after, walked to the market to buy potatoes, onions, beets and sour cream. She'd prepare a feast for Iskra and Yelizaveta. The medicine was wearing off and the pain in her cheek intensified.

Chapter Twenty-One

Evening
Tuesday, January 15, 1957

Anya was standing at the top of the apartment building staircase talking to Boris in the hallway when a young boy bounded up the steps and walked to her apartment and knocked.

"Who're you looking for?" Anya asked.

"Miss Anya—"

"That's me. What do you want?"

"I have a letter for you. The man said to wait for an answer. Can you read it, please?"

Over the boy's head she called to Boris. "I'll see you later. Sorry about your bicycle."

She opened the door and let the boy in, tore open the envelope and read Andrei's words quickly.

Received message. Be wary. Omar told me what happened,
but I imagine it's not everything—so desperately sorry for all you
endured because of me. I'll come to you when I can. Tell the boy,
yes, if you want to see me again.

The boy stood gawking about, waiting. "I have no tip for you."

"No need. He paid me handsomely. Your answer?"

She hesitated, knowing how dangerous it would be for both of them. What if I say no? He'd come to me anyway. She nodded. "*Da.*" She took the note inside with her and lit a match to it over the sink.

~*~

Late afternoon
Wednesday, January 16, 1957

Anya trooped in cold and tired. She'd been to a factory and to an office, but with no luck of securing a job. Yelizaveta was waiting for her. Anya barely touched her door and it sprang open. She told Anya that Andrei had chanced coming to her apartment, hoping to see her, but she wasn't there. "Where were you?"

"Job hunting. A factory, an office in a mechanic's garage. Then I went to the theater. I heard they're looking for a wardrobe mistress."

"Any luck?"

Anya shook her head. "Position filled."

"You gave him the key?" Yelizaveta said with a note of accusation. "I introduced myself to him. He's handsome in a rugged way. Your beau brought back the bicycle, a new lock and chain and gave me the key for Boris. Can you believe that? He said he knew he shouldn't stay, but walked into your bedroom. I peered in on him. He threw himself on your bed and messed up the covers, inhaling, as if he wanted to become inebriated with your fragrance, and with it, out of sheer exhaustion, fell asleep. Even I sensed your soap and powder scent. A gift from him, I suppose."

Anya smiled. "Would you like some?"

"After a half hour, I woke him, shaking his shoulder gently, but my words were harsh and told him to leave. He said he'd be back tomorrow. Well? Say something."

"What can I say?" Anya said, fidgeting with her hands.

"Then I'll tell you something. In a time when it's impossible, this man loves you."

Anya's head jerked up.

"Really. Loves you. He left you this." She handed over a package wrapped in brown paper. Anya opened it, knowing it contained food.

"Dinner," she said, her vision veiled with emotion from Yelizaveta's words, as she held up several sausage links.

Yelizaveta's hands flew to her cheeks, and then she pointed to the meat. "Forget the pretty soap and powder—I'll have some of that." Yelizaveta sniffed the meat. "Venison."

Dawn
Thursday, January 17, 1957

At the first flush of morning, Andrei opened the door with his key. Glad to have left Iskra with Yelizaveta for the night, Anya sat at the table sipping tea. She looked up, knowing it would be him. "Are you out of your mind coming here? I knew if I'd have told the boy No, you'd risk coming here just the same."

"Ah. You know me well." He reached and pulled her up and into his arms and squeezed her. "Don't fear. I lost them."

She pulled away from his embrace. Her eyes became large with fright.

"In the Metro. For sure."

"You can't be sure of anything. Thank you for the message with the boy."

"Thank you for not giving me up to that son-of-a-bitch Nikolai. Before they made a move to arrest me or take me in. Fortune smiled on us. Omar's wife gave me a French magazine with an article similar to the one you told Nikolai I'd given you. I left a copy of it on my desk. The rat must have taken the bait. He said nothing to me the next day, except to ask where I had been."

"And some ancient god smiled upon you because you had proof of your hospital visit."

"Quite the little investigator yourself. What's wrong with your cheek? Is that left over from your visit to the cells?"

"I tripped holding packages and Iskra's books. A misstep. I'm always turning around thinking that they must be watching me. What do you think you're doing?"

"Nothing whatsoever that someone completely insane for you wouldn't do—I'm taking off your clothes so I can love you till you beg me to stop."

"Insanity!" She giggled in spite of herself, shaking her head. "In that case, I give up. Here," she said, taking off her sweater and unbuttoning her pajama top, "allow me to help. But I beg you to be gentle. I'm still quite sore—"

After they made love, she nestled under his arm. They stayed in the semi-darkness as she told him of the inquisition and everything she went through. Then she sat up, repeating everything Yelizaveta told her of the searches, pantomiming her large neighbor with her booming voice. He listened to her every intake of breath, every syllable, never once interrupting her stream of words gushing like last year's snowmelt flooding the Neva.

He reached over and turned on the soft nightlight, and that's when his face showed the horror of what he saw in hers. "How can I ever make it up to you? All that you suffered because of me."

She hesitated, wondering if she should confess Nikolai's brutal aggression after the Kretsky interrogation. But seeing the pain on his face, which would turn to anger, she hid away the information like the rubles sewn in her coat.

In that instant, Andrei's eyebrows lowered and drew together, vertical lines appeared between his eyebrows, the bottom lids tensed, and his eyes froze in a hard stare. "I could cut Nikolai's heart out like the Mongol hordes did to their enemies for what he did to you." Thinking aloud, he said, "He thinks he's Spetsnaz, but he's definitely in bed with the NKVD. And some son-of-a-bitch on high protects him. What's the police got to do with that kind of interrogation and torture?"

His fury heated the room. To quiet him, she changed the subject. "That was so kind of you to bring back the bicycle for Boris and—"

"You were reckless to steal the bike and go out in the middle of the night. What are you doing now?"

"Getting us tea."

"Is your solution to everything a cup of tea? Are you British?" Over her shoulder she said, "Certainly better than watching you fume. There's nothing you can do about it. It's over. Now we must be watchful because your people know we're having an affair."

"I inferred you were a lesbian."

"You did what?" she asked and laughed.

Minutes later, she came back with a steaming cup, took a sip and handed it to him.

"Look in the pocket of my jacket. There's a packet of biscuits."

While he drank, she retrieved the biscuits. He lit a candle, turned off the light, and stood back from the bed until she took the cup from him and put it on the nightstand. "Sometimes," he said, "I wish on things, like falling stars, or the half-hidden moon, a squirrel in the park stashing nuts away for winter, or a leaf touching my shoulder. Sometimes snowflakes. Did you know that each one is different from the next?"

She sighed. "Everyone needs a Garin in their life."

Much later she said, "Take a nap. I'm going to accompany Iskra to school and then I'm going to apply for a tutor's job at a school nearby to hers. What time do you have to go to work?"

"I'll be in the office from nine to six. Can you meet me at the movie theater at seven? It would be better to go separately."

"And we should leave separately also and meet at the café on the corner. Then will you see me home?"

"We just missed a foreign film—Indian—thanks to Khrushchev's "thaw" policy, but there's a romantic drama with Nina Ivanova and Nikolai Rybnikov."

"A movie? How eccentric! And extravagant. I bet four people could eat for the cost of the tickets. Is it *Spring on Zarechnaya Street?*"

Nodding, he said, "I'll cook you dinner afterward at my place, if you can leave Iskra with our mother-in-law next door."

"Beast! I think she has a crush on you."

Chapter Twenty-Two

Nighttime
Thursday, January 17, 1957

After the movie and dinner, Anya took mental stock of everything in Andrei's miniature sparse apartment. She walked around, her hand sliding across the back of his overstuffed reading chair, as if to leave a specter of herself on it, so she'd be forever part of his unconscious world.

In the narrow bedroom, with the single bed, she unzipped her skirt and it fell to the floor, a circlet of black around her ankles. Anya stepped out of the material's corona and peeled off her blouse and slip. She stood before him, exposing not only every stealthy spot her body possessed, each cicatrize, every transgression, but also every love channel lit by the flame of one flickering white candle in a wine bottle. She knew he wanted her as much as she desired him in this time of uncertainty, so they both cast aside all concerns, because it might be the last time for this convergence.

When they finished making love, Anya burrowed beneath the covers and pulled his arm around her. "If you were David, I'd be your Bathsheba," she said, barely a whisper.

"Odd thing for you to say."

"I was reminded of the biblical story when I saw some old books."

"What were the books?"

"They had strange names. *Midrash* and *Haggadah. Talmud.*"

He sat bolt upright. "Wherever did you see those?"

"In a bookcase at a pawnbroker my ex—Grigory deals with."

"Is he a Jew?"

"Who? Grigory? No. Oh you mean the pawnbroker. I thought I told you so, although he doesn't advertise it. No long beard, side curls, or skullcap like in the paintings."

"What else did you see?"

"Grigory smokes hashish. Maybe the broker sells him that. But—"

"Yes?"

"An odd coincidence—he had ancient-looking *matryoshka* dolls, and some newer beautiful ones like the woman near the Church of the Spilled Blood gave me around the time Calina was killed. I think there's a connection." With that thought she decided for the time being to keep secret what she knew about the eyes in the dolls and the diamonds she'd found in Calina's kitchen. When would she trust Andrei enough to tell him?

"I don't want you going over there anymore—it's dangerous."

"Why?" She sat up.

"He's a Jew and could be picked up anytime for any reason. Anya, you've no idea how treacherous these bastards are. My friend Sasha is constantly on the lookout. He says any little misstep and they go for your jugular. They'll stop at nothing to get what they want—and that includes surrendering over their own parents for interrogation. Don't you realize that? Especially after what they did to you to find out what kind of paper I gave you?"

"Is that true?"

"What?"

"The pawnbroker can be picked up merely because he's a Jew."

Andrei nodded. "What if someone followed you there? What were you there for anyway?"

"I had to see Grigory."

"Why?"

"I needed money—"

"From now on if you need money I'll give it to you. I don't want you seeing him either."

"He's Iskra's father. Of course I have to see him—"

"Didn't you tell me he was a no-good bum? You said he doesn't work. Smokes hashish. He also could be picked up."

"When there are real criminals roaming around this city? Honestly?"

"In the State's eyes, he's one. He breaks the law. Daily."

"So your giving me money, makes you what? A saint, a pimp, a john, a mack?"

Andrei tensed. He got up and pulled on a cardigan. "Tell me about Grigory."

"I don't want to talk about him."

"Why not?"

"He's. He—"

"What?"

She threw her head back, her hair cascading down her back, haloing around her shoulders. "He broke my heart. I was young, but he has a cruel nature."

"Broke your heart. That's what you're afraid of. If you fall in love with me—I'll break your heart like he did."

"Don't be absurd. Our relationship is nothing like—"

"You're petrified. And shaking." He reached out to touch her.

She backed away. "You've already seen the worst of me. I can't sink lower in your eyes. But . . . how could you possibly love a creature like me?"

He didn't say anything, but the look on his face told her he didn't believe a word. Anger displayed itself in his bunched up fist and told her all she needed to know.

She couldn't help herself. Provoking him further, she jutted out her chin. "Here, I'll make it easier for the man who says he never hit a woman. Is it just me that gets your goat?"

He stormed out of his bedroom. She heard him gather up his belongings. He dressed in the kitchen. The next sound she heard was the slamming of the door. She stared at the nightstand where he'd left the key to her apartment.

~*~

Friday, January 18, 1957

That evening, Anya sat at the kitchen table counting out how much money she had left from grocery shopping. Her head snapped up as she heard someone running upstairs and stopping on her floor.

Someone banged on her door. She swept the money off the table into her hand and dumped it in her cup and covered it with a dish.

She stood behind the door. "Who is it?"

"The idiot who got huffy and left you last night."

"What makes you think I'll open up?" She mumbled the word *idiot* under her breath.

"Because you don't want a scene with me breaking it down."

She unlatched the lock and stepped back.

He grabbed her in his arms. She fit herself in the crook of his arm and looked up into the face of the man who was claiming a piece of the heart she couldn't protect. He sprouted a five o'clock shadow and she rubbed his chin. She writhed out of his hold, but he began kissing her face, her neck, her lips.

"You're rough and need a shave. My skin is sensitive and I have no lotion or cream."

"I'll bring some tomorrow."

"Promise?"

"*Obeshchay.*" He looked up. "Where's Iskra?"

"Playing with the baby one floor below."

"How long will she be gone?"

"Long enough for you to get what you came for."

He kicked the door shut and she locked it.

"What a fool I am not to realize we must savor our minutes."

Anya remembered the Gypsy's words, *To thieve moments to be with you.* At that, Anya had no recourse and caved into his arms. He picked her up and deposited her on the bed.

Later as Andrei dressed, he looked at her, pursing his lips.

Anya ran her fingers across his brow. "You look pensive. What is it?"

"Late one night, early December, I returned to the office to fetch some film, and saw Nikolai interrogating a guy. I did some snooping. Guess who the guy was?"

Anya threw out the question, "Tall, skinny, dressed in a black turtle-neck? A small scar above his lip on the left side?"

Andrei said yes, surprised.

Recognition washed over her face. "Grigory. What had he done?"

"Not so sure he was guilty of anything. Nikolai and Grigory. Their attitude and behavior was peculiar."

"What are you getting at?"

"The whole incident seemed bizarre. Too friendly to be a grilling."

"After Calina's murder, you'd mentioned the pawnbroker he's associated with so I paid him a visit. The unmounted earring found in Calina's hand—there was an exact pair in an internal showcase, mounted with small diamonds. And one similar mounting with a chain made into a necklace. That odd earring was probably from a set."

"And your cop friends didn't find the other one? That doesn't prove he killed his mother. The pawnbroker might have given them to Calina—didn't you know through your inquiries that she and he were lovers?"

"Hardly. Although now I'm going to do some more probing on my own. Tomorrow I'm going on a photo shoot and I want to explore—take a look. I've got a list of pawnbrokers and I'm adding his name to the mix in case anyone has objections. Do you know any of these other names? Do they sound familiar? These addresses?"

She took the paper from him, glanced to see if it had the correct one for Yasha, and pointed to another one. "Here, chief investigator, this'll make it easier for you. Absurd. Why didn't you ask me before? Of course I know Yasha's address. I don't know if he's connected to Nikolai." She tapped the paper. "After she was killed, I went to this other pawnbroker to retrieve something left by Calina. What I want to know is how come your big police officer didn't bring Yasha in for questioning already?"

"Good question. One I'd also like to know the answer to—want to come on the photo shoot with me tomorrow? What did you get from the other pawn shop?"

"Another doll." Anya busied herself folding a blanket, giving herself time to reflect. She had packed up that doll with the other two. She'd gone with Yelizaveta to hide them in the basement among Boris' equipment, unbeknownst to him. And just recently she added Iskra's "recovered" one from the canvas clothespin bag, Anya euphemistically called the "doll hospital."

"I'd love to accompany you tomorrow, but I've actually got an interview with a theater company that may pay off. Ludmilla, Calina's friend set me up."

"Come here," he said. "Let's forget the ugly world we live in and hide away in each other's embrace."

"You're such a romantic—it's hard to believe you're a real, live human being."

After they'd cosseted and coupled, Andrei smoked a cigarette in bed. Anya was in the crook of his arm. He kissed the top of her head. "I've been trying to build up my courage to tell you something, to ask you if you'd do something important for me."

"You need courage to speak to me?"

"My boss's wife—that is to say, Chief Vladislav Sergeyvich Linsky's wife is away and he needs a young beauty on his arm at an upcoming cocktail party. Nikolai suggested you." Silence reigned for a full minute.

"And like Peter in the garden of Gethsemane, you denied me, right? Nikolai," she said, "the one who arrested me." *Nikolai on top of her, cursing at her. Did he also offer up the rape scene to you, my love?*

Anya started shaking involuntarily. "What? I could almost laugh at the absurdity of this—you mean after he put me in prison and had me beaten with a hose?" *Would Nikolai deliver her up to have her submit to Andrei's boss?* She felt queasy.

Andrei didn't answer. He put out his cigarette and turned to look at her. "You'll never understand the devious ways of the party."

"If I refuse?"

"It's how things work. I'm sorry I got you involved in all of this. But I see no way out. For either of us."

She pulled her hair up and let it fall. "I'm anything but beautiful."

"Not to me. You could be ravishing with a new hairdo, make-up and a sensational evening dress."

"You're serious? You are. You're dead serious."

"Don't panic."

She flipped her hair in back of her ears. Shaking her head from side to side. "You're not kidding, but I'm petrified. Besides what am I going to wear, my coverlet?" She picked up the blanket and let it fall.

"I'd have guessed you'd be a bit more original. Don't worry I've got everything worked out. The Gypsy woman at Omar's is a dressmaker. She can make anything. She was a costume designer for theater."

Anya sat up straight with a vision of herself in a white tulle overskirt dancing in the corps de ballet of *Swan Lake*. She blinked. "Impossible. You've arranged it all already, haven't you?" She grabbed the heavy ashtray, spilling the contents to the floor and was about to bean him over the head.

He grabbed her arm and pulled it out of her hand. "Please. Hear me. This can save us. You. And me."

She folded her arms across her chest.

"Stop fuming and listen."

"Save me? The way I've already been saved?"

He made a move closer.

She put up her hand. "No more. Please. Never mind," she said, but she felt she was already acquiescing. "Does the dressmaker have white satin? I look great in white. I can fix my hair the way I used to for ballet performances and I certainly know about make up if I can get hold of the right materials."

"Let me know what you want and I'll bring you everything you need."

"My shoe size is 37. Nothing open or strappy. Not too high a heel. When is this affair going to take place?"

"A week from today—next Friday."

"Get me a pair of heels beforehand so I can practice walking in them again." She got up from the bed, stripped off her sweater. "I've lost a great deal of weight. I don't know my dress size."

"You needn't worry—the dressmaker will measure you and you'll look phenomenal." He stood and helped her back into the sweater that came to her knees. He pulled her into an embrace, but she gently pushed away.

"I want a sheath dress, strapless with a built-in bra, one strip of gauzy chiffon in smoke gray fanning out and going over my shoulder and hanging to mid-calf."

Andrei looked stunned. "For a poor girl, you sure know about fashion."

"Any moron can look at a fashion magazine to imagine how she'd appear in one of those gowns made for models." The thought of Nikolai ripping her dress off gave Anya tremors of panic, and she had to clasp her hands to stop quaking.

After Andrei left, Anya got Iskra from the neighbor a floor below her and went with her to Yelizaveta's.

"How about a cup of tea? I need to talk to you." Anya sat at the kitchen table and Yelizaveta made tea, while Iskra sketched and colored her drawings.

"Anya. Why so quiet? I thought you wanted to talk."

Anya confided the events that were to follow concerning her going to the diplomatic cocktail gathering with Andrei's boss.

"It's a good thing, no?" Yelizaveta sipped some tea.

Anya shook her head. "Andrei's treated like an underling, and they're testing him or using him."

"Don't look so glum. Either way, you get to eat caviar, drink vodka, listen to music and wear a pretty dress." Yelizaveta squeezed the tea bag into her cup and put it on a dish to save for later.

"Eat. Drink. All night while the music plays, I'll be wondering if there's a room upstairs of the banquet hall where I'll be served up on a platter to that fat bastard Nikolai. Or maybe both him and his chief."

"Oh blessed virgin! I never thought—"

Chapter Twenty-Three

Friday, January 25, 1957

Andrei watched Anya and the chief enter a high-ceilinged room with marble columns. The room was hot and filled with smoke. Comrade Chief Linsky made the rounds, introducing Anya as his niece to one group, while one of the men in smoking attire smirked. "Ah, the wife's away, I take it."

"In fact, visiting relatives on the Black Sea," another answered.

Each group of men had one or two who tittered behind a hand quickly brought to a mouth, or merely laughed out loud. The chief didn't seem to mind, but rather reveled in it.

Andrei observed Chief Linsky as he drank and smoked. He glided from group to group, talking and gesticulating. At one point, he made a pass at Anya, letting his hand slip from her elbow down to her hip and across her ass. She disengaged his hand and stepped aside, but too late.

Andrei tensed, cursing under his breath, about to make a move toward the scene. Sasha grabbed Andrei's arm, twisted it back, pushed and pinned him against a wall in back of a huge column. "Calm down, my friend. Not here. Not now."

"Where the fuck did you get such strength—" Andrei started to say.

"I'm thin and look weak, but I do body-building at home. If these bastards ever put me through what they put Anya through, I guarantee they'll be surprised at how much this skinny Jew can take," Sasha said, almost spitting the words in Andrei's ear with ferocity seldom heard.

"How do you know about Anya? I never told you."

"Let's say, our mutual friend Nikolai has a big mouth. Now if you keep your head screwed on right, I'll let you go before we're both found out."

Andrei nodded, felt the arm released and rubbed it.

"Don't," Sasha said. "Suck it up and listen to me. You're going to hate yourself when you hear this."

Andrei stood monolithically still, staring out across the ballroom floor to where Anya cajoled the chief. Music started and the next thing Andrei saw was Anya in the chief's arms gliding across the dance floor. As they twirled around, the chief stroked the side of her face with too much intimacy and she edged back from his touch, almost losing her balance. The chief embraced her tighter, pulled her into him, as she resisted, trying to keep her equanimity yet avoid the crush of his corpulence pressing against her.

Sasha looked out onto the dance floor. "Relax. She's in control and handling him well." Then he leaned closer to Andrei's ear. "Nikolai not only had Anya worked over in prison, but he paid her a cordial visit on his own when you were missing."

"What're you saying?" Andrei spit out between clenched teeth.

"He went to her place and raped her."

Andrei turned ghostly white.

"Ah, so she didn't tell you? Thought so. You've got a good woman," Sasha said.

"I'll butcher the bastard. Who knows?"

"Everyone in the office but you."

"How's that possible?" Andrei's eyes targeted his chief, darted around the room trying to locate Nikolai.

Sasha said, "If I didn't know better I'd swear you were a dragon— steam's billowing from your eyes, Andrei. Cool it, my friend. Nikolai left with somebody else's lady."

The boss made another pass at Anya. She ducked out of his seductive grasp, spilling champagne on him. She made a fuss of wiping it off apologetically, but Andrei read the boss's lips. "Clumsy bitch," he mouthed, pushed her away, did an about face, and stormed out. She poised herself, threw back her head, her lush hair falling from the neat French twist, billowing about her shoulders as she composed herself. She smoothed her dress, stood perfectly erect and sauntered toward the Ladies Room.

Andrei stared, following her with his eyes after the explosive incident. *God in Heaven, she's gorgeous.*

Sasha grabbed Andrei's biceps and squeezed. "Calm down, *zabijaka.* Your hot head will get us both eliminated sooner than necessary. Forget Linsky. Consider, instead, how you're going to make it up to our dear comrade. You're lucky the girl spilled her drink. Now she can leave— let's see she's escorted home."

Andrei sobered. "How?"

"Let me handle this. I'll volunteer. You'll owe me, but remember, you can depend on having an inside man," Sasha said starting to walk away.

"Who?"

Sasha pointed a thumb toward his chest. "The invisible man who held you against the wall."

Chapter Twenty-Four

3 AM
Saturday January 26, 1957

Anya was in a deep sleep when she heard knocking on the door. It woke her with a start. At first she thought it was part of her dream. She sat bolt upright. Andrei. No, he'd use his key. More insistent pounding. She didn't know for sure if it would be him, she prayed it would be, but at the same time, she was afraid it was him. Her hands began to perspire despite the cold air of the apartment. She tried to guess exactly how much of his boss's man-handling he'd seen. Quite a lot from the way he was banging on the door.

She opened the door, stepped back and put her hands in front of her face. "I'm sorry," she stammered. "It wasn't my fault."

"Couldn't use my key, so I banged with my foot. Should have put the package down. Sorry if I scared you." Andrei placed a large package on the table and grabbed her wrists and forced her arms down, never letting go. "I'm not angry with you."

"Your boss is an animal—you should've heard the things he said to me."

"I'm sorry I put you in that compromising situation." He yanked her forcefully into his arms and kissed her, kissed her, kissed her till she was breathless. He marched her backwards toward the bedroom. He stopped. "The child?"

"Yelizaveta read Iskra a story from the book you gave her and she fell asleep next door."

"I just need you to hold me, nothing more." So that's what they did on her rumpled bed for some time. Then she got up and started to move away. He caught her wrist. "That's not all, is it? Tell me," he demanded.

"What do you mean? I never saw your boss until tonight."

"Nikolai."

She drew in a deep breath.

"You know?" she asked barely above a whisper.

He nodded his head in a deliberate way as if he had the whole night to do it.

"Then I don't need to tell you." She yanked her hair into a pony tail with an elastic band.

"That's exactly what I need from you. Tell me."

"I didn't want you to know—afraid it'd enrage you, even if I wasn't sure you really care for me."

"What? What are you saying?" He pulled her down to sit next to him.

"Ouch. But how do you know?"

"My friend Sasha overheard Nikolai bragging he had you before the boss could."

She stiffened. "He forced me—forgive me." She buried her face in her hands, and muffled again, "Forgive me. I submitted to his savagery so it'd be less agonizing and after my prison ordeal, I feared he'd choke me—"

"*Ya yego ub'yu.* I'll fucking kill him. Then drink his bastard blood just so I can throw it up in his face." After he spat out the words, his lips pressed together with the corners down, nostrils dilated. He looked like a prize fighter, his lower jaw jutting out.

"This—" She raised her hands to his face. "This is why I didn't tell you. It means nothing—"

"Nothing! He's a beast and a fucking coward," Andrei shouted.

"Good! Now the whole neighborhood knows."

"How can you be so calm after what he did to you?" Andrei looked her up and down, his right hand falling in front of her and then bringing it back as if to slap her. She tried to grab his hand, but he pulled it away.

She slowly shook her head from side to side as if castigating a child with an almost inaudible, "*Net, ne delay etogo.*"

"No, don't do it? I'm in such a jealous rage. I could beat the living crap out of you. Tell me," he insisted.

Anya bent her head, tears ready to break the confines of her lashes. In an unhurried manner, she raised her head, her ponytail flipping back. She looked at him, shaking her head left to right, then steadying herself. "No worse than what I went through in prison." She hesitated a few seconds to let the words sink in. "A show of his power over me, maybe even over you if he thought I'd be stupid enough to tell you, and have you react like this—like you're doing now. You can't defeat the enemy if you demonstrate emotion. He's heartless. Hasn't got a soul. But you. You on the other hand, my beloved, are a precious human being."

Andrei wrenched her into him and cried into her shoulder. "I couldn't shelter you. I can't shield you, guard you—cannot even now—I fucking don't know how to protect you."

"Protection? There's no such thing. It doesn't exist."

"Sasha said we must leave Leningrad."

"Sasha from the office?"

"I trust him. I think he's right."

"Why?"

"Sasha stopped me from attacking the chief when he pawed you at the cocktail party."

"Ah. I see." She threw back her head, her dark hair whipping back like a horse's tail.

"That's not all. He's a Jew, and only under torture would he betray me, or I him."

She put her fingers over her mouth, and pensively rubbed her lips. "There's something more. Nikolai threatened Yelizaveta—"

"He'll never stop now till he gets what he wants. He'll kill her."

"Maybe. But maybe not her. He threatened to take Iskra from her when I'm not around—which is a lot."

"That fat bastard. He'll do anything." He pursed his lips and blew out. "And for sure, he's capable of everything—until he gets me."

"Not if you get him first?"

"Get him. How? What're you saying?" He drew his finger across his throat. "I'd be prime suspect."

"Why should you be? He must have enemies besides you."

"I don't know. I'll talk to Omar. There's got to be a way out—"

Anya disagreed with pointing both her thumbs inward and down. "Never. He'll hound you."

"Let me finish—I meant a way out of Russia."

"Ah, yes. Omar told me you would've gone but not now."

He looked up.

"Because of me."

He slumped forward and put his head in his hands and raked his fingers through his hair, looking at her, shaking his head.

She knew it was either because he didn't know what else to say, or he was afraid to say it.

"I'm starved," Anya said. "Any chance you have something to eat in that package you brought?"

"*Piroshki*—some sweet, some savory."

"It seems to me all we do is make love and then you feed me."

"Not such a bad thing, right?"

"Right." At the kitchen table, Anya tore open the wrapping, picked up one of the yeast buns and bit into the soft filling of mashed potatoes, mushrooms, cabbage, and ground beef. She finished chewing and stuffed the rest in her mouth and pushed the sweet ones towards him. "Sorry," she said with a mouthful. "I didn't eat at the party." She broke open one of the sweet ones oozing stewed fruit and jam and held it to his mouth. "You need sweets more—you're tense and strained. Eat."

He smiled despite himself and took a bite of the offering. "Make tea. Here," he pulled two sugar cubes out from his pocket, handing them to her, closing her fist around them. "You need sweets," he mimicked, "you're tense and strained."

After they ate and drank the hot tea, he asked if she had any vodka. She shook her head. The last drop, I drank after that brute left me. Sorry."

Andrei took out a flask from his coat pocket, and shook it. "Wonder of wonders and it pours like water." She got out the two mismatched glasses. They clinked and drank with a mock toast, laughed and kissed.

Later in bed neither of them could sleep. She snuggled in his arms. "We have to plan on something brutal, but for tonight let me speak a thing of beauty. There's nothing like the catharsis of poetry. The author of this poem spoke of his grandparents," and Andrei began to recite some of the poem:

> "They were early birds and never waited
> for crows to wake them up at dawn,
> but all was vain: however hard they sweated
> they would be swallowed by the harvest grown.
> They mowed, threshed grain, made hay and weeded,
> they did the house-chores and cleaned the shed;
> sufficiency of bread was all they needed—

the truth, they thought, was in the daily bread.
My great-granddad believed in bread devoutly,
and, having gone through miserable days . . .”

"What is this?" she asked.
"A poem by Yevgeny Yevtushenko."
"What's the title?"
"*Stantsiya Zima*. Zima Station."
His voice was low and sweet with something akin to honeysuckle wafting on a summer breeze with the words he recited. Then he stopped abruptly, like summer's end with a sudden autumn chill in the air. "It's extremely long and I only know little bits of it."
"Say some more of it. Please."
He kissed her forehead and continued reciting.

"I'd go fishing, fly a kite, and often
alone, bareheaded, I would take a stroll,
I'd wander, chewing clover, out in the open,
my sandals green from grass, from top to sole.
I'd walk along beehives and fresh black furrows
and watch the clouds floating, soft and white,
I'd see them, slightly trembling, stretch as far as
horizon, where they'd drown, filled with light.
I'd see a farmyard and, walking by it,
I'd listen to the horse's neighing,
and would fall asleep, tranquil and tired,
relaxing in a stack of hay.
I had no worries living life of ease then . . .”

He finished reciting and said, "The poet was praised by Pasternak."

235

"Who?"

"Another poet and writer."

"Why did you stop the poem?"

"It's long—pages and pages. I never memorized all of it." He took his arm from around her shoulders and puffed up the pillow.

She reached behind her and gave him her pillow, too, and then scooted down in the crook of his arm again, taking his hand and gently pulling it about her. "How do you know so much about the letters, poets, and literature?"

"My mother used to read poetry to me when I was little. Poems—the images carry you away from all your problems. I enjoy reading fiction, too, and going to plays—the admiration of the arts transferred from her to me."

"What happened to this poet?"

"Which one?"

"The one who wrote such beautiful memories in the words you narrated."

"Unsurprisingly he was ostracized for his individualism! What kind of society do we live in for condemning a poet for stating the Soviet borders are an obstacle in his life? He also wrote about his youth and recollections. They expelled him from the Literary Institute. He's probably under surveillance because he was banned from traveling."

"Where is it?"

"What?"

"Zima Station."

"Zima's a town in Irkutsk Oblast. Now you're going to want to know where that is, right?"

"Of course."

"Its position is situated where the Trans-Siberian Railway crosses the Oka River. Now shush." He gently put his finger over her lips. "I know. Your question now is where exactly is that?"

She bit his finger gently.

"Irkutsk Oblast," he said pensively, "is in Siberia. Enough. I'll not say another thing about its location unless we have a map and I can show you. And," he said with exaggeration, "I extract payment in something more than two hands filled with rubles and rubies." He took away his finger and kissed her gently at first. He looked at her and whispered, "Dark eyes. I want you." He put his mouth on hers as if to possess her very soul. Then turning her, turning her, turning them until they were one.

When Andrei had fallen asleep, it seemed as though Anya's speeding heart would be impossible to calm. Exhaustion made her try to surrender to the covering of night, but her mind was a merry-go-round of thoughts hurtling and converging in on one another. Finally she got out of bed and threw on Andrei's sweater.

"What's wrong?" Andrei reached for her arm pulling her back.

"Useless to sleep. My brain is a *karusel* of images and ideas. I keep envisioning ways to kill. I've never contemplated murder before. I'm edgy. Do you have a cigarette?"

He shook his head. "Out."

"Let's make some hot tea."

"The vodka might work better."

"It's cold. Stay in bed. I'll bring it."

She sat on the bed and they alternated taking swigs from one glass.

"You're so pensive," he said, brushing hair out of her eyes. "It's not like this is going to happen tomorrow."

"You're wrong. We must have a plan. Life can change in an instant. When you least imagine it, your world collapses—everything transmutes in seconds, alters in seconds."

"Come here under the covers."

"Tomorrow I'm going to meet Rada at the Levashovo Cemetery to pay respects to Calina. I need to sleep—tell me some more of the poetry so I can be at ease."

Chapter Twenty-Five

Saturday morning
January 26, 1957

Levashovo Cemetery was for those targeted under the Great Terror, where Jews, Assyrians, and others were buried. Somehow Anya's ex-lover Grigory had made arrangements to have his mother buried in a small plot the pawnbroker had for his ancestors in the Jewish sector. At the time, before she'd been interrogated in prison, Anya couldn't allow herself to think how he'd paid the man or what bargain he'd struck in order to secure a burial site for Calina. Grigory had told her that Yasha knew the gravediggers and all would be done as quickly as the body was released from the morgue. But all Anya could think of was that Grigory had made a deal with the devil. *Did Yasha kill Calina?*

After a night of semi-restfulness, Anya got up early, kissed Andrei goodbye, and took Iskra to school for her Saturday program. That left Anya time in order to arrive when the cemetery opened at 9 a.m. She took the suburban train from Finland Station to Levashovo. There she'd hop on bus No. 75 or 84 to the Gorskoe Shosse 143 stop. She caught the No. 84.

The day was frost-laden and windy. What was it like to have to suffer through a winter in Siberia? That morning Anya packed a thermos of hot tea in her rucksack to go to the cemetery to pay her respects to Calina. Anya had been imprisoned when the funeral took place, and this was the first time she went to the gravesite.

Even with directions from one of the groundskeepers, it took her about twenty minutes to locate the burial place and when she did, she sat for several minutes on a workmen's plank nearby staring at Calina's final resting place, until the dampness began to torment her legs. A shadow appeared that made her jump slightly and turn.

"Sorry. I didn't mean to sneak up on you like that, but you looked like you were praying," Rada said.

Anya stood and embraced her, kissing her cheeks three times. "Are you by yourself, Rada?"

"Ludmilla came yesterday, but she couldn't get away again today. I told her I'd bring a flower today."

Anya looked at the lone chrysanthemum with some green foliage surrounding it.

"Thanks."

"No need. Calina would get a big laugh out of this—I filched it from one of the ornate graves with lots of flowers. They won't last in this cold anyway—they'll freeze just like these poor corpses."

Anya smiled. "You're a treasure."

"Did they find the murderer?" Rada took hold of a small metal container from a nearby grave. She took one glove off and put it under her arm. With the bared hand, she took the flowers out, tossed them on a pile of other dead flowers, and put in her offering. She set it at the top of the fresh mound of dirt near a small marker, but no stone. She put on her glove.

Anya and Rada each bowed their heads whispering farewell. Rada kissed her hand and blew it toward the gravesite.

Anya adjusted her head scarf and looked around. They were completely alone.

"Rada, my Iskra said there were two men there the day Calina was killed. What if I told you the police won't help, but I think I know who killed her. Would you help me bring justice for this fine woman?"

Rada's eyebrows went up, and then seemed to settle back for what she was going to hear. "What are you inferring, my dear?"

"An eye for an eye. I trust you with my life because you know I loved Calina, who was more caring than her own son. Can you help me?"

"This is so unexpected—I want to see Calina's killer suffer as much as she did." Rada started slapping her arms and marching in place.

Anya leaned in close. "I doubt that the guilty party would ever be judged or condemned. He's protected. What would happen if someone accidentally gave a person an overdose of morphine?" she asked barely above a whisper.

"Impossible to procure from the hospital—under lock and key, and the nurse in charge, we call her the demon or Rasputin. Let me think. Perhaps on the street. Isn't your ex into drugs?"

"Not sure. He may be hooked on heroin." Anya hesitated. *How much should she reveal?* "I can't ask his help. I'm almost certain he's involved somehow."

Rada's eyes grew large. "That villain! You don't think it was him?"

Anya took a step back and rubbed her chin. "Not even that gutter-snipe Grigory could have bludgeoned his own mother." She shook her head. "Not his hand, but somehow I feel he's complicit, connected."

"Let's walk. We've got to keep moving or become gelid."

"There's an old rural run-down dwelling with a brick *pechka* inside. The men had a small fire going before the workers left with their shovels. I was lost and followed them until I found my way here. I saw where they were going. The ground must have thawed enough—to dig a grave with a backhoe. The dirt was mounded on both sides of an open grave. They're going to bury a wooden casket and shovel in the earth on top. What gruesome work."

"Over there," Anya said nudging her chin in the direction. "I have some biscuits and a thermos of sugared tea."

"Good," Rada said and slapped her purse. "I brought vodka."

They walked arm in arm to the remains of what had been a peasant's home. Anya peered in a dirty window. Empty. The door was unlocked and a small, almost extinguished fire of birch and pine burned low.

Anya pointed. "They cook their meals on the stove, keep warm, and hide out for naps, but good thing they're working now."

Three rickety chairs were near the stove. Anya took off her scarf, and Rada removed her hat and gloves and shoved them in her pockets.

They moved the chairs even closer to the stove, using the third chair as a table. They took out their provisions and laid them on the chair between them. Anya poured tea into the thermos top that served as a cup. Rada poured the vodka into the thimble top of her flask. She downed her shot and gave one to Anya. Without a word, they repeated their drinking. Then took turns eating and drinking the tea.

"You're so preoccupied. What is it? Afraid they'll come back?"

"Hell no. I can handle some workers with my vodka. But wait a minute. I'm thinking of something I learned. You'll need to get very close to your victim—how big is he?"

"A monster. He towers over me in height and in strength. He's a giant."

"Could you stab a needle into his neck? Could you do that? An injection of—"

"A drug substance?" Anya rubbed her arms.

"No, no—you'd need way too much of that—ah!" Rada shook her head. "I know. *Khloristyy kaliy.*"

"Potassium chloride?"

"An overdose stops the heart. I don't want to know who it is—the less I know the better for you."

"How can I get it?"

"You can't. I can. My concern. Best you stay uninformed." Rada stamped her feet.

"When can you get it to me?"

"Let me think a second. How about here? Could you manage this coming Tuesday?"

"*Da.* Certainly. Can you get the time off?"

Rada nodded. "I'll bring brandy—it warms better than vodka. I steal it when no one's around the drug cabinet or from a doctor while he humps one of the nurses."

"How will I get a syringe?"

"If I'm getting you the vial—I'll also get a syringe for it. Pretend you're stabbing an orange with a needle. It's easy. But you must get it in the neck on the first try. Now tell me, how Iskra is doing without her *babushka*?"

"When she's not in school, I leave her with Yelizaveta, my dear neighbor."

After some quiet conversation and when they'd finished their slight repast, they tidied up, moved the chairs back, and left. The women linked arms and walked to the entrance.

They kissed at the gate.

"Tuesday," Anya said.

"Same time."

Chapter Twenty-Six

Sunday, January 27, 1957

Anya heard the key in the door. She leaned against it. "Wait, I'll open it."

Andrei came in, leaned forward and kissed her. He asked Anya if she knew how to prepare *shchi*.

"Doesn't everyone? I stole cabbages to make soup from backyard gardens during the Siege."

"Close your eyes then, and I'll work magic," Andrei said, wriggling his eyebrows up and down.

Anya smiled and shook her head; then watched him. Without taking off his heavy jacket, he took from behind his back a package and placed a paper bag on the table. "Here are the makings of *shchi*," he said with drama and a wink. Exaggeratingly slow, one at a time, item by item, he pulled out the ingredients for the soup: an onion, three carrots with feathery green tops, two potatoes, a jar of sauerkraut, and a few pieces of meat."

"Stop!" Anya screeched. She picked up the meat. "Please don't tell me this is left over from the war and is human."

"Not many people admit that cannibalism existed—"

"*Da.* It's so unpatriotic and bourgeois, isn't it?"

"But so true. No, my love, this is pork," he said and took the meat out of her hands.

She pursed her lips. "From a butcher shop?"

He shook his head. "Outside of town, there was some nasty business at the Red Partisans Collective. Nearby there's a minuscule farm—

practically non-existent, but the guy still thinks of himself as a *muzhik,* a peasant, so I bribed him."

"You're Jewish—you don't eat pork."

He took off his jacket. "If you grow up religious, no, but remember I was raised hungry and Russian."

He washed his hands at the sink, and pulled out a pot from under it. He tossed the meat in and rinsed it under cold water.

"Your job is to clean and cut the vegetables. If you do a good job, my sweet, I'll let you have sour cream to top the soup." He put the pot on the stove, lit it, turned around and pulled from his inside pocket a twenty-faceted thick drinking glass filled with *smetana,* sour cream. "Two birds with one stone. Now you have a glass for your neighbor."

Anya took hold of the glass tumbler, and turned it around in her hand. It was the standard one found in schools and hospitals. "Not sure I'll be so willing to part with this— when filled to the brim it measures 250 ml, approximately a cup. I can use it in my own kitchen as a measure—that is if you continue to support me with food so I can cook."

"How do you know that measurement?"

"Doesn't everyone? I worked in a school cafeteria for a while when I was pregnant with Iskra."

He hugged her, kissed the tip of her nose. "You're so full of information, we should get you on the force."

She pushed him back gently. "Here's something else, Calina used the glass as a round cutter for her dough to make *pel'meni* and also grew seedlings in one of them."

"How about *varenki?*"

"She made those, too," Anya said, a note of sadness in her voice. Her eyes pricked with tears.

"Here, here," he said. "Don't fret. I promise I'll find the *prestupnik.*"

"Criminal? You mean killers!"

"Perp. Murderer. I don't think both men killed her—only one." He pulled her back into his arms, lifted her chin and kissed her. "I'm famished. Lower the flame for the meat. Got salt?"

She reached for a shaker and handed it to him.

"Not enough. Get some from our dinner guests—your neighbor and Iskra." He tied an apron around his waist. "I'll wash the cabbage."

Chapter Twenty-Seven

Late morning
Monday, January 28, 1957

Andrei was in the office when he heard a scuffle. He waited till every-thing was quiet and then walked down the hall to see what it was all about. He scrutinized Sasha's office. Empty.

Sasha would never have vacated his office unless he'd been forced. Andrei slipped in and took a cursory gaze about. Desktop cleared. Open drawers empty. His eyes came to rest on a tiny piece of paper barely visible and stuck in the corner under Sasha's desk, He quickly retrieved it, stuck it in his pocket, and left.

Back in his office, Andrei perused the folded paper with numbers, and realized it was the code that they'd set up but had never used. It also wasn't typed, which meant Sasha was in a hurry.

After work, Andrei would go to Anya's and get the storybook he'd given to Iskra to decipher the meaning.

As soon as he got to Anya's, he asked to see the fairytale book he'd given Iskra, silently thanking Gorky for saving Russian tales. Anya brought the book back from Yelizaveta's where Iskra had left it. He sat down at the kitchen table, opened the book, and turned to the story "Alenouska and her Brother."

"What is it?" Anya asked.

"It's a message in code from Sasha, but how did he know I'd see it? It was sticking out of an edge of his desk. He was obviously in a hurry or he'd have typed it on someone else's typewriter." He whispered,

"Chapter, page, line, words," and began to write as he scanned the words:

- 13 4 6 7 long journey
- 4 8 5 8 or dead
- 5 6 7 9 beware wolf
- 6 6 9 5 burnt footprint
- 6 7 5 6 brother leave

"Anya, give me a minute to work this out. Long journey sounds ominously like Siberia. Dead—his worst fear. Beware wolf seems obvious. Sasha's referring to Nikolai. Burnt footprint?" Andrei said. "I wonder if that means Sasha burned everything or I should set a match to anything that might be remotely considered incriminating." He scowled at the last two words: brother leave, which could only mean, get the hell out before it's too late. He handed the paper to Anya. "Read it. Then burn it along with this," he said, handing her a small sheet with numbers on it.

Chapter Twenty-Eight

Morning
Tuesday, January 29, 1957

Anya waited at Calina's grave as she'd promised to get the needed hospital supplies from Rada. Anya felt jittery and kept turning in different directions at the slightest sound. *What if Rada was unable to procure the necessary instruments from the hospital?* Finally the nurse appeared and they greeted each other with affection.

After the two women showed their respects, they moved away from the gravesite toward the shelter house where they'd been the week before. As soon as they entered, Rada emptied the contents of her bag on top of a wooden crate that served as a table. There were several items in the package Rada had brought. She displayed the drugs and syringes she'd obtained from the hospital.

"I thought there'd only be two things," Anya said.

With care, Rada took out a small bottle of brandy, opened it and said, "Drink."

Anya obeyed and felt the liquid burn going down her throat and felt her eyes bulge.

Rada took a hit of the bottle, closed it and stuck it in her purse. Next, she pointed out the cache of goods. Anya saw a vial with a tiny rubber stopper in it, an ampule of liquid she thought was Potassium Chloride, and two syringes. Rada spoke quietly but fast. "Perhaps, if he's a big man, you're going to have to render him unconscious first."

Anya shook her head and started to say, "Impossible, I'll never—"

Nina Romano

"No details—that's your problem. This vial contains a barbiturate. You're to stick the needle into the vial without taking off the top. Extract the barbiturate—"

"What's a barbiturate? A kind of drug?"

"A sedative which will depress the central nervous system—you inject it into a vein in his arm to relax him."

"I'll never have the chance—I won't be sleeping with him."

"Too bad. Maybe you should so you could get him drunk first and after when he's snoring, suffocate him."

"Please. We haven't much time."

"Then, here, let me show you the method *in case.* Take your arm out of the coat sleeve." Rada rolled up Anya's sweater and tapped on the inside of her elbow, demonstrating how to find the vein and perform the *vpryskivaniye.* "You can inject him—it'll only take a few seconds to relax him. You can use the same syringe—you certainly don't have to worry about germs." She laughed. "But as a precaution, I gave you a second syringe."

"In case of what?"

"If you break the needle or drop the first one. Snap off the glass at the top of the ampule—be careful not to cut yourself, use a cloth to snap it off. Insert the syringe and draw out the liquid. Inject it in that same spot on the victim's arm."

"There won't be time to use this. I'll have one chance, only one opportunity, and it'll be a mere few seconds to jab him."

"In that case you'll have to thrust this into his neck." Rada waved her hand in front of her face. "Save the barbiturate. I can't very well return it. Now let me show you the other."

A loud voice from one of the gravediggers yelled outside the window, "What do you think you two are doing in here?" Anya rolled down her sleeve and put her coat back on.

250

The man barged through the door. Rada stepped in front of Anya to give her time to collect the items and put them in the bag.

Rada thrashed her arms upward, moving around like a theater actress. "You must excuse us—you see my friend was overcome with grief about her mother. I'm a nurse. I took her in here to revive her. She turned white as a specter—she may be pregnant. You see I gave her some medicinal brandy." She dipped into her coat pocket and held the flask in front of him, bait on a hook for a craving worker.

"You must be frozen—it's such a beast of a day out and you work so hard. Would you care for a nip? I have a cup. Let me pour some." She tipped out a little, stopped, looked up at his face, greedy with desire, and said, "Oh, that won't do—you're a big strapping man, you need a little more." She topped off the cup, handed it to him, and shoved the flask in her coat pocket.

"We really must go now," Rada said, taking Anya under the arm and bustling her outside.

The two women ambled back towards Calina's grave. Rada broke free of Anya's grasp. "It's easy. Watch. She picked up a twig and made as if to stab Anya at the side of her neck near the jaw bone and a little in front of the ear. "Simple, but jab it in deep. Make sure you hit the carotid artery."

"How will I know?"

"The carotid runs down on both sides of your neck. Put your two fingers under where the jaw-bone goes back toward the ear like this. Do you feel that? There's an internal and an external carotid. Stick either of them." She dipped inside her purse and took out an illustrated picture and handed it to Anya.

"I ripped this out of a medical journal, but don't keep it. Get rid of it on the way home."

Anya took hold of the paper. "What if he fights me?"

"If he's huge as you say, he could grab you into a stranglehold—be sure to plunge deep, sink it in with force, and step away fast."

"What if he pulls it out?"

"Did I not say, *deep*? Now study the picture." Rada pinged the paper with a thumb and middle finger snap. "I have a feeling we'll not meet again on this turf."

"Not just in this cemetery, or in *Piter* or all of Soviet Russia. You were a true sister to Calina and I give you heartfelt thanks on her behalf."

"Goodbye, dear friend. May God forgive you and be with you."

On the way home, Anya pictured Nikolai, Yasha, and Grigory each holding the fire poker. It was impossible to see Grigory in a stance posed to strike his mother. It was equally impossible to envisage Yasha holding the deadly instrument. The figment figure she imagined who could wield it was Nikolai. She wanted it to be him. She'd relish killing him. But how could she know for sure he killed Calina?

Would she have to involve Andrei to somehow lure Nikolai to the apartment? Should she be alone or with Grigory?

At home, Anya got the key from Yelizaveta and went to retrieve the dolls from Boris' mess of hardware and gadget closet. Anya put the dolls under her bed. When she returned the key, Yelizaveta gave her a knowing look. "It won't be long now, will it?"

Anya placed the framed picture of herself in the ballet costume into Yelizaveta's hands. "If you need money, there's a bill in here."

After she'd put Iskra to bed, Anya didn't have an orange so she practiced injecting first an onion, and then a boiled potato. She practiced several times and felt confident she could do it. Andrei came in just as she slipped the killing tools under a dish towel, thinking at first chance she'd put them away properly.

The first thing he said to her was, "What's that old expression: 'Beware of Greeks bearing gifts?'" He pulled a package from behind his back and set it on the table. Then he kissed her quite formally.

"Shsh. I've just put Iskra down for the night. She had a nightmare and I had all I could do to calm her down."

"What was the dream about?"

"Calina. Apparently Iskra saw more than she admitted the day Calina was killed."

"What do you mean?"

"There were two men that entered the place—remember how she mentioned the shoes? She kept pointing to the cop's sturdy shoes. One of the men wore brown boots."

Andrei sat down at the table, took out a pencil, and jotted down something in a pocket notebook.

"Shall I check on her to make sure she's asleep?" he asked.

"I gave her chamomile tea. She's out cold."

"Bless her. Then there's nothing to stop you from opening these gifts."

Anya tugged at the cord, and when it didn't give, took a knife and cut it. She removed the paper wrapping. Her eyes and mouth opened wide, and took hold of a pair of boots. She immediately put them on and pranced up and down in front of him. "Beautiful soul! How I have yearned for such foot coverings!"

"You'll need them to travel."

She got the inference but ignored it. Then she reached for a small red box, tore it open. "I can't believe my eyes—Belgian chocolates! And what's this?" She took hold of a tiny tissue covered cylinder. She unrolled the tube and yelped, "A lipstick? Where in the name of Holy Mother the Virgin Mary did you get this stash?"

"One more thing." He reached in and pulled out a jar of face cream and handed it to her. She read the label Lancôme Nutrix, and almost dropped the jar as she flung her arms around his neck, squealing with joy and raining sweet kissing pecks all over his face.

He put on a sheepish grin, shrugged his shoulders. "I stole it from a huge basket of goodies the chief received for his wife. He barely looked at it. He's so used to getting *Vyplaty.*"

"Payments. Indeed. What luck, my darling thief."

"Oh, and this," Andrei reached into his inside vest pocket and plucked out a rolled-up pair of sheer silk stockings. "For you, dark eyes, light of my life."

Anya shrieked and unfurled the stockings like flags. "I don't have a garter belt! And I certainly can't pin these to my knickers!"

"I'll have to work on that—do they come in sizes? Colors?"

"White. Small, but if you can't find that get me a medium any color—I can alter it, if you please."

"And lastly . . . this." From his coat lapel he plucked out a wilted red rose. "It's not the golden rose of Lancôme, and it's not even in the most perfect state, and a rose could never be as flawless as your lips, but it's a sign of my devotion to you. I swear. Sorry it's crushed and secondhand."

Anya threw back her head, pulled away her arms from around his neck, and laughing, opened the cream pot and smeared it all over her cheeks. "I feel like a kept mistress of the old regime! What's your name? Let me guess. Prince Andrei, is it? How exquisite! Where's my Fabergé egg?" She kissed the rose, set it in a glass of water, and placed it in the middle of the table.

Andrei pulled Anya onto his lap. "I'm going to stay here until we leave."

"I don't want to talk about this now."

"We must. I'm no longer going to my office. Nikolai will come after me and this is the first place he'll come looking. After tonight, Iskra should sleep at Yelizaveta's."

Anya lifted the towel covering her killing instruments. "Either you shoot to kill or I'll use this."

"What is it? Where did you get it?"

Anya explained about the meeting with Rada. Next, Anya told him of her murderous intention. "I'm not a good soul, and now I'm taking on the spirit of an avenging angel. The devil will own me." When she finished, she wiped away tears coursing down her creamed cheeks.

"It may be the end of us as well and we won't be able to travel—"

"You mean escape. If you want out of this—now is the time to say so."

Andrei shook his head.

"Here's your murder case whittled down." Anya quickly went over the route she discovered about how the diamonds were smuggled out of Leningrad through the dolls now in her possession.

"I'm all ears," Andrei said, in an astonished voice.

"I'll take the painted diamonds out of the doll's eyes and sew them in Iskra's clothes. If we pull this off and can get away, I'll give a portion of the stones to Yelizaveta, but as a fail-safe, leave Iskra's packed clothes for her to use for the child if we don't survive."

"You're not only a keen investigator, my pet, but a strategist as well. I want him dead just as much as you do. But—"

"It goes against your religion."

"My new religion is you."

Chapter Twenty-Nine

11:47 PM
Thursday, January 31, 1957

Andrei was in a dream sequence of a soft sleep when he heard banging on the door. He shook Anya, already dressed in her ballet togs for comfort and warmth and shoved his legs into his trousers, stiff with cold. Walking toward the kitchen, he pulled on a sweater, placing his gun in the small of his back beneath it. He took a deep breath before he opened the door with caution, but someone behind it kicked the door with enormous force, knocking Andrei sideways to the floor.

Without a word, Nikolai and Sasha roughly dragged Andrei to his feet and slammed his wrists into handcuffs. Andrei's eyes went wide with surprise to see Sasha, confusion muddling as Andrei tried to sort out the possible reasons, but also his own predicament now registering.

Anya entered the kitchen as the scuffle ended, and the man with Nikolai whom she recognized and was shocked to see, grabbed and twisted her around to tie her hands with cord he snatched from her table's open catch-all drawer.

Nikolai sent Sasha down to the car, berating him for forgetting the other pair of handcuffs. Then he closed the door, brandishing a pistol, indicating that Andrei should sit at the table.

Anya fixed her gaze on Andrei, making a slight imperceptible movement to the right with her head, then moving her head slightly to the left, hoping he understood it to mean: Don't. Andrei made a hesitant and clumsy pass to sit at the table but was clearly away from Nikolai's gun, when Anya, taking advantage of Nikolai's attention toward Andrei, whirled her right leg and foot in a perfect forceful arc, knocking the gun out of Nikolai's hand.

A tussle ensued. Up and off the chair like a raging bull, Andrei butted his shoulder into Nikolai's chest for a sports tackle. Then Andrei's head struck upward for chin contact and next rammed his forehead into Nikolai's.

Anya kicked the gun away from Nikolai's reaching hand. She crouched, bending her knees, and picked it up. Turning her shoulder halfway, she lifted her hand from behind her back, cocked and fired the gun, the bullet grazing Nikolai's leg. He bellowed as loud as the report from the shot, which was louder than she expected despite the fact it was mounted with a suppressor.

"Not at all silent," she said, surprised.

Nikolai howled like a wounded wolf. Anya slid her right foot back to thrust it forward and deliver a powerful, solid kick in Nikolai's face. He fell to the floor. Anya dropped the silencer out of reach of both men. With her hands still tied behind her, she took hold of a knife from the opened drawer. Andrei's outrage, too much for him to contain, repeatedly kicked the downed man, who had already passed out.

"Stop it," Anya barked.

Andrei ceased the vicious kicking.

She placed the knife on the table and then did a contortionist move bringing her arms down in back and stepping over them so that her hands were now in front of her. She sank to her knees and took the keys from Nikolai's vest pocket, stood up to unlock and release Andrei's cuffed wrists.

She held her hands up. "Cut the rope."

When she and Andrei were free, the foot soldier burst through the door as Andrei opened it. Sasha looked shocked. "I heard a shot and thought you'd be dead."

Nina Romano

"Thanks. I don't know how you're going to get out of this, Sasha. Thought you were already in Siberia by now or buried in unhallowed ground."

"Would have thought so too, but got a promotion instead. They hung some poor schmuck from homicide."

"Schmuck? You mean *tupitsa*?"

"Exactly. As in *chmo*. There wasn't time to let you know what was going down. A long shot, but I'd hoped you would've found my coded message—"

"I did."

"I couldn't let you know the way things righted themselves after they made me clear out my office. Things turned three hundred and sixty. Don't have a clue why Linsky chose me. I'm certain Nikolai wanted me in Siberia or dead because I'd witnessed him killing the old woman in the apartment, although even Nikolai must've changed his mind, knowing I'd be of value and still able to do more of his dirty work."

Anya pointed at Sasha's feet. "Brown boots. Not a cop's shoes. Iskra saw. You were present—"

"A witness, but not a murderer." Sasha said, in lieu of an apology.

She bent and picked up the gun. "I wasn't certain, but now I'm sure I want him dead." She faced Andrei. "Are you going to kill him or shall I?"

"How'll we get him out of here? Roll him in your Bokhara rug and throw him over the banister down the stairs? Unless you've a better idea."

"And what? Bury him in the basement? Mmmm. I could get the key from Yelizaveta. She keeps an extra one for Boris. Although—"

She leaned over Nikolai and rolled up his pants. "He yowled like a beast, but it's only a flesh wound. Andrei. You might think you knocked him to kingdom come, but he's coming around."

258

"What're you doing?" Andrei asked.

"Deciding whether or not to clean the wound."

"Why?"

"To make it look like something other than a strafe from a bullet."

"Are you going to sew the hole in his pant leg, too? No time."

"We're not going to shoot him—this silencer has a loud report and one shot's already been fired." She wiped her fingerprints off the gun and with his jacket lapel replaced it in Nikolai's shoulder holster. "As much as you'd like to carve his heart out—you're not going to use my kitchen knife to do it. Too messy and I'd probably faint."

She went to her purse, pulled out the syringes Rada had given her and held them up to the light. She put the vial and ampule on the table. "This'll make it look like he had a heart attack. We won't need to waste my antique rug. I was planning on giving it to Yelizaveta when we leave. We'll dump him over the railing and he'll sail down the stairs after an apparent heart attack."

Sasha nodded in silent approval.

Nikolai started to moan.

"He's all yours. Oh, and by the way," Andrei turned. "This is Sasha."

She nodded. "Fine time for introductions. We met at Calina's apartment and again at the diplomatic party. He drove me home."

"Under the arm or in the pubis to hide the injection site?" Sasha asked, pointing to the syringes.

"Armpit," Andrei said.

"Neither. Not in the back of the head either. I'm drugging him the way I was taught. Then, I'll plunge the syringe into the carotid." She pulled the charger back and let a little of the liquid out into the sink and ran the water.

Andrei pushed up the sleeve of Nikolai's jacket and unfastened the button of his cuffed shirt.

Anya picked up his arm and drove the needle into the vein at the bend inside the elbow. "*Da. Da. Ty svin'ya,*" she said, and repeated, "you are a pig," and spat in his face as his moaning ceased.

Nikolai lay motionless—his breathing shallow. Anya put two fingers to his neck, then stabbed him deep into the spot Rada had shown her.

Nikolai breathed his last and Andrei buttoned the shirt and pulled down his jacket sleeve. He heaved the dead man up and over his shoulder. "Open the door, Sasha. Help me lean him over the banister. How will you get out of this mess?"

"I was never here. He came alone," Sasha said as they maneuvered the body out the door and doubled him over the banister. "One question, brother, did you ever find the diamonds?"

Andrei looked back at Anya, standing under the door lintel.

Sasha looked at her, nodded, clicked his heels, and did a slight bow.

Sasha wiped his hands on his coat. "Nikolai recruited me a second time—perhaps the reason for my promotion. I had to liquidate someone for him—a pawnbroker. Sorry to say, Andrei, he was one of our own."

Anya drew in a sharp intake of breath. "Yasha," she murmured.

Before Andrei came back inside, she heard him say to Sasha, "Now leave us, my friend. Invent a great tale for Linsky, but always watch your back." Andrei embraced him. "One more thing. Who killed the doll-seller?"

"Grigory. He, too, was on Nikolai's hit list to eliminate. I would've done the job but, by dumb luck, he wasn't at the pawnbroker's when he was supposed to be. Off the hook now. I could care less to pin Tamara's murder on him. I'll be too busy in charge of investigating Nikolai's accidental death."

"Grigory doesn't know you were present when Nikolai killed Calina?"

"No. And too strung out on drugs to understand he was to blame or that Nikolai killed her."

"Are you going to accuse Nikolai of being an enemy of the state or complicit in a smuggling game?"

"He's Chief Linsky's favorite henchman. Weren't you told never to speak ill of the dead?"

Andrei smiled.

Descending the stairs, Sasha put the Orthodox cross inside of his shirt collar. "*Shalom.*" He looked up at Andrei. "You have a gun, but take his, too. It'll look like a theft and you might need it."

"*Da.*" Andrei removed the holster and gun off the dead man leaning over the bannister.

Once again inside, Andrei shook Anya by the shoulders. "Don't tell your neighbor you're leaving. Tell her I'm taking you away for the weekend to a friend's country place."

"I'll tell her it's your family's—"

"Don't say that. We are going to the abandoned dacha if possible. What she doesn't know, she can't give away if questioned." Now. We'll go down and out, but not together—it'd be best to leave separately. I'll go first with Iskra."

"Where are we going?"

"Omar's."

"Yelizaveta will know I'm leaving. I must say goodbye, give her my key and tell her to take what she wants from here. She's been like a sister and a mother to me."

"*Da.* Of course you must. And the *Ketubah?*"

"Yelizaveta has the scroll. She's made a toy bear for Iskra to serve as a hiding place for it. She was afraid it would ruin or get stolen from the outside drain gutter."

Andrei opened the tap and guzzled water straight from the faucet.

He turned to see Anya packing a *matryoshka* doll and rummaging through a box of buttons. "What the deuce are you doing? Packing another doll, collecting buttons?"

"These are the keys to our freedom—they cost Calina her life." She held up colored stones. "They're painted diamonds—like the ones in the doll's eyes. Smaller ones inside the doll."

Disbelief swathed his face as he gawked at the new doll. "And that one?"

She stopped packing. "From the other pawnbroker. Calina left it there for safe-keeping."

She looked up. Sadness veiled her eyes. "The price was her life. Have you figured the smuggling connection totally now?"

He nodded. "I've mapped it out. There were diamonds in Nikolai's cigar case at the Chinese border." He handed her the gun and holster. "Pack these, too. He took his gun out from behind his back. My holster is in the bedroom. I'll get it. Collect the syringes and stuff to throw out, but not here—take them with you and we'll get rid of them elsewhere."

After he got his belongings from the bedroom, Andrei went to the staircase rail, hoisted up the corpse, and dropped Nikolai over as Anya knocked on the opposite door.

Yelizaveta opened the door. "Is the bastard dead?"

Anya pointed toward the bottom of the stairs.

Yelizaveta gazed in the direction of the stairwell and spat. Anya gave her the apartment key. "Help me. Put the child's hat on. Give her the bear, too." Anya put on her coat and strapped a rucksack to her back. She hoisted Iskra's packed clothes in her arms and shouldered the child's rucksack. Andrei carried a suitcase, a duffle bag, and wore an army knapsack. He asked the sleepy child if she could walk. Iskra yawned as he took her hand. He nodded thanks to Yelizaveta and went down the stairs. Anya grasped her friend and begged her not to cry.

"I'll send word when we're safe. Pray for us." Anya reached into her pocket and handed Yelizaveta a new pair of mittens. "I sewed a cache of diamonds into the palms. Pawn them. Yasha's dead."

Yelizaveta gasped and covered her mouth with her hand.

"I put Calina's other pawnshop ticket inside. Never give your own name."

They embraced again. Yelizaveta signed a cross over Anya.

Carrying her gear, Anya made her way quietly down the staircase in her new boots. When she reached the bottom, she stepped over the sprawled out body. Anya glanced up to see the smiling, tearful face of her friend.

Chapter Thirty

2 AM
Friday, February 1, 1957

As Anya knocked on the door, soft strains from a balalaika reached her. Andrei had told her about his Romani friends—these Gypsies were raised Russian Orthodox—but Omar loved Jewish music. The song being played was a happy one, but she was unsure of the origin.

When she and Iskra entered there was an abrupt pause in the music.

"Oh please don't tell them to stop playing—it was such a joyous tune," Anya said.

"*Fraylich.* An old Jewish song," Omar raised his hand and the music recommenced. He ushered them to a corner table in the back.

Anya took off her coat, hat and scarf, and then helped Iskra out of her coat and an extra layer of clothing.

"Please. Make yourselves comfortable. You're waiting for Andrei?"

Anya nodded. "He's parking the car far from here. He said you had a safe place."

"I'll bring a samovar for tea, and something to eat."

Anya touched his forearm and shook her head.

"Payment? I owe Andrei my life. I can never repay what he did for me. And you are now his charge and he yours. Correct?"

She smiled despite the grave situation. "More than correct."

Iskra was now wide awake. "Such pretty music, Mama. Where are we going?"

"On a journey. Like in your picture books. We're going far away to live happily ever after." Out of habit, she crossed her fingers behind her back for telling one more lie.

Andrei came in, an uneasy display of nerves, as he took a seat next to Iskra. Omar also sat at the table.

"We're going to be hunted."

"By Nikolai?" Omar asked, turning his face toward Andrei.

Andrei shook his head. "Not when they find his body at the bottom of the stairs in Anya's building."

Omar raised his chin. "Your involvement?"

"I didn't shoot him—"

Anya interrupted. "I gave him—Iskra, my love, go over closer to the musicians and listen to their song." The child rose and walked away. "I stabbed him with a lethal injection that'll make it appear he had a heart attack and fell over the railing from the top of the stairwell." Anya was visibly shaken. She'd just admitted to murder.

"Are you a nurse? How did you come by this?" Omar lit a cigarette.

"I'm not," Anya leaned a little closer, "but I'd rather not say."

"Of course. It was indiscreet of me—I need not know." Omar's nod was in slow motion. Anya had committed murder, but something in his voice sounded a bit like admiration. He faced Andrei. "Have you a plan?"

"There wasn't time to alert you. Somehow I thought we'd have another day. If you'll have us, we'll stay here and then we'll go to my grandfather's dacha. Will you contact the priest, Vadim, to tell him to ready a part of the old place for us? We won't stay long. Here a day, and there, perhaps three. We're going to Finland. My father's brother escaped Stalin and now lives outside of Helsinki."

"How will you get to Finland?" Omar crushed his cigarette and raised his hand slightly for the waiter. "Warm milk with honey for the child, and champagne for the table."

"Extravagant, my friend," Andrei said.

Nina Romano

"Warranted as a farewell. After you leave for Finland, we may never see each other again in this lifetime. Tell me how you'll travel."

"I'm depending on you to give us false documents."

"You'll have to stay here two nights. A rush job. I can have them done. We'll need your photos. I have to contact an excellent forger, but even he cannot work a miracle in less time. And I'll need to visit our religious friend beforehand."

"When will you go to see Vadim?"

"Tomorrow I'll dress as a priest and meet him in the small village, Malen'kaya Finlyandiya, outside of Pushkin. He'll get your dacha somewhat habitable—around seventeen kilometers distance toward Krasnoye Selo. He'll make arrangements for the three of you."

Andrei turned toward Anya. "Vadim had been friends with my father and knew Omar during the reign of terror and persecution under Stalin. He's used to caring for fugitives—we won't be anything new for him. I remember Vadim with affection and hope the holy man is well and thriving."

"Tell me about Pushkin," Anya said.

"Pushkin's a town on the Neva Lowland," Andrei said.

"On the Neva River?" Anya asked.

"The left bank."

"May I give her my impression, Andrei," Omar said.

"Of course. Please." Andrei said.

The waiter set the milk down on the table, opened the champagne, and poured for them. They clinked glasses and all sipped the bubbly liquid.

"Pushkin. Beautiful, lush landscape—hills, ridges, orchards mingled in with valleys, plains, forests, farmland. A perfect place to build a dacha—near to *Piter*. Natural springs that birth streams and ponds.

266

You'll love it and the surrounding areas. Too bad you'll be there only a short while." Omar sipped from his glass.

"You paint a lovely picture. And *Krasnoye Selo*?" Anya asked.

"Much the same," Omar said.

Andrei waved his hands. "But what's spectacular is the little hidden settlement, the arbors and dells of *Malen'kaya Finlyandiya*—Little Finland—probably not even on a map. It's precious."

"You both speak of it with great affection. I can't wait to see it." Anya beckoned Iskra to return to the table for her milk.

Andrei shook his head. "You'll be sorry to leave it. Maybe we can find a similar countryside in the actual country of Finland."

Andrei leaned toward Omar. "I have to call Sasha to see him tonight. Need to borrow a car."

Omar sat up straighter. "It's a risk."

"I must go to my apartment and meet with Sasha," Andrei said, his voice insistent.

After Anya and Iskra were settled in a back room of the café, Andrei left his car and took the borrowed one. He drove to his apartment to make sure nothing incriminating was left behind. He didn't turn on the lights but used his torch to discover a ransacked place, furniture slashed and the guts spilling onto the floor. "Nikolai's neat work," Andrei murmured and went to police headquarters.

~*~

Andrei entered his office, took the picture of the dacha from is desk blotter, and stuck it in his breast pocket. Sasha waited in his office. Andrei went in and closed the door. "You saw what Nikolai did to your living quarters, but he didn't find anything. And here we meet. What safer place could there be for someone evading the law?" Sasha said.

"How did you get in so deep with Nikolai?" Andrei asked.

"Sit. You're jittery and making me nervous. Nikolai had clout and threatened me after I'd overheard him making plans with Grigory. The rest, a trip up, followed by a fall into steeper and deeper crooked wells."

"And next I want—"

"Before I knew it he and I went to use some scare tactics on Calina because she was holding out goods from Yahsha, Grigory, and him."

"Goods. You mean diamonds?"

"Exactly." Sasha smoothed a stack of papers, opened a drawer, and put them inside. "Nikolai lost his temper and got rough with her and the next thing I know we're covering his tracks while investigating the murder he committed."

"Did you know the child was under the bed?"

"If Nikolai had known, she wouldn't be breathing." Sasha lit a cigarette and handed one to Andrei.

"And your cut?"

"Of a sudden, Tamara had no stones, and although we searched Calina's, we found none. I'm lucky to be still vertical and breathing and talking to you. Anya did me a huge favor ridding me of a migraine headache. Didn't she tell you of the agonies she suffered at the hands of that ruthless bastard while she was a guest of Hotel Kvetsky? Do you have any idea of the countless atrocities? "

"All I ever wanted was to get into the police force and now I'm hunted—forced to leave Russia, an accomplice to murder, a killing I'd gladly have committed."

"What twisty paths we find ourselves on as we travel life's journey."

"Two more things I need to take care of before we leave. How much of a security watch are they going to employ to find Anya and me?"

"I'll cover for you now I'll be stepping into Nikolai's shoes. I'll take care of the *doktor* in autopsy—only the two of us will be present. If he finds needle marks or an infinitesimal puncture on the inside of Nikolai's arm or neck he won't report it."

"Or perhaps say he was hooked on drugs."

"Impossible with merely one mark in the crook of his arm and another in his neck."

"What about the strafe on his leg coming from a gun?"

"It'll never make it into his notes because he owes me and will conveniently omit all of those findings."

"What about security when I plan to leave *Piter?*"

"Not my detail. I've no idea who monitors exits. Andrei, listen. It's best to have your hospital doctor friend call the chief to say when you were assaulted it caused more serious problems and you'll be out from work for a few days. Arrange that tomorrow," Sasha said.

"I want to attend the pawnbroker's funeral with you."

"No burial tomorrow, Saturday. It'll be Sunday, but why wait and chance it?" Sasha ground out his cigarette.

"To tie up loose ends."

A worried expression creased Sasha's brow. "As far as this office is concerned, the pawnbroker's case is closed—a break-in and theft. The matter's solved."

"Solved? The doll seller?"

"Of no consequence, sorry to say."

"How can I ever repay you?"

"Get out of Russia. When you're settled elsewhere send me a postcard to my home address—nothing written on it. Nothing but a stamp. I've got no one—nothing to keep me here, but I do have family in Israel. That's where I'll go—to the Wailing Wall to repent killing a brother Jew."

Chapter Thirty-One

Sunday, February 3, 1957

Andrei was at the cemetery in advance of the scheduled burial. He wanted to attend the funeral in case Grigory showed up. Even though he might not recognize him, Sasha would signal Andrei to be certain. He stood apart and out of sight from the group of mourners. He had attached a Russian M39 SLR Screw Mount Lens to serve as a telephoto lens with large focal length, not to take pictures but to view the attending mourners. He was struck by the thought that he'd be stealing government property because he had full intention of taking his camera and equipment with him. What if he were stopped before gaining entrance to the ferry, or his car searched?

He scrutinized the group of mourners and his thoughts led him back to the present. Would it be likely that Tamara's murderer would attend his partner's funeral? Who knew what darkness was in the heart of someone who could kill for money or material gain?

Deep in concentration, Andrei had been gazing down. When he looked up, he saw Sasha nodding and then tilting his head to his right. A skinny, tall man all in black. Grigory. Andrei recognized the perp Nikolai had been interrogating that late night in the office—the night Andrei had returned for the forgotten film. But there was something more. He realized by this man's size and gestures, he was the assailant who had accosted him on the bridge. Andrei stiffened and touched his shoulder recalling the aggressive stabbing. He hadn't linked his attacker to the perp because despite being thin, he was much stronger than he looked. It had been close to sunset. In the struggle Andrei had tried to pull off the thug's face mask without success, but saw a pronounced scar on his neck. During the assault on the bridge, Grigory hadn't been in his usual attire, he'd worn an expensive short coat and a fur hat, his face hidden by a balaclava. But now his scarred bare neck proved his guilt. Why had Andrei never thought to connect the attacker to Grigory, and why hadn't he ever asked Anya if her ex had a scar on his neck?

His attention refocused as Andrei listened to the ending words of the Mourner's Kadish: *Oseh shalom bimromav, hu ya'aseh shalom aleinu v'al kol-yisrael, v'imru: 'amen,'* grasping some of the meaning: He who creates peace in His celestial heights, may He create peace for us and for all Israel; and say, Amen.

Well after Yasha's burial concluded and none of the grievers or curious were left, Andrei, who wasn't religious, adhered to the old tradition he'd been taught by his father, symbolizing the resurrection of the Dead. He yanked some snow-covered dead grass and tossed it over his shoulder whispering three times, "And may they blossom out of the city like grass of the earth." There was a small fountain in a niche in the wall overgrown with ivy and behind a privet hedge sparse of leaves, where Andrei, checking to make sure he wasn't followed, washed his hands.

From the cemetery, he went to Calina's apartment. Could he pull off his plan? He banged on the door and cocked the gun. Footsteps on the other side. Silence. He knocked again loudly. "I have a message from Anya."

The door opened slightly and Andrei shoved it, burst in, and faced Grigory, raised and fired Nikolai's weapon, blowing a hole in Grigory's chest. "Scumbag, you'll never beat another woman or impair another child, mine, or anyone else's again." Andrei touched his shoulder, summoning up the pain he'd suffered from the stab wound.

He cleaned the weapon of his fingerprints with a handkerchief, tossed the gun near the victim. Leaving the apartment, he pocketed the handkerchief. Premeditated, cold-blooded murder. He had no remorse whatsoever, and only a tiny niggling idea crept into his mind—how would Anya react to the fact that he killed the father of her child? Andrei wouldn't be confessing this anytime soon.

Chapter Thirty-Two

Wednesday, February 6, 1957

Three nights later the threesome arrived in the priest's village—fretful, but rested and not hungry or thirsty, thanks to Omar. Dressed in priestly garb, a voluminous cassock, with a long flowing beard, Vadim greeted Andrei affectionately, pulling him into a smothering embrace. Andrei had always thought of him as a giant when he was a boy, and although he was tall and broad with a husky voice, he was only half a head taller than Andrei.

Andrei had recounted to Anya the story of how the priest had been happily married, when tragedy struck and his wife was killed in a farming accident. He entered the seminary and became the local priest and very good friend to Andrei's grandfather and father. Under Stalin, the Orthodox Church had flourished and the priest had openly celebrated the Divine Liturgy. The situation of tolerance of the church and religion was in a thawing period after Stalin and with the beginning of Khrushchev until now.

After they had taken tea, Iskra fell asleep on a reading chair while Vadim explained things had gradually changed and the position was now ripe for even more oppression under the new leadership. The priest stated his opinion, saying Nikita Sergeyevich Khrushchev was ready to start a new wave of persecution and intolerance toward the Church.

The older people of the parish were still under the guidance of the priest, who surreptitiously gave them the Holy Eucharist, and even celebrated the Divine Liturgy in different hidden places around the countryside.

"I was just about to change to street clothes," Vadim said.

Nina Romano

"Please don't. Not just yet anyway." Anya, who wasn't the least religious, told the priest she wanted to take Communion.

He looked at her askance. "Only those Baptized," he started to say—

"How many times do you need Baptism? She reached over and picked up a pair of scissors on a small linen cloth-covered table, which also hosted a candle stick with a lit candle, and a long-handled spoon. She cut a snippet of her hair and dropped it on the table.

"I trust God with my fate. I've suffered martyrdom of my body in so many forms I've lost count—I've been consecrated by blood not just by water, by desire, too, wanting God's grace. But I've committed a grievous sin—" she hesitated, and then blurted out, "the cardinal sin of murder and beg forgiveness. I'm not sorry the man is dead, but I do regret taking a life."

Andrei looked at her, shock on his face he tried to cover with a cough. "Let's leave Iskra asleep in the rectory. We'll go with Father to the sacristy."

The priest looked at her with something that she perceived as a new understanding. She watched him as he walked into the sacristy to take out the chalice. He poured in some wine and dropped in the bread.

He blessed the chalice and mumbled a prayer, turned and walked toward her. As he approached, her stance became rigid. He stood very still and then nodded, making a sign of the cross upon her forehead. He picked up a cochlear from a covered table, and with the long-handled spoon, dipped it into the cup and took out some bread and wine.

"If God damns you, then so am I, witness and guide, damned, but I forgive you in His holy name, and thus does He forgive."

Afterward they collected Iskra and the priest took them to a room in back of the church where he served them hot soup in wooden bowls with brown bread. He poured Anya and Andrei each a shot of homemade vodka, left the bottle on the table. He patted Iskra on the head, and asked in a soft voice if she would like a sweet.

The child's eyes went from dull to shining-bright but she shook her head to mean no, her fear evident.

"It's all right, Iskra. You may have a sweet if you'd like," Anya said.

The priest went into the refectory and brought out a small dish laden with gingerbread. "But first, you must eat all of your soup."

The child dug her spoon eagerly into the bowl, scooping out chunks of fish.

"Take it easy, Iskra, my love. The sweets are not running away," Anya said.

As they ate the last of their repast of soup, the priest told them it was Lohikeitto, a Finnish dish made with hunks of salmon and potatoes, drenched in a creamy broth with butter and fresh dill, served with rye bread.

"It's delicious," Anya said. "Sweet onions."

"Also leeks," the priest said. "It's one dish I make myself. I prepare a broth of the fish skin, wilt the leeks and onions in the butter, add the salmon—then add cream and dill last."

He can tell I'm nervous. He's trying to put me at ease by giving us the recipe. "No wonder it's so tasty," Anya said.

Andrei eyed the bottle of vodka, and the priest nodded acquiescence. "And here," he said, pointing to a basket filled with bread, butter, lingonberry jam, honey, eggs and bacon. "This is for you tomorrow morning." He covered it with a fringed linen towel and set it on a sideboard.

"How can we ever repay you? Shall I wash the dishes?" Anya asked.

"Leave everything. Women from the village will become disgruntled if they think you usurped their positions. You've no debt with me. Omar has settled everything. We'll talk tomorrow. I'll show you to your lodgings. For tonight you'll stay here." He made an expansive gesture with his hand. "Tomorrow we're having a little bazaar to raise money for the church. So for recompense, you, Anya, and dear Iskra will help to decorate the rectory. Of course, this is forbidden, so all the people who donate or attend are completely complicit. It's a wonderful celebration and it has been going on for such a long time that it's almost considered secular, pagan even, and has nothing to do with the church."

They got up from the table, picked up their small belongings and followed the priest out the door as he doused candles and small lights.

"Iskra, do you know how to dance the troika?" Vadim asked.

"Dancing? To music?" Iskra's eyes brightened.

"And much more," the priest said.

"Like what?" Iskra stopped walking and looked at the priest.

"Gaming, gambling, races, and indoor bandy."

"What's that?"

"Hockey."

"Will there be children?"

"Many. Some come with their babushkas."

"My babushka is dead. She was beaten to death."

Now it was the priest's turn to stop in his tracks.

Surprised her daughter knew how Calina was killed, Anya hunched her shoulders and motioned upward with her hands.

"I see," the priest said.

"No." Iskra shook her head. "You couldn't have," the child said flatly. "You live too far away from where it happened."

"I'm stunned she understood so much," Anya said, an apology in her voice.

"A case unresolved by police," Andrei added, "but we now have all the puzzle pieces."

"This way." The priest indicated a long, dark hall. He held a candle in front of himself. "Follow me." They reached a circular staircase and mounted one at a time as the steps were steep and narrow.

"It might be terribly cold. The building is old and drafty, but we'll light a fire. Sleep all together on the rugs and blankets I've laid near the fireplace. I've stored some wood nearby but I couldn't take the chance of leaving a fire already underway. There's water to drink in a pitcher over there on the wrought iron table, and those three wooden buckets over there by the fireplace. There's a night jar in the corner. Of course there's water in the cistern back of the church, covered with a tarp and a wooden wheel. There's a bucket and rope alongside. You'll have to crack the ice—I've left a long metal rod if you need it, but I wouldn't attempt it at nighttime." He lifted a tea towel covering the basket on the mantle. "There's unblessed sacramental wine and bread here in case you get hungry tonight." From his vestment frock's pocket, he handed a flask to Andrei that Anya guessed contained vodka.

"Bless you, Father," Anya said, and took the priest's hands and kissed them.

"And you, my dear." His long beard belied good looks hidden beneath.

The priest turned to light some candles on the mantelpiece, and told Andrei he could start a fire now, but to make sure to douse it in the morning before walking out onto the verandah and to use the outside stairs down to the unkempt, secluded garden.

As an afterthought the priest said, "It'll be too soon for you to leave the day after the celebration. There's much to do beforehand."

"Tomorrow, we'll speak about when would be the best time," Andrei said.

"Rest well." Vadim made the sign of the cross over them before leaving the room. He closed the door.

277

"What a handsome man to give himself up to God in a country of heathens," Anya said.

With Iskra cuddled near the fireplace, Andrei sprawled next to Anya. "We have to drive back to Leningrad, I'm afraid. Road blocks may be set up. The ferry runs only twice a week."

"How long is the ride to Helsinki?"

"About fifteen hours. It leaves in the evening."

"Will you meet with Sasha again at Police Headquarters?"

"Not sure," he said and pulled out his wallet and placed it next to him.

"You parted well with Sasha?"

"Well enough."

"I almost forgot." She reached into her pocket and handed him a folded card. "Omar gave me this for you—a forged Militsiya identification card. Put it in your wallet. He said you'll need it if you intend to take your gun with you." She smiled. "Congratulations! You finally made it into the police force, and just think you didn't even have to join the party."

He looked it over, winked, and stuck it in his wallet. He put his arms around her.

"Omar also gave me a new license plate for your car—it's in my rucksack. You're to have the car painted in the next village. A Gypsy friend will come to pick it up for you tomorrow."

"What time?"

"Before noon, but he cautioned that none of his people are ever punctual." Anya told Iskra to snuggle close, kissed her head, and made a cross over her like the priest had done. "Good night and dream well, my child."

The candlelight gave the room an eerie look and Anya shuddered. "Can the priest be trusted?"

"Can anyone, except you and me?"

"I believe he can, but would he hold up under torture?"

"He'd never be taken alive. The hunters of the community would see to that. Vadim shares all of their hopes, dreams, sins, and secrets."

Anya kissed Iskra again lightly on the forehead and the sleepy child wriggled over her mother to settle in between them. Hugging Iskra, Anya leaned over to kiss Andrei.

The fire had taken hold, and they set about making themselves at ease for the night in the strange surroundings.

~*~

Thursday, February 7, 1957

In the morning, Anya watched the priest. He was a passionate man in all things—his love of the Divine Liturgy was obvious as the look on his face was beatific as he dipped the long cochlear into the wine and scooped out the bread and wine, the transubstantiation into the body and blood of Christ. He venerated the Eucharist. Anya received again, and Vadim smiled.

Later, while Andrei was seeing to the painting of the car, Vadim took Anya and Iskra sleighing on a troika, the three horses abreast gliding over snow, the tinkling of bells, the sound of the wind sluicing through the denuded frosty branches of the trees. They went at a stable clip sliding over hills, slipping through valleys, skidding huge gullies, skating some flat terrain.

When they returned, cheeks rosy with the ride, they helped with decoration and then went for tea in the rectory and met Andrei.

Before the church festival got underway, Vadim left to oversee the last minute details, and Anya and Andrei talked about the escape from Leningrad to Helsinki.

"Once we cross the Gulf of Finland, we'll be like fish out of water. Do you speak Finnish, Andrei?" Anya asked.

"No, but I speak Estonian and they're very similar. The location of the port of Leningrad is on the western verge of Vasilevsky Island, separated from the mainland by a fork of the Neva River. There's an underground train line that runs from the south of the city to Primorskaya station—about a thirty-forty minute unencumbered walk to the harbor. I can do this if you drive the car—I didn't think of this till now. Can you drive a car?"

She shook her head slowly.

"I'll teach you to drive in Finland."

She smiled.

"If they search for us, they'll be looking for all three of us together, or me alone and you with Iskra. So we'll change that by me taking Iskra and you going alone. You'll have to walk. Leave all your belongings with me. I pray my forefathers will watch over us and the guards won't search the car."

"I'll put Iskra's doll in her rucksack. I've sewed the loose diamonds into the hems of my skirts. How do I meet you on the ferry?"

"The train and then the longer walk, or the little city mini-busses, the *Marshrutkas*, that make the trip—a hop and a skip over one of the island's four bridges—they drop passengers within minutes of the ferry terminal from stops across the city. For you, the bus and the shorter walk."

"You'll make it a game for Iskra so she won't get upset?"

"Indeed. Oh and I've set an appointment for you later with the wife of the man who painted my car. She'll cut and dye your hair. And you'll wear these." He handed her a pair of horn-rimmed glasses.

She put them on. "Clear lenses. Thank heavens I can see, although, I probably look like an old schoolmarm."

"You're charming." Andrei poured a second cup of tea.

"Mama looks funny," Iskra chimed in.

When Anya came back from her hair appointment, Andrei said she looked like an American flapper from the 1920s.

She fluffed her bob. "You hate it?"

"It'll grow back," Andrei said.

Exhausted from the dancing and gaming at the church bazaar, Andrei picked up Iskra and signaled Anya it was time to leave. "We're staying here tonight. Tomorrow we'll drive to see the family country house seventeen kilometers from here. Less than an hour."

~*~

Morning
Friday, February 8, 1957

Anya and Andrei left Iskra to play with some of the village children. When they arrived at the dacha, the wind picked up and blew snow flurries, making it seem as though it were actually snowing around the dacha—an apparition of a dwelling from another epoch. They climbed the steps to the verandah and peeked in the windows.

"I wish we could have stayed here but it's in such a state of disrepair that Vadim couldn't get it habitable for us on such short notice. But come here and look out across the snowy fields."

"It's breathtaking," Anya said.

"Look across the wide expanse," he said.

She took hold of his arm and leaned her head on his shoulder.

"Imagine how it looks with a curtain of undulating blue above and puffy white clouds moving at a summer pace languidly across the sky. The trees in the distance a deep green, the broken fences, brown and weathered, enclosing in a plot of wild grasses and variegated wild flower heads dancing in the breeze."

"You love it here and you'll miss it even though you've never came back to see it in all these years. I fear you're already grieving the loss of ever seeing it again."

"I have it forever painted in memory and evocation." He kissed the top of her head. "I can give this up without regrets, but never you. You've melded with my soul. I feel as though I've known you for a lifetime. Perhaps from another life, a divergent time."

"You live for the beauty of wild things."

"That's why I adore you."

Chapter Thirty-Three

Back at the church, while Anya and Iskra waited in the newly painted car sporting a stolen license plate, Andrei said farewell to Vadim and Omar, who was also at the rectory.

Andrei embraced and thanked Vadim and the priest blessed him.

Omar ensnared Andrei in a bear hug. "Maybe not again in this life, but perhaps in another realm, we'll meet again."

"You're no longer in my debt—you've repaid a life for a life. I'm grateful to you for mine," Andrei said, overcome with emotion.

Omar approached the car and wished Anya safe travels. He slipped her a piece of paper. "In case they ask questions at passport control. You're visiting a dying aunt at this address."

"A thousand thanks," Anya said, and extended her hand.

Omar took her hand and kissed it. "Keep well and be safe and happy."

They arrived in Leningrad in time for a meal at a small tavern near the ferry station. Anya left her meager belongings in the trunk of the car and stuck two wrapped bottles of vodka underneath the front seats. She only took her newly forged documents, passage money with her for the ferry. She'd walk to the pier and Andrei would drive Iskra onto the ferry. Andrei made sure the child knew this was a game and said she was to call him, *papachka.*

"Are you going to be my daddy?" Iskra asked.

"Do you want me to be?"

"Oh yes. I love my storybook. Maybe you'll get me another one and read to me like Babushka Yelizaveta."

Andrei smiled and tousled her hair. He turned to Anya. "Please, darling, change your expression. You look guilty of a crime. If anyone stops you for any reason, keep your head up and look them straight in the eye. Kindly don't spit at them."

"How can you joke at a time like this? Can't you see what a wreck I am?"

"Precisely. Take a deep breath. Remember, Vadim forgave you, so will your Christ crucified."

She kissed Iskra and touched Andrei's cheek. "Be safe, my loves."

"See you on the ferry. Look to see if the car made it on, but don't come to us until after the ferry has left the shore."

Anya bordered the bus, arrived and took the short walk to the kiosk to buy her ticket. She got on the passport control line behind boisterous students, grateful for the diversion.

"Business or pleasure?" the control guard demanded.

"Pleasure."

"Pleasure? What kind? Where will you stay?"

Anya cleared her throat. "Not really pleasure. I'm visiting a dying aunt. Here's the address." She pushed the paper towards him.

"*Da. Da.*" He shook his head, and gave her back the address. He detached a portion of her migration card, and yelled out, "Next in line!"

Relieved, she walked to the concession stand. With the money left over she bought a packet of Jubilee tea cookies for Iskra and put them and the change in her purse. Wanting to run, she forced herself to walk as slowly as possible to the ferry. Once aboard she went up the stairs to overlook the cars pulling on.

Sure enough, the guards with huge police dogs were searching cars. Her heart plummeted and her legs shook. How will Andrei explain his police camera and equipment? Andrei's car was the next one to be examined.

Andrei and Iskra were out of the car. One of the uniformed men rooted around in the *bagazhnik*. Iskra was getting agitated and started to cry. Andrei picked her up and patted her back in an attempt to soothe her. He walked around the car to the trunk and asked the guard something, and then set the child down again in the front seat. He pulled out the crushed velvet teddy bear Yelizaveta had made to conceal the *Ketubah* and handed it to Iskra.

Was he out of his mind? But the child seemed immediately placated.

Next, Andrei gesticulated like a mad man. He pulled out something from his wallet and showed the patrol guard, who looked it over and passed it to another officer. His hat was off. He tossed it in the car and raked his hand through his hair. He put his hands together and in prayer-like supplication, waved them up and down. He then pointed to Iskra, and said something to the guard.

Anya brushed tears off her cheeks as she could swear she read the response word *contraband* on the sentry's lips.

Anya started to run down stairs, thought better of it and went back to her place on the fence railing. Andrei was no longer standing by the car. She had the fleeting notion she was going insane, when Andrei stepped out of the control booth with his camera around his neck, smiling, and shaking hands with the officer in charge. He put the camera in the back seat, slammed the trunk and got behind the wheel to drive onto the ferry.

Anya knew she wasn't supposed to go to meet them until after the ferry had pulled away from shore, but in her frantic state, she ran down the stairs to the car park area. She located his car and jumped in the back seat. "What happened?"

"Did I not tell you to stay put until after the ferry got underway?"

"Are you insane giving Iskra the teddy bear under the noses of the border patrol? What did you take out of your wallet? How did you convince the guards the camera was yours?"

Andrei turned to Iskra. "If your mother will stop badgering and interrogating me, I might be able to answer her."

By her puzzled look, Iskra was uncertain how to respond, but then Andrei smiled at her and she relaxed. He turned toward Anya. "I told them it was a gift from my father's friend, Chief Linsky, and showed them his card with the words 'Enjoy the camera on your vacation, dear friend' written on the back."

"You didn't!"

"Oh but I did. Now where is Vadim so I can confess?"

Anya leaned across the front seat, flung her arms around him, and kissed him fiercely. She pulled her face back from his. "There's vodka under your seat. I'm glad they didn't requisition your camera—or that."

"*Na Zdorovie!*" Andrei said, and took a swig out of the bottle.

"Cheers!" Iskra said.

"Amen." Anya said.

~ Fine ~

Glossary

Azoy, bruder, vi'zenen di tingz mit ir? Yiddish, So, brother, how are things with you?

babushka: 1. an old Russian woman or grandmother. 2. a kerchief or scarf (this is a western variation of the word)
babushki: grandmothers
bagazhnik: trunk
bab'ye leto: Indian summer
bol'shoy vystrel: big shot (this doesn't seem to appear in a Russian dictionary. Seems to be a transliteration in meaning from American English)
Bozhe moy: Oh my God
Bratva, the brotherhood (More or less. Specific meaning or gangs or the mob. Criminal insinuation)

chebureki: (a kind of street food), a deep-fried turnover filled with minced meat and onions, made of a round piece of dough which is folded over giving it a half-moon shape. Chebureki is a national Crimean Tatar dish. It can be made with other fillings, like potatoes.
chertovski sumasshedshiy: hellishly crazy
chmo: Yiddish, schmo

da: yes
dedushka: grandfather
derganyy: antsy, nervous, panicky
der'mo: crap
dobroj noci: goodnight

dobroye utro: good morning

doktor doctor

dorogaya: darling

dva: two

Glavnoye Upravleniye Ispravitelno-trudovykh Lagerej i kolonij: Gulag. Soviet system of forced labor camps

goniff: Yiddish, thief

goryachaya golova: hothead (Seems to be a transliteration from American English)

goy: Hebrew and Yiddish, a "Sabbath gentile" or non-Jew

idti: go

karusel: carousel

kasha vernishkes: buckwheat groats with noodles, an Ashkenazi Jewish dish

KGB: Komitet Gosudarstvennoy Bezopasnosti, translates to "Committee for State Security"

khloristyy kaliy: potassium chloride

khrushchyovka: an apartment in a block, not a communal one (Named after Khrushchev plus a name for a Russian slum.) A 5-6 story apartment block stamped all over the Soviet in the 1950s-60s. Run down.

konechno: of course

mal'chik: boy

malen'kiy: little one

malyutka: baby girl, old fashioned

malyshka: baby girl

mama: mama

mamasha: mama, a crude way of saying mom, usually not your own mother. It would apply to a large woman of lower level of society between 50 and 60 years old.

mamushka: mommy

мать: Mother (formal) You would say Mat' with a soft "t."

mat: check mate in chess or Russian coarse swearing, considered worse than American ubiquitous fuck and shit.

matryoshka: hollow wooden nesting dolls

medovaja lovuska: sex trap, honey trap

ment: cop. Slang. Derogatory

mentovka: cop shop

Militsiya: police force. Literally militia.

moya dusha: my soul

musor: garbage

na zdorovie: cheers. Literally: to your health

net, ne delay etogo: no, don't do it

niet: no

NKVD Narodny Komissariat Vnutrennih Del: The People's Commissariat for Internal Affairs.

obeshchayu: I promise

o bozhe: oh christ

odin: one

O, Khristos: Oh, Christ

Oseh shalom bimromav, hu ya'aseh shalom aleinu v'al kol-yisrael, v'imru: 'amen': Mourner's Kadish in Hebrew: He who creates peace in His celestial heights, may He create peace for us and for all Israel; and say, Amen.

Ostorozhnost: caution

pechka: stove

pekarnya: bakery

pel'meni: Russian meat or other stuffed dumplings

piroshki: baked or fried buns, some sweet, some savory

prestupnik: perp

puzhalsta: not at all

politsiya: police

politseyskiy: policeman

pirozhki: baked or fried yeast-leavened boat-shaped buns with a variety of fillings

podklyucheniye: connecting, hooking up

pozhalujsta: please

prestupnik: criminal, perpetrator

prestupniki: criminals

psikh: crazy, psycho

razvaluha: car that's falling apart as it goes

razvalina: applies to houses as well as other things falling apart

Rosiyane: people living in Russia

Russkie: are people of Russian nationality as opposed to Jews, Ukrainians or Germans living in Russia

rvota: vomit

sharovary: sweat pants

shchi: cabbage soup

shivorot-navyvorot: topsy-turvy

*shkvorni:*king pins

sookin syn: son of a bitch

spasibo: thanks

spokoinoi noci: goodnight

spokjnoj: goodnight

*tolstya*k: fat man
tovarishch: comrade
tri: three
tsigane: Gypsy from the Hungarian *cigány*
tsyganskiye shirokiye shtany: Gypsy wide pants
tualet: toilet
tupitsa: jerk. Stupid. Intellectually dumb.

ugolovnoye delo: criminal case

varenki: Ukrainian dumpling, any filling
vot: here
vyplata: payment
vyplaty: payments
vpryskivaniye: injection

ya obeshchayu: I promise
yob'tvoju mat: fuck your mother

zaddik: Yiddish: saint
zakouska: singular, Russian hors d'oeuvre
zakouski: plural, Russian cookery—hord'oeuvres, tiny open sandwiches spread with caviar, smoked sausage etc., cold dishes such as radishes in sour cream, and all usually served with vodka. Russian antipasti. Hot and cold dishes served before the main dish.
zakusit': to have a snack
zaplatit': payoff
zheltyy kress-salat: yellow cress

About the Author

Nina Romano earned a B.S. from Ithaca College, an M.A. from Adelphi University and a B.A. and an M.F.A. in Creative Writing from FIU. A world traveler and lover of history, she lived in Rome, Italy, for twenty years, and is fluent in Italian and Spanish.

She has authored a short story collection, *The Other Side of the Gates,* and has had five poetry collections and two poetry chapbooks published traditionally with independent publishers. She co-authored a nonfiction book: *Writing in a Changing World.* Romano has been nominated twice for the Pushcart Prize in Poetry.

Nina Romano's historical *Wayfarer Trilogy* has been published from Turner Publishing. *The Secret Language of Women,* Book #1, was a Foreword Reviews Book Award Finalist and Gold Medal winner of the Independent Publisher's 2016 IPPY Book Award. *Lemon Blossoms,* Book # 2, was a Foreword Reviews Book Award Finalist, and *In America,* Book #3, was a finalist in Chanticleer Media's Chatelaine Book Awards.

Her latest novel, a Western Historical Romance, *The Girl Who Loved Cayo Bradley,* Book 1 of the Darby's Quest Series, a semifinalist for the Laramie Book Awards, has been released from Speaking Volumes, LLC.

Romano spends her time between Florida and Utah when she isn't traveling, and is currently at work writing on Book 2 of Darby's Quest.

Nina Romano is most thankful to readers who kindly leave Amazon and Goodreads reviews—reviews are what help market books.

Acknowledgements

I extend heartfelt thanks, as always, to Jane Brownley, who spent considerable time reading this manuscript, draft after draft.

I'm ever grateful to reader/reviewer Anita Dow for her careful readings, impressions, insightful reflections, comments, and suggestions.

Sincere thanks to special author/readers, Marni Graff and Melissa Westemeier, for their close analysis of the manuscript and observations.

Many thanks to my wonderful historian friend, teacher Cris Edwards, who is now reading the final version of this work from above in celestial realms.

I'd like to offer my thanks to mystery writer Sue Coletta who generously read and commented on the autopsy scene.

For her generous support and friendship, I'm grateful to Cynthia Hamilton, wonderful author of the Madeleine Dawkins mystery series, for having read and blurbed this novel.

While visiting Russia, sailing on the Volga River from Moscow to St. Petersburg, I was fortunate enough to meet Ph.D. Assistant Professor Vladimir Kalmykov of Dobroliubov State Linguistic University, Nizhny Novgorod, Russia. I was able to interview and discuss with him my plans for writing this novel and many of the details contained herein. I wish to thank and acknowledge him for this informative interview.

A note of indebtedness . . . I read a great deal of background material in the form of novels from wonderful authors Jason Mathews, Tom Rob Smith, Daniel Silva, David Benioff, Paullina Simmons, and Helen Dunmore, who wrote *The Siege*, which served as contextual material about Leningrad during World War II before the time period of this novel. Previous to reading these authors, I read the many wonderful

Russian classicists: Tolstoy, Pasternak, Dostoyevsky, Turgenev, Chekhov, Gogol, and the 1970 Nobel Prize winner, Aleksandr Isayevich Solzhenitsyn.

Last, but certainly not in the least, blessings and heartfelt gratitude for my husband, Felipe, who took me to Russia twice and who listened to me talk about the characters inhabiting the world of this novel—all my love and a thousand thanks.

Upcoming New Release!

NINA ROMANO'S
STAR ON A SUMMER MORNING
DARBY'S QUEST SERIES
BOOK 2

After a deathbed promise to her mother to further her education, Darby leaves her father and brothers behind on their New Mexico ranch, travelling east where she completes her studies. Now, with a letter of acceptance to teach in Colorado, she intends to finally reunite with her beloved.

An unexpected and sorrowful event undermines Darby's plans to immediately join him, their reunion jeopardized by a startling complication, her cowboy's disappearance.

Months later, to help search for her man, Darby hires a Ute tracker to guide her on the treacherous journey, following a trail through wild Mescalero territory and into Mexico.

Has Darby fallen under the spell of the alluring tracker, while fearing he'll make good on his promise to kill the man she loves in order to keep her? Will Darby ever again see the man who changed her life? Or will her dreams fade like an evanescent star on a summer morning?

For more information
visit: www.SpeakingVolumes.us

Now Available!

NINA ROMANO'S
THE GIRL WHO LOVED CAYO BRADLEY
DARBY'S QUEST SERIES
BOOK 1

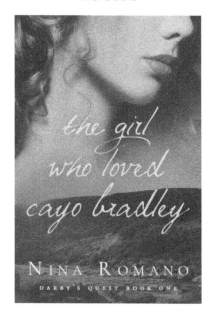

**For more information
visit:** www.SpeakingVolumes.us

Now Available!

BETH GROUNDWATER'S MYSTERIES

**For more information
visit:** www.SpeakingVolumes.us

Now Available!

LYNN SHOLES & JOE MOORE
COTTEN STONE MYSTERIES

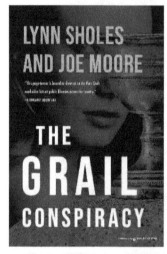
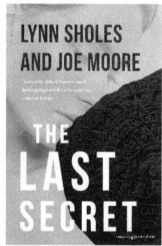
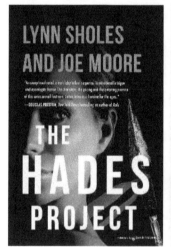
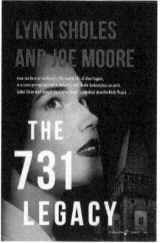

For more information
visit: www.SpeakingVolumes.us

CPSIA information can be obtained
at www.ICGtesting.com
Printed in the USA
LVHW032043240223
740350LV00020B/139